ASHES

A POST-APOCALYPTIC FAIRY TALE

J. R. DEVOE

Dark Tide Publishing

First Edition: November 2024

Cover by MiblArt

ISBN 978-1-0690223-1-8 (paperback)
ISBN 978-1-0690223-0-1 (eBook)

www.jrdevoe.com

To my Father,
For the Name

CHAPTER I

DEKA

Every night the stars come out to taunt me.

Their scattered arrangements in the black sky are sparse and unfamiliar, and serve as a constant reminder of how far from Earth we've come. I could stand for hours watching them cross the sky and see a cluster no bigger than seven, let alone the bulging seam of white light that marks the center of my home galaxy. The blue star that gives this planet life seems to fly through empty space, a lone speck of dirt in a cold dark universe.

I give this planet's surface a good look over from atop a sea wall of platinum dunes. We could certainly have done worse. Daylight always brings lavender skies over crystal blue water that washes over glittering wet sand of pink, purple, and blue. This place couldn't be farther from the wasteland I grew up beneath, with its toxic air and polluted sea, but still...

We cannot stay here. This thought plagues me day and night, all day every day, as I waste away in paradise. It's crazy, I know. I should be dead, yet I've ended up here — a sanctuary of peace in a universe ravaged by chaos.

It's been seven nights since we fought the Watchers on the Great Pyramid. Seven nights since the slaughter that sent many a human and even more intergalactic fae to their graves. I should savor the bliss of these peaceful days, but disharmony finds me too easily here.

Making matters worse are the nights. They're twice as long as Earth's. Nya tells me it's from the planet's slow rotation, but I swear the opposing days are only half as long. It's just another anomaly that torments my frazzled mind. If only I could adapt as well as my fellow humans.

Laughter echoes from down the beach, where Marlok chases Ko Skadia into the sea. They plow through rolling surf and then stand firm against crashing waves. My war chief splashes water at Ko Skadia playfully. The dust-making Elder responds by picking him up by his waist and slamming him into the water.

Marlok's head remains submerged, his hands clawing at Ko Skadia's arms as she holds him under water. Ko Skadia ignores his struggle for air and continues holding him under. Her clenched teeth and determined expression reveal there's no play involved here.

I jump up, muscles tense with panic. This isn't good. Nya told me her elder's mind had not accompanied her body to this planet, that she's the shell of the person she once knew.

Both of Marlok's hands disappear underwater as Ko Skadia pushes down with all her might.

I sprint toward the rolling surf to save my war leader. My feet splashing the fizzing tide line announces my approach to Ko Skadia, who looks up in alarm. She bares her teeth in warning, and it's enough to stop me dead, for what am I to do against such a destructive being?

Luckily I don't have to find out.

Ko Skadia rises and splashes onto her back, her arms flailing as she tries to keep her head above water. This struggle goes on for a few seconds, until she sinks to join Marlok beneath the water. The surf rolls unbroken over where they'd both just disappeared.

My heartbeat pounds on my eardrums. I'm about to shout for help when Marlok erupts from the water. Ko Skadia clings to his front, her legs wrapped around his waist and hands locked behind his neck. She pulls his head into her shoulder to choke him out from the front. At least, that's how it looks until she flings his long locs back and presses her lips to his.

Marlok embraces her kiss like he's been waiting for it his whole life. He spins slowly in the waist-deep water, where blue moonlight shimmers over the choppy surface.

I shake my head in disgust. How can he play around like this knowing our people have been left to face the Watcher army alone? The portal transit must have jarred his good sense. He'll recover his wits soon, and when he does, I'll be sure to remind him of the time he forgot about his responsibility as our colony's *Master of Defense.* He'll want to get home at once, which is why my work here is of utmost importance.

I look to the sky map at my feet. When we find this planet's gateway, we'll need to know our position to align it with Earth. That's what Mora tells me. Each gem and ruby scattered across the flattened sand corresponds with a star in the sky above. Nya told me the red rubies represent dwarf stars, which burn cooler than others. This had surprised me because I expected red to mean hotter. There is much about this universe I do not understand.

Nya also tells me my eyes don't see their colors as hers do. She sees their energy, which to her means their color. She says they're not actually white, nor blue, or even red. Each star has its own unique color, which is mind-boggling when paired with her claim of there being an infinite number of stars. That means there's an infinite number of shades. An infinite number of blue, an infinite number of yellow, and an infinite number of green...

Green... Like the color of Nya's eyes.

Her laughter dances through the air and illuminates the shadows around my heart.

I turn to see her sitting upon the dune wall to my left. Huxley crouches on the slope below her and blows through a sea shell. His breath squeaks out the other end, the high and farcical noise at complete odds with an over-sized human like him.

The strange noise sends Nya rolling onto her side in laughter. A warm sea breeze blows her brown hair, and Huxley seizes the moment to admire her while she isn't looking.

He's falling for her. And worse than that, Nya is not opposed to it.

A wave of jealousy rocks my gut, tossing my belly like an awful spell of sea-sickness. But it's more than just jealousy that's got me all wound up.

Seeing Marlok and Huxley flirt with the fae has a magnetic effect on my teeth. My jaw clenches so tight it bulges and aches. How can they treat this like a holiday?

The answer comes swift and clear: *Me*, that's how. They

expect me to figure this all out on my own, and they either put too much trust in my ability, or they don't think I have a sliver of hope at succeeding. Either way, success or failure is all on me.

"Nya."

She perks up at my voice.

"Will you help me?"

"Of course," she says.

She gives Huxley's shoulder a friendly squeeze, then glides down to join me.

"What do you need?"

"More stars," I say.

"You got it!" Her bright smile and wide-eyed enthusiasm takes me aback.

I watch her curiously as she whizzes along the beach berm, head scanning the ground for precious gems. She plucks a ruby from the sand, then an emerald from nearby. Then another. And another.

One of the first things I noticed about this place was the abundance of rare stones. You can't walk ten feet without stepping on a sapphire or ruby. When I'd flattened the patch of sand here for my star map, all I had to do was rearrange the gems already lying in the sand to get me started.

Nya returns with an armload of jewels. She dumps them along the map border and awaits my instructions.

I look to a faint red dot rising over the ocean horizon. Comparing it to the small wing-shaped constellation to its right, I return to my map and point to a cluster of glittering sapphires near the bottom edge. "There — dwarf star."

Nya picks a ruby and places it where I'd indicated.

"A little to the left," I say.

She moves it two fingers' width.

"A bit more."

She huffs and gives the ruby a flick.

I roll my eyes and shift my attention to our position at the center of the chart. Something is off.

"This doesn't make sense." I hug myself and rub my chin. A sapphire near a silver border branch a third-way down the star map has raised my suspicion. "I could've swore this was the pole star yesterday."

"You're overthinking it," Nya says.

"I'm not."

"You are!"

Nya's anger shakes me. The intensity in her eyes is enough to rattle anyone, but the hands clenched at her sides are what get me. I've seen what those fists can do. After all, the first time I ever set eyes on her she'd dusted a drilling rig with her bare hands. At the time I thought she used magic or advanced technology, but that all changed on the Great Pyramid. The way she pulverized those blocks with her bare hands, each punch blasting away ten feet of stone before her... Such power from a being her size had blown me away.

Nya traces my stare to her fists. Her eyes soften and her fingers uncurl. She steps close to me, careful to avoid disturbing the stones scattered across my flattened patch of sand. I know what she's thinking. *He's making freedom seem like such a chore.* The frustration in her eyes says it all.

She wraps her hands around my waist and presses her head to my chest. Her soft hair and warm breath on my skin sends a hot tingle through me. I find my hands rising to embrace her, to pull her close, and the pleasure I get from this warmth comes with its even share of shame.

Tears blur my eyes from the guilt swelling inside my chest. "I can't just leave them."

Nya's body tenses against mine. My pain over this gives rise to anger in her. It grows every time we have this fight. No matter how many tears I shed into the night, she won't share this pain with me.

A scratch tickles my throat, and before I can cover my mouth, a cough erupts from my chest.

I release Nya and turn away, knowing full well what's coming. I cover my mouth with one hand and cough until my skull throbs and my vision blackens. This goes on until I run out of breath and nearly pass out.

When the fit passes, I pull my hand away to see black blood spattered on my palm.

"You're just adapting to the atmosphere," Nya assures me. Again.

"Sure, nothing to worry about. I'll be fine in a few days."

Nya gives me a wide smile, completely missing the heavy sarcasm laced in my words.

I return my attention down to the shifty star map.

"You listen too much to your mind," Nya says.

"I don't," I say, and resistance comes easier now that I'm free of her distracting embrace. But I infuse some lightness into my voice, and a smile comes naturally with it. "It's cosmic navigation, for godsakes."

"Exactly! It's way too vast for your mind to comprehend." Nya points to the sky with one hand and taps her belly with the other. "You have to let your heart guide you. It never forgets where your home is. It's the surest way. But it's not the *how* you should be worrying about right now—it's the *should*."

My chest tightens and my cheeks burn. She'll not convince me that my people are dead until I see their bones with my own eyes. We survived the demon hunts for fifteen years. Just because a new army of them arrived does not mean we are doomed, especially with open rebellion from Nya's folk distracting them. The fight on Earth carries on in our absence. We cannot abandon them. Though, I do feel Marlok will need some convincing to leave this place.

He and Ko Skadia walk toward the far end of the beach holding hands. He seems to think he's died and gone to Heaven, and part of me wonders if I should rob him of this ignorant bliss. But it's not all paradise.

He bends over and bursts into a coughing fit. Ko Skadia hovers over him, looking very unsure about what to do.

Nya can't hide her concern either. When she notices me watching her, she shakes off her alarm and forces a smile. "You'll both be fine in a few days," she says.

A voice echoes from beyond the dunes, near the forest. "Search party returning!"

I scramble up the dune and down the other side toward the purple forest edge, where four Ori hustle out to meet us. Our Fori and Ori allies have been searching tirelessly for the portal gate, which so far has eluded us. From the whispers of the Ori I've gathered this is not only unusual, but borderline miraculous.

I stop at Mora to hear her report. Nya hovers nearby, listening intently.

"Nothing," Mora tells me.

My shoulders slump and I hang my head. "Did you check the caves Sheffa told us about?"

Mora's eyes flick to Nya as she fidgets with her forging

apron. "Just rock walls," she tells me. "Sorry. We'll send another party to the far side of the mountain in a few days."

I hug myself and saunter back up the beach berm. Nya's flittering wings tell me she's close behind.

"You should be out there helping them," I say. "The Ori can't cover as much ground as you."

Nya whirls in a half-circle to face me while blocking my path. "Sheffa is a better flyer than me," she says scoldingly, "and she's been non-stop in her search. Give her some credit, will ya. You've got—"

I raise a hand to demand silence. Nya gives it to me, and I catch her suppressing a victorious smile. She knows I hate letting her go on a rant, because she can certainly go on and on and... well, you get the idea.

And it's usually now when the headaches kick in. By the pressure already building behind my right eyebrow, this will be worse than the last one, which had been worse than the one before that.

My belly squirms at the promise of pain to come.

I crouch atop the dune overlooking my map and rub my temples. Nya assures me it's my body adapting to the atmospheric pressure, but this does little to comfort me when I'm in the midst of a spell.

"You should get some sleep," she says. "You'll think better after some rest."

This I do not protest. I give the map one last look over, to ensure I have everything right to memory, then make my way back toward my bed in the tree line. But I'll find no rest there. Urgency shall haunt me until we find the gateway back to Earth and return home to save my people.

CHAPTER 2
NYA

The first thing I learned about death is that one man's hell can be another's paradise.

I smile into a warm sea breeze, trying my best to ignore Deka's sulking that wafts through the night air. Though these cries are not physical, they weigh heavy on my heart nonetheless.

I sit cross-legged upon a silvery dune, watching Deka stomp toward the tree line, his shoulders slumped in defeat. Why can't he be more like his war leader?

In the distance, Marlok and Ko Skadia run naked across the beach and into the retreating tide. They splash and wrestle in the waist-deep water, their laughter rising loud in the midnight air. I've seen them play like this for days on end.

Part of me pities Marlok. Deka's war chief has fallen for a shadow, an echo of the great Entropath that once wreaked havoc across the realms. Although she exists here in body, her mind is lost.

He picks my Elder up by her waist. She wraps her legs around him and presses her lips to his.

I squirm with embarrassment for them. It's a tug-of-war concern for me. One moment I wonder how he can care for her fragile state; the next, I fear for his life, for if her consciousness returns she will shatter him into a hundred trillion particles.

Watching the way she melts into him though, this threat seems a long way off.

Behind me, Deka cusses in his walk to the tree line.

It takes all my strength to bite my tongue when he goes on like that. I'm not sure if he's in denial, or if he really hasn't considered the likely chance that every *sapien* on Gaia has perished. That his entire race is now extinct. With all those Watchers trapped on his home planet, it wouldn't take long for Jexa to wipe out his colony.

I want to tell him the few humans here are all that remain of his race, but I don't have the heart. Besides, looking at his star map, I'm actually worried his endeavor might succeed. I'd assumed my destruction of the Capstone had caused a warp in space-time that deposited us here, but now I'm not so sure.

As the fog cleared from my mind in the days following our arrival on this planet, a startling possibility had revealed itself to me. If I'd truly succeeded in destroying the gate key, we'd all be dead. I didn't have the energy to do it, even with Ko Skadia. And there's something else.

I have this sense that the Capstone possessed a form of consciousness. That there was an element of sentience laced through it. It identified me as a threat and worked to eliminate me by undoing my bonds. But when all my allies anchored me I actually stood a chance, and that drove it to desperation. It shot us through the energy stream and dumped us here, somewhere far away and where I'd have too hard a time returning to finish the job.

Imagine, a thinking block of gold. Sounds crazy, I know.

Deka breaks into another coughing fit.

I hug myself and watch him stagger along the path toward the amethyst-colored trees. He'll be fine. Whenever we arrive through a portal's membrane, it alters our DNA slightly to harmonize with the new planet. If this environment were too harsh he'd have died already. Even Mora agrees.

The planet I'd worked before Earth had given me the worst cold. My head was so stuffed full of snot for a whole five years, that eventually I had enough and went rogue. A year of dry desert air did the trick for sure, and was well worth the scolding Jaleera had given me for it.

Oh, Jaleera. My heart sinks. I never thought I'd see the day where I'd actually miss a Watcher. It's sick, I know. But looking back at all my playing around that she'd put up with, she must have truly loved me. She never punished me the way my Fori and Ori cousins got it. And now that she's gone, I realize just how much I'd come to see her as a mother figure. She was my guardian and protector until her awful death.

A wave of nausea rocks my belly. *What am I thinking?* That Capstone must have scrambled my neurons, because I am messed in the head if I'm missing *any* Watcher right now. Though, if she's sharing an afterlife alongside Jexa's other victims, it must be worse for her. Whatever misery they are experiencing, at least they are among their own. Jaleera is an enemy to them all and will find no peace among them.

I look around my own surroundings, to the glittering sea under a glowing moon, to platinum sand sliding down silky dunes. A warm breeze blows my hair back from my face and caresses my skin. If this is death, I hope it's for eternity.

I wait until Deka disappears into the tree line, then get to work.

I flutter down and hover over his gemstone map. Deka is already suspicious of the sapphire he'd placed as the pole star, so I mustn't touch that one again. Too risky. Instead I rearrange a cluster of rubies to change their north-south orientation. It's a good start. I've noticed him using specific stars as directional anchors, so I can't touch them directly, but I can rearrange the stars nearest them to throw him off.

I move an emerald and then scatter a swirl of purple dust. Leave the borders but disrupt the center. He'll thank me for this in the future.

I rub my hands together and laugh deviously to myself. In doing so I realize how sinister I must sound, but I don't care. Deka will become so frustrated that eventually he'll give up and accept that this is where we belong now. Then we'll all be free to enjoy ourselves.

Yes, this will work, and I'll be the one everyone thanks for breaking his resolve. If anyone can do it, it's me. For I am Nya —*Destroyer of Gemstone Galaxies!*

I float back and land at the map's edge to survey my work. The general shape and layout of the chart appears untouched, but the minor changes are what matter. Yes, this should really throw him into a fit.

I will break you, Deka. I will wear down your determination and force you into a life of peace and abundance, and one day you will thank me for it.

But that's still a long way off. I yawn and stretch both arms out wide. Now it's my turn to retire.

I fly out over the retreating surf and whiz to an arched rock that sits beyond the low tide line. Atop this three-hundred foot boulder sits my damp nest of purple leaves.

Sitting on my knees, I clasp both hands in my lap and stare up at the night sky. And for the first time in all my lifetimes, I pray.

"Oh heavenly creator of all that is good and light, please forgive me." These words sound strange leaving my mouth. "Forgive me for all the Sparks I've forsaken, and forgive me for the misery I've forced upon the living. Know that for as long as I continue to live, no other shall fall to darkness by my will. I shall serve only to guide those who are lost back into your light."

I stare at the pinholes of white, partly awaiting a response. Praying for a sign. What's out there? I'd go almost anywhere to escape the ghosts in my mind.

The stars, for all their brilliance, fail to entertain me for long. So I lay my head down and prepare to face my demons. They've not found me up here yet. I suspect that's due to the water crashing against the rock beneath me, which allows me to rest without crossing into the realms of dream.

They'd started our first night here. All the souls lost in the battle, those I'd led to their deaths, now search for me in the netherworld. And like how Jaleera once said my light shines bright wherever I go, on this planet my flame continues to attract a good many moths. Some of those lost souls blame me for their fate; others beg me to save them; a few come simply to torment me.

"*You did this to us,*" they say, "*and soon you shall be among us.*"

But it is not they who truly haunt me.

Always in the background is a little Fori who says nothing. She just stands there, alone in the Dark, and watches me with the saddest eyes I've ever seen.

Oh, Jinny! How I miss her. I'd do anything to hold her again, to ease her suffering, but when I approach her in my dreams her companions swarm me. They issue their pleas, cast their blame, or make their threats until I lose sight of her. It's awful!

Since I'd moved my nest to this rock, I've been spared these unpleasant visits. Though, this sleep deprivation has left me ever so tired. So tired that no amount of crashing waves may keep me from crossing over to the dreamworld on this night.

My eyelids slide down so easily that it takes all my effort to lift them again.

Okay, I say, resigning myself to this fated encounter. I'm coming. I'll see you all soon, and maybe this time I'll get close enough to Jinny to tell her I'm sorry.

"The *sapiens* are dying!"

The voice invades my sleep with words worse than Jinny's silence. Her claim rattles me so deeply that my wings spring me from my back to my feet before I can open my eyes.

On the beach below, at the low tide waterline, an Ori paces frantically while hugging herself. Mora must have sent her as a messenger, which means she must be busy, perhaps tending to the ailing humans.

I zoom overhead without a word to her. To my right, a violet glow over the horizon signals the coming dawn.

A column of grey smoke rises from the tree line and guides me to a cluster of spectating Fori, who watch their Ori cousins race about in a frenzy. At the center of this commotion lies Deka, and he does not look good. His eyes are open but they stare blankly skyward, with all his effort directed to his breathing.

Mora dabs sweat from his brow with a wet rag. When someone alerts her to my presence, she glances up at me.

"I tried, Nya." She hangs her head and shakes it in defeat. "They can't stay here."

"What's wrong with them?"

She shrugs and gives me a befuddled look. "Spores. Low atmospheric density. High atmospheric density. Parasites. Who knows?"

I hug myself and chew my thumbnail.

"It's time," Mora says, and the desperation in her voice tells me our holiday here is over.

I turn and kick sand, then belt a bloodcurdling screech at the pre-dawn sky. It's a cry of frustration and fury, of claustrophobia and fear. Just when I thought we'd caught a break...

When I turn back to Mora, she watches me expectantly. My outburst has sent a few Ori and Fori hiding behind trees, but it's not my wrath they need fear.

"Uncover the gate," I say. "We're going back to Earth."

CHAPTER 3

NYA

A planet teeming with swarms of Watchers is the last place I want to be going, but we have no choice. Our only alternative is to allow Deka and his people to die here, and I'd sooner die myself than let that happen.

I watch helplessly as the Ori load him onto a litter. He looks so bad! His skin is slick with sweat and, although his eyes are open, they fail to notice any of his surroundings. But the way his dilated pupils dart around suggest he's processing some visual stimulus.

I crouch beside him and take his hand. He squeezes so tight he almost breaks my fingers, and it takes great effort to keep myself from squealing. Luckily his sweaty skin allows me to slip free from his grip.

"We got him," Mora says as she takes her place at the head of his stretcher. "Go open the gate — Sheffa knows where it is. We'll come back for Marlok and Huxley."

Sheffa grabs my wrist and launches into flight, dragging me up into the sky along with her. She guides me over purple forest toward a conical mountain that looks so much like a volcano but is not. This obvious place had been Deka's first guess as to the gate's location, and he'd been right. And if the cone slopes weren't so silty and difficult to climb he'd have gone looking for the gate up there himself.

Luckily the search party had reported its location to me first, when Deka was nowhere near, so I could order they keep it hidden. They did not protest this measure. They've enjoyed our life here as much as I. But I know pretending to keep looking annoyed them to no end, and it actually took some threats to keep them at it.

As we approach the flared-out mountain base, which rises from the shimmering canopy of violet leaves, I'm expecting the awful feeling that always accompanies my arrival into a gate's Anomaly. But, as we keep flying, my wings keep me in the sky. No falling through a void and crashing to the ground, just as Sheffa had claimed. Instead we fly right up the slope to the flattened mountaintop.

Okay, so, this is strange. I've never had such smooth access to a gate, and this leaves me wondering if my search party cousins have been playing some sort of trick on me.

But no. As we crest the mountain peak—with its truncated top perfectly flattened and capped with fine, powdery dirt—I see clearly they were not mistaken. I'd dared not come inspect the site myself before this, as doing so may have raised Deka's suspicions, but there it is, sitting dead center of the mountaintop.

The dirt around the trapezoidal altar had been recently cleared away by my search party, but only a bit. It stands waist high, but I know its sloped sides run all the way to the ground like a great pyramid. Whoever this planet's Consul is, they believed it necessary to cover the gate to keep it concealed in plain sight. Why they did this is a quandary for another time.

"Where's the key?" I say.

Sheffa whizzes to the far edge of the mountaintop. There she scoops away dirt to expose a golden pyramidion.

I breathe a sigh of relief. It's only about six feet high. A few Fori should be able to drag it across this flat surface of fine dirt and shimmy it up onto the altar.

"It was just sitting here," Sheffa says, "right next to the lock."

"Of course it was," I say, coming to a realization. This gate wasn't covered for concealment. It's so the key can be easily seated by a small party. And for Deka's sake I am grateful.

We waste no time getting to work. A Fori team arrives with hauling straps weaved from vine, which they lash around the golden pyramidion. It takes only six of us to drag it to the altar. Seating it does require a bit more skill, but with some grunting and cussing, and even a few fists raised in frustration, we manage to heave it up onto its seat. All we have to do is slide the key to match all four corners with those of the square altar-top below.

We shimmy it into place, working it back and forth, until Sheffa stops and hovers back in fright. "Wait!"

We all stop and look at her.

"What about the Alignment?" she says.

I look to the dawn sky. The only star in sight is this planet's blue sun peeking over the horizon. My haste hasn't allowed me to forget this crucial step, but none of us knows how to align a portal opening anyway. Our only hope is that the gate will send Deka and his folk back to where they belong. When I'd tried to destroy the Capstone on Earth, I swear it connected with me on a conscious level. I'm sure it's what delivered us here. If it had meant us harm, there's no shortage of places it could've sent us for a quick death... or eternal suffering... or somehow a combination of both. And there's something else.

I've developed the strong suspicion that the Alignment isn't actually a physical arrangement in space. It very well may be the will of the gate opener that decides what gate it connects to on the other end. Think about it. How else could Jexa have reached back through time to pull her dragon lord from the past? Perhaps it's not a physical law that keeps us in linear time, but one imposed on us by some physical entity. Someone high and mighty, who possesses a strong command over the physical realms. Someone like the Magister. Or the Magister's master, if there exists such a being.

"Don't worry about the Alignment," I say, and I lean my shoulder into the golden block for another push. It doesn't budge.

I step back and notice I'm now alone in seating the pyramidion. Sheffa's fear has spread through her Fori sisters, who now hover away from the key.

Sheffa shakes her head at me, her face scrunched with fear. "Somethin' ain't right about this, Nya."

She's right. There is much about this place that doesn't make sense, but Deka doesn't have time for us to investigate the mysteries of this planet.

"If we don't set this key," I say, "the *sapiens* are going to die. For them, there is no restart. Their deaths are permanent."

I see in the eyes of my Fori cousins they don't care all that much about the fate of Deka and his people. To be honest, I don't blame them. If we actually succeed, we'll be patched into a planet full of Watchers. Swarms upon swarms of them. How long could Deka expect to last there?

Longer than here.

"We'll just dump them through," I say, "then we'll shut the gate."

I must have a quirk that reveals when I'm lying, because not one of the Fori seems convinced of my commitment to that plan. They all exchange doubtful looks with each other.

"Fine," I say.

I hover back from the pyramidion, then fly hard against its sloped side. My impact slides the block in a twisting motion, one finger-width closer to matching its corners. A few more of these hits should bring it close enough to activate the gate.

When I fly back for another go, I see Sheffa and her sisters exchange rattled looks. Their hands are clenched into fists and I know they're wondering if I'll dust them if they try to stop me.

"Do it," I say, calling their bluff.

Sheffa notices her fists and loosens her fingers. Her eyes soften as she gives me a pleading look. "We'll fly far and wide to look for medicine," she says. "We'll search the whole planet if we got to, scour every cave, visit the highest mountains..."

"They don't have that much time," says a voice from behind me. It's strange in its manner, yet familiar in its sound.

I turn to see my Entropath Elder standing at the edge of the mountaintop.

"Ko Skadia!" I shout in relief. It's so nice to hear her

words. Ominous as they are, I welcome them over the childish laughter from her playtime with Marlok. She's all the ally I need, because no Fori would dare stand against her. You'd need a whole army to defy The Hammer. "You're back!"

"No," she says in her approach.

I give her a puzzled look. Coming from another I'd assume she was joking, but Ko Skadia is not known for her humor.

"I don't understand," I say. If she isn't here, then to who do I now speak?

"Nya..." says Sheffa from behind, her voice trembling. "Look at her eyes."

I do, and the sight of Ko Skadia's all-black eyes sends me stumbling back until I trip over a dirt mound.

"Who...What..." My mouth moves, but I have no control over the sounds coming out. *What devilry is this that approaches?*

My Elder spreads her arms wide and walks past me, to the gate key. "They call me the *Mistress of the Pyramid*," she says.

Looking to the fine sand covering this planet's gate, I venture a guess. "You're the guardian here. The Consul."

Whatever possesses Ko Skadia stops at the gate key and presses a hand to its golden face. In the polished surface, I see a reflection that does not resemble the figure casting it. Her wings are long and feathered, yet not wings at all. They're a colorful garment that hangs from her back and attaches to her wrists to give the appearance of wings. Black makeup lines her eyes which, in her reflection, are not all-black at all.

They're clear as ice and look right through me. The frigid stare freezes me in place.

"You forged the Capstone," I say, standing slowly.

"I *am* the Capstone," she says.

I'm not understanding this until she smiles at me. *The consciousness I'd felt...*

"You could have destroyed me," the Mistress says.

"I tried."

"A weak effort on your part. Your heart wasn't in it, not entirely, or you'd have succeeded." She stares longingly at her own reflection. "There is nothing you cannot do when you put your whole heart into something."

I think she's right. Even though I'd put everything into separating the Capstone's bonds, there must have been a small part of me that held back—the part so desperate to see my home again. Or an overpowering reluctance to obliterate the friends who'd gathered about the Capstone with me, offering to share my fate.

"So what happened?" I ask. "Where is this place?"

"I created this sanctuary for you, to rest and regroup. For your fight is not yet over."

I don't like the sound of that.

"There are souls trapped in a timeline in which they do not belong," says the Mistress. Her stare in the reflection darkens. "My partner—the Lord of Eternity—warns of disastrous consequences should this energy imbalance endure."

I'm really not liking where this is going. In fact, I may throw up in my mouth. My chest swells with pressure. "You're saying we have to clear the Watchers from Earth? But Jexa managed to summon so many of them... anyone we left behind, my army... the Watchers probably destroyed them!"

The Mistress nods gravely. "I sense the loss of your army, and a strong presence of darkness before you."

And there it is — I just threw up in my mouth. The taste of bile is foreign, as this enzyme is used to digest organic energy sources. It has been years in the thousands since my species required this function to survive.

"But they are without their leader," the Mistress says.

"Where is she?" I ask, recalling Sheffa's recount of Jexa gliding through me. I'd assumed the Marshal had missed the gate jump and remained on Earth.

"I've confined her to a realm where she can do no harm. But I cannot hold her there forever. It takes all of my strength to maintain that prison..." She winces, then continues. "She will be released, and..."

Her face twists with strain.

"So what?" I say. "The Watchers are without a leader, but we're without an army."

The Mistress of the Pyramid turns to lock eyes with me. "But you are not without allies."

My instinct is to say something sarcastic, but curiosity keeps those words at bay. Instead I say, "Who?"

"The former custodians of Earth are not yet gone, as you've already seen. But you've encountered only a small number of them."

My intrigue must be showing, because Ko Skadia's possessed mouth curves into a devious grin.

"In a land to the south," she says, "a great human civilization still thrives. Their location has kept them safe from the extermination tactics of your masters. Until now, that is. But when the swarm reunites with their queen, she'll see those three million humans for the threat they are, and with her new army she will rain death upon them like an apocalyptic meteor shower. Yes, those humans are mighty, but they are unaware of the dark storm building on their horizon."

Did she say three *million* humans? "Then I just need to warn Deka's southern kin so they can prepare for the attack."

"Your role in this war will not be so subtle. Only the one who unites them can command them in this fateful fight, and that will be you."

My teeth clench in anger. "You know what happened to the last person who told me to lead a rebellion?"

"The sooner you accept this, the easier it will be."

"Fine. I'll go kick the hornets' nest again. Why not?"

This, of course, is a lie. If that *sapien* civilization survived the Watchers this long in the open, they'll be strong enough to take the fight to them. Little ol' me won't offer much help they can't do without. I just need to make sure they get the message so they're prepared. Besides, Earth is their planet. It's them who should bleed for it. I'll be a glorified messenger, nothing more. Maybe a puppet master if it comes to it.

"So," the Mistress says, "you are ready to go?"

Honestly, I'm not. Even if it's just as a messenger.

"You can stay as long as you need."

I cast my gaze to the silvery sand that lines the distant glittering sea, where my nest of safety sits upon the arch rock island. Suddenly the colors of this place appear brighter. The air smells so sweet and fresh, as if it's always about to rain. Even the seawater tastes like grapes. I discovered this while swimming in the ocean during what had felt like the first of endless swimming sessions. How can I leave this paradise for Earth?

Maybe I won't have to.

A reckless idea pops into my head. Can we just dump the *sapiens* through the gate and then close it?

I'm working up the nerve to ask this question, but the Mistress must be inside my mind as well as Ko Skadia's.

"You arrived here together," she says, "and so you shall leave together."

Now, in this moment, I realize I should have spent more time swimming in the sea. And maybe I still can. Deka might get better. There's no telling if his return to Earth will even help his condition.

"Open the gate!" shouts Mora from the slope beyond. Her huffing and grunting rises louder to match each ominous beat of my heart. When she crests the hill at the head of Deka's stretcher, I see his face is soaked with sweat and the shade of copper, and his wheezing has become a high shrill.

My choice is clear. This place will be no paradise to me with Deka's body rotting in the ground beneath my feet.

I turn to the Mistress and say, "Take us back. Get us to Earth."

"Easier *done* than said," she says with a mocking bow, then pushes her pinky finger against the Capstone's nearest corner. Somehow the heavy pyramidion slides into place with such ease that I'd have more difficulty nudging a small stone. But I don't have time to marvel at her strength.

My eyes spasm and my vision flickers. Ko Skadia's body wavers like a mirage, or, more like a distant object on a blazing hot day. I rub my eyes in hopes of clearing this effect, but when I remove my fingers the wavering becomes worse.

And it gets stranger when another phenomenon joins the mix.

Rather than a bulbous portal opening overhead, a dark net falls from the sky. The Fori and Ori scream and shield their heads. I throw up both hands and infuse them with a high frequency to burst apart whatever falls on me.

The net stops and hovers twenty feet above us. Its dark lines, evenly spaced and straight, form a perfect grid. Though, a closer look reveals it's not actually a grid. It's more like... the edges of rectangular blocks.

I squint to focus and see that, yes, that's exactly what they are. The lavender sky darkens to brown ceiling blocks, while black lines give shape to stone walls enclosing the mountaintop.

Is this how the transits always are? I've never made a jump between planets while awake, so I have no idea. Or maybe I'm hallucinating. Maybe I inhaled a toxic spore or stepped on a barb that injected me with a psychedelic toxin.

A quick look at my companions' faces reveals I'm not the only one experiencing this phenomenon. Sheffa's frazzled eyes dart all around in panic. Mora clings to my side and wraps her arms around my waist, though she doesn't seem to notice she's doing it as she watches the world close in around us.

A rancid stench blows away the sweet mountain air. It is a mix of smoke and death, the tang of blood and the rot of flesh.

Then we're underground, me and my cousins crammed together in a windowless chamber with a vaulted ceiling. Deka and the *sapiens* are nowhere in sight.

"Are we back?" says Sheffa, her voice echoing. "Is this Earth?"

"*You never left,*" booms a woman's voice. It rumbles through the chamber's only exit, and carries with it the same authority as that which had commanded Ko Skadia's voice. I see now Ko Skadia sprawled on the floor in the far corner, still as stone.

"Where are you?" I say to the Mistress. "You have a lot of explaining to do. Show yourself!"

"Why must you see me to hear my words?" answers the voice. "Must you look upon my face to trust that I am real?"

"There's a lot you can tell by looking into someone's eyes," I say, and this reminds me of Ko Skadia's ink-black stare. The memory sends a shiver through me, and I doubt seeing the Mistress's physical being will offer me comfort, so I don't press her on it. "Where are we?"

"Inside the Great Pyramid," echoes the voice. "I brought you here before you could destroy the Capstone. I..." She pauses as if in search of the right words. Or she has the words, but she doesn't want to share them. "At first I did it to protect Earth's primary gateway. I've since come to realize my error in doing so. The battle upon the steps above had not been enough to stir me from my slumber, but your attempt to shatter that which is not to be shattered succeeded in waking me from the darkness of eternity. That is why I spared your lives. I made for you a sanctuary where you could rest, because, as I have said before, your fight is not yet over. You must finish the job you started."

"Destroy the Capstone," I say.

"Evict the Watchers through the gate, then destroy the key. Yes."

"Sure, no problem," I say with much sarcasm. "Just tell me where Deka is and we'll get right to it."

A scream blasts down the corridor. By the frequency of the echo, I can tell it's from a distance above, and also who it's coming from.

I sprint through the chamber exit and down a level passageway. The walls glow with enough blue energy to illuminate the way, which leads me to a junction of a diagonal shaft. Forward leads down a sloped passageway of similar size. The upslope side behind me is a grand gallery with an astonishingly high ceiling.

A scream of terror thunders from the far end above. The gallery's acoustics rattle through me and knock me off balance.

I quickly recover and bolt up the great corridor. As the blood-curdling screams increase in intensity, my hands feel awfully empty. My time in that false paradise had allowed me to leave my guard dangerously low to the point I felt comfortable without a weapon.

The grand sloped passageway levels through a choked entry. A crimson glow lights the room, where the *sapiens* gather at the far end. They stand around a rectangular altar, on which Deka thrashes and writhes while Marlok and Huxley hold him down.

"Deka," I say from across the room.

Deka's arms and legs lock stiff, then his arched body sinks to lie flat on the altar. Tears streak the sides of his face as he stares blankly at the ceiling. Even in the dim light, I see something different in his eyes. Something that was once there is now missing.

And something else has taken its place.

CHAPTER 4

DEKA

It's the rudest awakening you could ever imagine. One second you're falling asleep in an alien forest, the rustle of purple leaves overhead and the crashing of distant waves lulling you into oblivion... and then you're hit with a blast of white light.

This brightness cannot be ignored, and my eyelids do nothing to dim the glow. My whole body feels as if I'm sinking—like I'm drowning, only... I can breathe. Yet it's not air that fills my lungs.

I slide through a tunnel of vibrant light. Colors I've never before seen streak by in a rainbow passage, stretching forward and back without end. But I see it is not I who is moving.

A kaleidoscope of light spins around me. Dark bands interrupt the sliding tube at increasing intervals. The streaks of light shorten between blackness to form segments of color separated by bands of black. Each section displays a wheel of images that flicker past like the flipping pages of a book, an ancient and endless record containing more knowledge than one mind could ever remember. But rather than written words to pass on information, there is something far more profound conveying this knowledge.

Emotions.

My heart flutters and races, stops and then starts as the scenes flash by. My belly tightens and then twists as events impress upon me feelings of joy that are swiftly smashed by waves of dread, and everything in between.

In this manner I experience each event like a memory, though not of my own. Not in the traditional way of seeing memories, anyway.

This flurry of information is like a collection of memories from my people, a library which has cataloged every event. Though I've not experienced most of what I'm seeing personally, it was a part of my experience nonetheless. It's like I'm accessing a collection of knowledge, like I did when reading the words of my mother's books, except on a much grander scale.

I don't have long to ponder the intricacies of this experience. Before I know it, the images slow down. Or, my focus sharpens on those of importance to me. I'm able to hone in on certain scenes that a deep part of me knows I need to see. Scenes like...

A steel ship, in the shape of an upright cylinder, lifting up from the ground in a blast of orange flame and smoke. As the vessel rises high into a clear blue sky, I fall away from it at a rate faster than its ascent.

Backward I fall, through the rainbow tunnel of light... Until a passionate voice stops me.

An angry man shouts from a stage at a cheering crowd. The scene wavers and shifts to transform the crowd into soldiers marching in neat ranks with great purpose, a feeling of hope and determination giving power to each of their heavy steps.

I jolt forward... to where bodies lie piled in a ditch. A toxic cloud fills my lungs and chokes me. Grief and despair smother me. I need to get out of here, so I do.

I slide forward a bit more... to where a fountain of fire pushes a mushroom-shaped cloud into the sky. A shock wave sweeps across the landscape and blows me away, and I feel the effects ripple beyond the confines of this space and time.

Backwards again, tumbling back through what I now know is Time...

Despite the constant motion and mental havoc, I realize what's happening. I'm searching the collective memory of my people for something, answers to questions I don't know the words to. A time that will help save us in the future? People who will understand what's happening and can assist us? Am I to pinpoint the exact moment in history where we lost our way?

Well, if that's the case, it must have started long before the age of steel killing machines rolling over bloody trenches before me.

I whiz backwards, falling deeper into the past... watching my people devolve in technology, but not so much in other ways. In some respects this regression accompanies great progress.

I see humans worship the Sun in the sky and the ground beneath their feet. They pray to nature in all its forms, connected in a way long forgotten by their descendants. Seeing how they interact with the world is so foreign to me that I feel like an alien on my own planet. They live with truths that my ancestors have shamefully forgotten. And it's not only that.

The neighborly spirit shines bright here. People not only lived closer to the land, but also to each other. Yet, no matter how much harmony and laughter brightens one page, there is always blood and violence smearing the next. An endless history of bloodshed doesn't surprise me. The roots of our nature run deep and wide.

What really gets me is an ever-abundance of resources. They were good to the land, and the land was good to them. This world is unfamiliar to the harsh planet my people have struggled to survive on. The contrast hits me hard in the stomach. How could they have been so unhappy with so much to enjoy?

Ahead I go...

Men in steel suits ride in neat lines upon horses. They clash with an opposing army, their barbaric weapons unleashing a bloody mess upon the earth while leaving scars in humanity that shall haunt us to our end.

Backwards I go again, farther than before, until I come to an abrupt stop. It's as if I've hit a boundary to my time shifting—the far end of the spectrum. There's like a glass barrier preventing me from sliding too far back. Perhaps beyond this border lies a sensitive time where my trespassing may induce irreversible consequences.

Yet, what could make our future any worse than the days into which I was born?

I find myself watching a scene that would seem far less intriguing than those I just witnessed. A young girl ushers goats toward greener fields. And a boy in a boat jigs for fish in a river nearby. Aside from paler skin, he could be me. Grey smoke rises from stones huts along the bank, and the smell of burning wood reminds me of the day Mali died.

How many years lie between this day and then? Is there anything I could do in this moment to change my dear friend's fate? Oddly enough, this is not something I give much consideration, for something else seizes my attention.

The world is quiet. I sense more people alive in these days, yet the planet is more silent than in my lifetime. Only now do I realize there was a static, like an electrical interference, in the atmosphere of my time.

The girl guiding the goats suddenly stops. As if sensing me watching her, she turns to meet my stare. At first there is fear. Then, as if recognizing an old friend, she smiles at me and kneels. She lowers her head in a sign of respect.

I do not know how to communicate with her, so I just watch. Some time passes before she grows restless enough to lift her gaze. When she does, her stare shifts past me, and her fear returns.

Her jaw goes slack. She rises on shaky knees and holds up her walking stick defensively.

A growl rises from behind me. I shift my focus to my rear in time to see a one-eyed wolf pounce through me and onto the girl, and there's nothing I can do as the beast rips out her throat.

CHAPTER 5
NYA

Though Deka's eyes are wide open, with not even a blink, it takes a long time for his attention to come to us. He scans our faces gathered around, shaken and confused.

I drop to his side and take his hand. "You're all right, Deka. We're back on Earth."

Both of my claims are false. We'd never left Earth to begin with, so we can't be 'back'. And he is not all right. None of us are. Not yet, anyway.

As I help him sit up, his frown turns to a hard wince. He shakes like a leaf in a hurricane, and his grip nearly crushes my hand.

"He'll be fine," assures the Mistress's voice from some unseen place. "You know what you must do, Nya."

"Where's Skadia?" asks Marlok.

Everyone looks to me with uncertainty. We've all seen how poorly these *sapiens* deal with death.

"She's resting below," I tell him.

Marlok breaks away and bolts toward the exit.

"Wait!" I say. "There's more of your people on Earth—a great human civilization to the south."

He skids to a stop in the doorway and turns to face me, unable to resist.

"They are strong and can help us defeat the Watchers," I say. "We just need to get word to them."

"You know where they are?" Marlok asks, skeptical.

"South."

He spreads his arms. "It's a big wide world. South could be many places."

"Well, if they're mighty enough to have survived the Watchers so long, they should be easy to find. Thriving civilizations make a lot of noise."

Marlok scoffs. "We survived this long. Would you call us a thriving civilization? They're probably hiding underground in caves too. Maybe *that's* how they survived so long."

Anger heats my chest. Why do these *sapiens* have to be such naysayers? "Three million humans hiding underground wouldn't go unnoticed."

Marlok roars with laughter. "You hear that, Hux? She thinks there's three million of us left."

Huxley smirks to indulge him, then offers me an apologetic look.

"Come on, Mistress," I say to the ceiling. "Give me some help here!"

"South," comes her voice. "Head south and you will find them."

"See!" I say to Marlok.

He gives me a quizzical look. "See what?"

"Didn't you hear? She told us to go south."

His frown deepens. Then it hits me: he can't hear the Mistress's voice.

"So an imaginary voice tells you to lead us south," he says, "and we're supposed to listen? Forget it. We'll be exposed in the open for too long."

I huff in frustration and look back to the ceiling. "Could you be a little more specific? You're not giving us much to go on here."

"I cannot see them directly," the Mistress tells me. "I can only sense their presence and strength, and that they are due south of here."

Marlok stares at me expectantly, clearly deaf to the Mistress's voice.

"She says to trust that it's south."

He folds his arms and lifts his chin. "Well, I hope you forgive me if I'm a bit skeptical of your imaginary friend. But we risk too much in the open."

"He's right," Deka says. Though his mouth speaks to me, I can tell his mind is elsewhere.

He sits up with my help. His face twists in pain, and the despair in his eyes tells me he's badgered by ominous thoughts. "I've seen Africa on maps. It is too vast to travel safely. It may take us weeks to reach the south end, if we are lucky."

"Maybe if you were doing it on your own," I say, an idea taking shape in my mind. It's time to get my sea-dwelling cousins more involved in our struggle. "A dozen Nixies could haul a boat around the whole planet in a fortnight. If they can find a fresh whale carcass to hide you in, then even better." I look to Mora for support. "Right?"

Mora folds her arms and looks to the ground in

contemplation. Marlok and Huxley watch her, awaiting her assessment. The *sapien* war leader seems to have developed a respect for her opinion. He will approve of my plan if she does.

She looks up and meets my imploring stare.

"This seems like a time-sensitive thing," Mora says. "Could you not just fly there and deliver the message? Why must we all travel that great distance?"

"They won't believe me!" I say. I look to Marlok as I point to the round scar between my ribs. "Remember how you welcomed me?"

Marlok winces at my reminder, and for a second I see a flash of regret in his eyes.

"Maybe them southerners is more civilized," Sheffa says.

"Hey!" says Marlok with a condemning jab of his finger. "Just because we live in caves doesn't mean we're not civilized."

"Ain't the walls around you that makes a people sensible," Sheffa says. "Maybe them other folk don't need to eat living things to survive."

A dense energy settles over the chamber. Deka buries his face in his hands, no doubt reminded of his friend Mali getting killed over slaying a deer.

I place a hand on his neck and press my forehead to his. "I'd not ask this of you if I didn't think it was our only chance. If you know a better way, I will do it."

He sniffles and wipes his nose, then swings his legs over the altar and stands with great effort. Taking a look around at the walls, he narrows his eyes as if studying each bump on the stone and groove in between.

"Our boats are still on the riverbank," he says. His tone tells me he is certain of this.

He looks straight up and squints at the ceiling. "There are Watchers on lookout above. Two of them."

I look up to try to see what he sees, but it's only stone.

He surveys the floor at his feet, then the walls all around.

I watch him curiously. "How..."

He raises a hand to silence me. His face is heavy with anguish, almost pouty. "Just believe me."

"There must be more."

"There are. They're fighting to the East. There's a big battle happening there."

"Okay," I say, and I look to Sheffa. "You up for a game of *Flee the Watcher?*"

Sheffa wrings her hands and looks around as if the walls are closing in on us. She crouches and hugs her knees to her chest.

In this state she will only slow me down. "Go with them to the boats," I tell her. "I'll lead the guards away. Mora, when the river pushes you onto the sea, summon the Nixies. Tell them what's happening."

Mora nods her understanding, but she appears uncertain about the plan. Yet she must see it's our only chance if she won't speak further against it.

"I'll meet you at the *sapien* sanctuary," I add, and I refrain from including the *'if it's still there'* part that I so fear. "There we'll form a peace envoy to travel south." To Mora, I say, "What's the best way out of here?"

She looks down the passageway we came in through. "That's the main shaft, but there's no draft coming up. It might be blocked, but I noticed a vent in the other chamber.

It had decent air flow." She sizes up our group. "But none of you will fit, so our options are limited. We can only hope whatever obstruction is down there is easily removed. Follow me."

To Deka, I say, "You ready?"

He rubs his eyes and looks like hell, but, considering he's just come back from near death, I'd say he's doing okay. And he doesn't resist when I take his hand and pull him along to follow Mora out of the chamber.

We walk the sloped floor down through the grand gallery and on past the switchback that leads to the lower chamber.

"Wait," says Sheffa. She points back down the shaft toward where we'd arrived. "What about Ko Skadia's body?"

Marlok gasps. "Body?"

Mora takes his hand and gives him a solemn shake of her head. Marlok crouches and rubs his hands through his hair.

Sheffa has raised a good question. Whenever I'd come across a dead Fori or Ori I'd just report the location to the nearest Hive. Then they'd bury it and have a ceremony with music and storytelling and hope their next incarnation brought them back to the same planet. But I've never come across a dead Entropath. Only one of us gets assigned to a work area, and we're not to cross each other's boundaries.

"We can come back for it," I say. "And we'll give her a good burial, and we'll play music and tell stories about her bravery."

Mora shakes her head ominously. "We don't bury dust maidens."

This takes me off guard. I'd never considered what would happen to this body after I'm done with it. "What do you do with them?"

"The Watchers take 'em," Sheffa says. "They have to dispose of 'em 'coz you's bodies is different. But now the Watchers..."

"Are our enemies," I remind. "Once we defeat them, we'll come back and give Ko Skadia a proper send-off. I swear."

My assurances do little to settle Sheffa. She stares down the passageway with great trepidation, as if fearing Ko Skadia's spirit won't rest until her funeral rites have been performed, and shall haunt all those who have failed in that duty.

"Snap out of it, Sheffa," I say, and I'm surprised at the sternness in my voice.

She gives me a surprised look, then nods.

We continue down the sloped passageway until a heap of crumbled stone blocks our way. The Ori pat the walls to our left and right. Their small hands test the stone as they make their way back up the passageway toward where we'd come from, until one says, "Here."

Mora joins her in feeling the stone. "There's a secret tunnel in there," she announces. Then she steps aside and says to me, "Care to do the honors? Our hands command dirt and soil easy enough, but stone..."

I release Deka's hand, unsure what my energy may do to him when I raise my frequency, and press a hand to the wall.

Everyone watches me nervously.

"Try not to bring the whole place down on us," Mora adds, obviously referencing my attempt to destroy the pyramid during the battle.

I press hard into the wall, feel the dull hum of its limestone, and send a disruptive vibration through its bonds.

The block slumps into a pile of dust, with the finer

particles whirling into a void beyond. I jab to blast away the block below to make a nice doorway for the taller *sapiens*.

Mora slips through first and leads us down a level passageway. It seems to go on forever, so much that I start walking along with my head down until I bump into her. She stands before a stone plug at the end of the passage.

"On the other side of this wall is the outside world," she says. "The *real* world. We leave this pyramid, and we're back in the fight."

I set my face with a stern look and crack my knuckles to show everyone I'm ready. But I'm not ready. I've seen too many times in the darkness of my mind what lies outside—a field of bodies contained within a moat of blood, where crows pick at the remains of those I've forsaken.

Cold sweat slicks my skin.

"Nya?"

I don't even know who says my name. "Just give me a minute."

"It's been ten."

I search the nervous faces around me to contest Mora's claim, but they nod in agreement. I've been standing here for ten minutes.

Without further ado, I give the stone a light tap with my fist.

The block slumps into a pile of dirt around my feet. A dust cloud swirls in its place, and I hold my breath in anticipation for whatever sight awaits us. Of the many questions I'd failed to ask our omnipotent host, how long we've been in here is now among the most pressing.

Part of me has been dreading a flood of sunlight, for that will complicate our escape. Instead I pray for darkness, or at most a hint of moonlight. As the dust cloud clears from the rectangular hole, however, I get none of that.

Smoke scorches my throat. The haze is so thick I can't tell if it's night or day.

As my eyes adjust, the source of the smoke comes into view and leaves me breathless. To the West, where there once stood a great forest, now lies blackened ground.

Someone whimpers behind me. I turn to see Sheffa staring outside, her bottom lip quivering as devastation waters her eyes.

I crouch in the opening for a long while, unable to force myself out. The Watchers have burned out all the hiding places for our remaining rebels, leaving only heaps of ash where there once stood trees.

Blue smoke forms a veil over the scorched earth like low-hanging clouds, with ash drifting like snowflakes through the air. A bright orange glow lights up the western horizon, where a great fire consumes the creations of my Fori cousins.

I place a comforting hand on Sheffa's shoulder, but she shrugs it away. Her look of despair hardens to anger. "They's gonna pay for this," she says through clenched teeth. "Every. Last. One of 'em." Then she meets my stare. "I's coming with you."

I nod and try to disguise my relief. We've already wasted enough time in here, so I peek out through the rectangular hole and up the pyramid.

Two Watchers sit at the apex in place of the Capstone, their stares set Eastward, and they don't so much as twitch their necks to look away. The heavy haze is too thick for us to see what they're looking at from here, so I shift my gaze to the ground, where a surprise awaits me.

We must have been in this pyramid for quite some time, because there's not a single body in sight. I'd believe we arrived in a different timeline if not for the massive pile of weapons barricading the foot of the moat bridge. But the absence of a sand drift around them tells me they've not been sitting there long. The pile blocks access to the bridge, with all the pointy ends aimed outward like a steal porcupine lying on its side, its belly facing us. If we're careful we should be able to slip around it without getting nicked.

Crimson light breaks through the clouds overhead and glints off sharp steel. When I look up, a scarlet disk burns through the haze to tell me it's midday. The black smoke up there is so thick I'd mistaken it for night sky.

Clever Watchers. Not only does burning the forest eradicate Fori hiding places, it also cuts them off from their energy source. They must risk rising above the smoke for sunlight, where there no doubt waits a swarm of Watchers. But this may actually work in our favor. If we can't see up, that means they can't see down. Which means Deka's boats have a better chance of slipping away.

"We'll arm ourselves from the pile," I tell Sheffa, and it takes great effort to keep the quiver from my voice. "Pick something sharp and light."

"What if they don't follow?" Marlok says from behind.

"What if a meteor falls 'n smacks you on that thick head of yours?" snaps Sheffa. "Look around, you ape. Ain't nothin' about this is ideal. We ain't good in *any* way. All we got is a bit a hope that Nya's plan works. It ain't exactly safe what we's gotta do out there, is it?"

I'm inclined to interject, to settle Sheffa and provide hope for our *sapien* allies, but I can't. Any words of assurance would be lies. Everyone here knows that. Marlok just has to accept his weight of the risk, and I see he's struggling with this. The fight is out of him. It's the same with Deka. Like the smoldering forest outside, the fire in his eyes has turned to ash.

I take Deka's hand. "You can do this. You've gotten through worse."

He frowns at me in a manner that suggests it is not doubt in himself, nor in his mission, that gives him pause. To me it seems like he's wondering if it's actually worth it. He's seen something on his return that robbed him of hope. He needs to see his colony to spark his fire once more.

"Deka..."

"Just lead them away," he says with an irritated shake of his head. "We'll meet you at the caverns."

Something is plaguing him, and I will find out what once we've reunited at his colony.

I look to Sheffa and say, "Come on."

NYA

I climb out onto the pyramid's West face and slide down the twenty levels toward the ground. The patter of Sheffa's feet on stone tells me she's right behind me.

We're halfway to the ground when sniffling and whining stop me. I turn back to see Sheffa covering her mouth, her watery eyes fixed on the scorched earth between here and the southern horizon.

I climb back up and place a hand on each of her knees. "You'll get your revenge," I tell her in as low a voice I can manage. Nodding up the pyramid, to the distracted Watcher lookouts, I force a smile and say, "It starts with them two up there."

Sheffa looks back up the pyramid and narrows her eyes. Like so many of us, she has seen that our immortal masters can be killed. She has felt their warm blood on her skin and heard the last breaths of a good many.

When she turns back to me, the despair in her eyes has been replaced with fierce determination. She slides past me and leads the way down the remaining levels.

From the bottom step I confirm that there really are no bodies in sight. Not even a single bone or strand of hair remains to tell of the carnage that had wrought so much blood upon this sacred ground.

At least there'll soon be two.

Sheffa and I run side by side across the moat bridge. Though I try to make my footfalls as light as possible, each step sounds like a deafening slap. Luckily my frequent shoulder checks assure me that the Watchers' focus remain East.

We round the pile of weapons at the bridgehead and begin pilfering the best pieces while facing the pyramid. From here, the most awe-inspiring sight seizes my attention.

A huge crater sinks the pyramid's west face. Over the center is where I'd been standing when the Aeri attacked us, right before I went on my rampage of blasting away blocks. But there's no way I did all that damage in such a short time. My punching spree must have weakened the structure through to the inner passageways, which eventually collapsed. But still...

"You went full *Berserk*," Sheffa says. She too admires the damage from behind the weapon pile.

I hardly remember my rampage at all, and I certainly didn't have much control over it once I got going. If the Butcher hadn't stopped me I'd have brought the whole pyramid down. I'd tapped into a power that now gives me goosebumps, and it emboldens me for what I must do next.

The pile of weapons is such a hideous mess of deathly devices that just putting a hand near risks cutting a finger off. It takes great dexterity to grab hold of a platinum spear shaft without gashing myself on a razor-sharp blade, and even more to pull the weapon free of the pile without causing a clamor.

I feel the spear's frequency and determine it's a good match for my fighting vibration. I'm whirling it around to test its balance when something in Sheffa's hand catches my eye.

My hands go numb and the weapon falls from my grip, and it's only luck that keeps the blade from chopping off my toes.

I wrench the round plate from Sheffa's grasp and hug it to my chest. The unblemished shield had belonged to Jaleera, my Watcher guardian who had defended me until her dying breath, and then to her successor, Jinny, the fiercest Fori to have ever lived. This shield had drawn more blows meant for me than I dare to count. I probably owe this object my life as much as anything that still exists.

Tears burn my eyes and roll down my cheeks. I hug the shield tight against my chest to stifle my sobs, yet they still sound unbearably loud.

Jinny, I cannot tell you how sorry I am.

A horn shakes up the haze.

I jump with such fright that my skin feels like it may burst from my bones.

Up the pyramid, the two Watcher lookouts bounce down the steep face toward us at remarkable speed.

I hand Sheffa the shield and recover my spear. Despite the speed of the Watchers' descent, they still have a long way to go. We must let them think they have a chance to catch us, so I search for another weapon to give them time.

Sheffa glares up at the approaching Watchers. She raises a short sword and screams, "You'll never defeat us rebellers!"

I raise my spear to back up her claim, but stop midway.

Sheffa notices me giving her a curious look and says, "What?"

"It's *rebels*," I say.

She frowns at me with deep confusion.

"It's not *rebellers*," I explain. "We're *rebels*."

Sheffa turns to square off with me and points her sword at the Watchers scrambling down the pyramid. They're still a way off, so we need to make a good show of it.

"Is you really tryin' to fix my speakin' *now*," Sheffa says in disbelief.

At the pyramid corner to our left, six Watchers race from the north side and sprint toward the moat bridge.

My leg muscles tighten like harp strings, and if not for the pyramid's gravitational Anomaly I'd have sprung into flight already. "Well," I tell Sheffa, "we may not get another chance."

My next thought is, *How did Deka miss those?* Odd, because the real question should be, *How did he know those other two were up top in the first place?*

Sheffa gasps and breaks into a westward sprint, and I'm hot on her heels.

The Watchers are remarkably fast runners. The only time I'd ever seen them run had been over this very ground, when they were retreating from the arrival of my Entropath sisters. But even their frightened state during the great battle hadn't seen them run this fast.

The Watchers have been training in the Anomaly, I conclude. *They've been expecting another fight here.*

I sprint hard over barren ground toward the scorched forest. My legs lighten with each footfall away from the pyramid until my knees spring me higher with each step. As I near the Anomaly border my feet bounce off the ground. My wings sense the change and instinctively flutter, eager to take flight.

Clinking grows loud behind us. I risk a look behind to see tailored steel plates covering every bit of Watcher skin except at their reptilian eyes.

Their armor gets my heart thumping. Sheffa doesn't stand a chance at landing a lethal blow with her sword, so it'll be me against all six.

I dig my feet in and race faster, and ten more paces has my feet kicking freely through the air. Wind whips my hair as I rise into the sky. When I look back I see Sheffa not far behind me, and the Watchers right behind her!

I fall back to join her and match her speed. Our only chance to beat them is together, and, with their armor, this will be a monumental task.

CHAPTER 7
NYA

I'm not sure if it's fear giving us unnatural speed, or the heavy armor slowing down our Watcher predators, but they fall farther behind by the heartbeat.

This isn't good. I slow my speed to allow them to close some of the distance. Sheffa notices and falls back to join me.

Smoke chokes me and forces me into a coughing fit, but I dare not rise into clear skies. Who knows how many more Watchers roam above.

When our six pursuers close half the distance between us, we increase our speed slightly to maintain a buffer. A bad move, apparently. Watchers aren't known for abandoning their targets, so it's a surprise when half of them peel back toward the pyramid.

A knot twists my belly. By my estimation, Deka and the others may be just arriving at the pyramid base, assuming the lookouts haven't given them any trouble.

"We have to make a stand," I tell Sheffa.

Worry floods her eyes. But all it takes is one look down upon the heaps of ash to harden her expression. She tightens the shield straps around her forearm with quick, jerking movements, determination growing fierce in her eyes once again.

I explain to her what I want her to do, and though I see she thinks my idea is pure madness, she simply nods and turns her shield toward the enemy as instructed. I hover behind her as she lifts her knees to her chest and ducks her head to make herself as small as possible behind the shield. I hold my spear shaft horizontally, gripping the middle so that an even amount sticks out to my left and right.

The Watchers reach us in a few quick heartbeats. Their arrowhead of three makes straight for Sheffa's shield, just as I'd hoped, so I prepare to swipe them with my spear in their passing.

The Alpha at center lines her spear with the shield's left side, which will spin Sheffa enough to expose her to the Watcher at her right wing. A fine plan if it were any other shield.

The spear tip gets not within three feet before it swerves hard left, deflected by the shield's diamagnetic field.

The Alpha glides past Sheffa's left side and into the tip of my waiting spear. I make a solid connection with her shoulder plate, but the vibration I shoot through bounces right back up my arms. I fumble my spear but manage to recover it as the Alpha glides on by in shock.

The spear shakes fiercely in my hands as I make a startling realization, one I'd not factored in when I planned to square off with them. Her armor... it's made of titanium.

I can't dust titanium!

I whirl around as the next Watcher swoops past Sheffa. I

swing wide and smack the side of her helmet with a vibration that should jar her real good.

It works. Sure, she's still in one piece as she tumbles toward the ground, her wings working instinctively to keep her from crashing below, but she buzzes aimlessly in a stupor, her head snapping all around as she tries to orient herself.

The Watcher I'd not yet made contact with circles Sheffa, who spins to remain facing her with her raised shield, which successfully deflects every spear jab.

Before intervening I check for the Alpha, and turn in time to see a flash of steel swipe at my head. I bat it away, but she's quick with a follow-up. *Ting... ting-ting... ting.* I block each swipe with a satisfying clatter, and though I take each opportunity to send through a different vibration to loosen her hold, her grip remains firm.

I release my spear and let it fall to the ground. The Watcher watches it briefly, allowing me all the time I need to reach out and grab her spear shaft. We lock eyes as she pulls me in close. She wrenches on her spear while I send a high frequency rattling through its shaft. She shudders like with an electric shock, armor rattling loud, and yet, despite her convulsions, the determination in her eyes remains hard and her grip tight.

I let go with one hand and jab at her face. She jerks her head back, but not far enough to avoid the two fingers I've aimed at her eyes. Her blood-curdling scream is enough to jar my spine into convulsions.

She releases the spear with one hand to cover her eyes, but I don't try to yank the weapon free. Instead I heave the spear left, which spins her enough for me to latch onto her back. Her wings flare against my chest, but it's no use. We fall.

Her heavy armor ensures she drops belly first. Her two large wings flex futilely, confined within my hold, right up until I release her twenty feet from the ground.

My buzzing wings halt my plummet. The Watcher's might have done the same if not for the burden of her titanium armor. Instead she hits the ground in an explosion of ash.

As the black cloud clears to reveal the Watcher's face-down body, I give thanks to Leeta. That's the second time the fire-diving Elder's daring technique has saved my life.

In the sky above, both remaining Watchers circle Sheffa while taking jabs at her with their spears. They've singled her out as the easier target in hopes of eliminating one of us to flip the odds. She moves her shield to deny them, but I see by her frazzled eyes she's struggling to contain her panic. Luckily, when I speed up to her rescue, she has enough sense to not announce my approach with a stare.

Instead, Sheffa flies backwards away from me. The Watchers follow her with their backs to my advance, but Sheffa can't fly in reverse fast enough, and one eventually loops behind her. She arrives behind Sheffa as I come up behind her partner, who in turn spins and shoves her spear out to greet me.

I slap it away and crash into her. My shoulder connects with her breast plate, and the impact rattles my vision. As the Watcher spins to right herself, I give her helmet a smack with my palm, which rings like a bell and sends her falling stiffly toward the ground, unconscious.

Seeing me as the greater threat, her partner rises above

Sheffa and dives down to crash into me. This move takes me completely by surprise. She slugs me in the belly with an uppercut, right to my heart, and for a second all I see is spots.

I fight through the suffocating pain and grab her gold collar, but she jabs me in the ribs to create space between us. The hit blows the wind from me and drops me a few feet, until I grab her ankle. I squeeze her platinum shin guard with both hands and freeze my wings, and my weight added to the burden of her armor are too much for her.

We fall, but this descent is much slower than my previous success at this. That is, until Sheffa lands on her back. The three of us plummet toward the ground, with Sheffa on top and me underneath. I'm barely able to escape from under the tangle before we hit.

I kick off the Watcher to separate and crash into a heap of ash. A clatter announces the arrival of my armored enemy nearby. A cloud of soot blinds me, but swishing ash and squeaking metal joints suggest the fight is not yet over.

Loud grunts and rattling metal lure me deeper into the ash bloom. It's a short trudge to the scuffle, but the ash clogging my throat and the sight of Sheffa straddling the Watcher leave me breathless.

She swings a broken antler down at the Watcher's face, pumping out a squirt of black blood with each strike. Sheffa huffs and gasps with each rabid stab, of which there are many, but her opponent's outstretched arms suggests she's already dead.

"Sheffa, that's enough."

She ignores me and continues her downward swinging. The squishing blows churn my belly, so I grab Sheffa under the shoulders and haul her away, taking great care to avoid stealing a look at the Watcher's face.

Sheffa thrashes in my hold. I lose my footing and fall with her to the ground. We land on a mat of ash, but Sheffa doesn't try to get up. Her body relaxes and her angered heaving softens into sobs. I hug her from behind as she cries in the remains of the trees she'd helped nurture from birth.

I'm not sure how long we lie like this, but it feels like too long. When I feel a respectful amount of time has passed, I peel myself away from her and stand. "Come on. We have to get to the *sapien* caves."

Sheffa crawls to her knees and stands. She's remarkably composed and requires only a quick pat down to dust the ash from her body, and a wipe of her nose to clear the snot from her sobbing.

"You good?" I say.

She nods, and when I fly up into the sky she is right behind me. We hover where we can see the outline of the three pyramids through the haze.

"Think the others got away?" Sheffa asks.

"We'll find out when we get to their caverns."

Sheffa notices the strain in my voice. She gives me a look over and her eyes flash wide in alarm. "You're hurt!"

She's right. A slit between my ribs reveals the blow to my chest had been with a knife. Blood streams from the wound, carving a trail down my soot-smeared belly. The more attention I pay to it, the worse it burns. But it could be worse. The first blow had found my navel, directly over my heart, and had been delivered by only a fist.

"I'm fine," I say, which is true. A bit of sunlight will have me completely healed in a few days. "We need to—"

A shiver rolls up and down my spine. I know this feeling too well to mistake it for anything else, and when I look back toward the pyramids, my fear is confirmed by the sight of three Watchers speeding toward us.

I feel the heat of their glares. This trio who'd abandoned the pursuit earlier won't let the deaths of their warrior kin go unchecked.

Sheffa's wings buzz excitedly as she holds Jaleera's shield in front. "We gonna fight 'em?"

"No. Let's lead them on a chase."

And so continues our Westward flight. All I can do is hope Deka and the others make it to their boats.

Assuming their boats are still there.

CHAPTER 8

DEKA

The lookouts on the pyramid are supremely interested in Nya's escape with Sheffa. The two Watchers have made their way back to the apex, where they watch the westward escape with intense fascination. Neither notices us crouched on the pyramid's south side to their left. Their captivation had allowed our group of fifteen to slip out of the exit right under their noses and make our way to the adjacent side.

I myself had been unable to look away when the first group caught up to Nya. From here they looked like quarreling flies. Nya and Sheffa appeared as black dots, which I'd have mistaken for drifting debris if not for red sunlight glinting off the Watchers' armor for reference. The brief clash just ended with the remaining three falling to the ground together.

I watch the black ground for movement. Smoke burns my eyes, but I dare not blink.

Is Nya hurt? Killed?

The image of her falling to her death makes me sick. What was the last thing I said to her? Something about there being only two Watchers to worry about. How could I have been so wrong?

Wait, that's not at all what I should be asking. '*Why had I been so sure?*' is the better question.

Two figures rise into the sky over where Nya had fallen, and my hope rises with them. My eyes water from the smoke, so I rub them to ensure they are not deceiving me.

A horn blast from above confirms my suspicion: the Watchers still have some fighting to do.

The second group of three are almost back at the pyramids when the horn sends them spinning around toward the two *rebellers*, as Sheffa had called themselves. The two black dots in the distance fly away, leading the three Watchers toward the western horizon.

I watch the chase for as far as the smoke screen allows.

"*Deka!*" hisses Mora. She's paused at the east corner of the third level. Everyone else is crouched on the ground, leaning close to the stone, waiting to cross the open toward the river. To our boats.

My belly twists with worry. What had made me so sure the boats are still there? The same thing that convinced me only two Watchers guarded the pyramid.

Just ask Nya and Sheffa how right I was on that one.

It's so strange. When I was inside the pyramid I'd been so certain. I didn't even question it. Where had that confidence come from? I'd been right about the two lookouts above, sure, but I'd missed the six patrolling the base. So far I'm two-for-eight. Not good odds, but at this point we have no choice.

Mora grabs my wrist to pull me away. I do not resist, because a quick look at the pyramid's west side reminds me that Nya can take care of herself.

I'll never forget the sight for as long I live. My war party and I were climbing the pyramid's East face during the battle, hoping to avoid detection from the Watchers until we gained the high ground, when the whole pyramid started shaking. This jarring was different than the rumbles of the gateway's energy stream. When we'd made our way around to the West side to join the fight, the sight of Nya obliterating chunks of stone with her bare hands had left me awe-struck. She'd have brought down the whole pyramid if not for a four-armed Watcher pulling her away. That beast would have strangled Nya to death if Marlok hadn't put an arrow through its eye.

Mora and I scoot along the bottom level of the south side, toward the East. Our party of thirteen awaits us on the ground. They huddle tight against the eastern base, with Marlok standing back and squinting toward the apex to keep an eye on the lookouts, who are still keeping a close watch to the West. It's open ground between here and the river, but it's our only chance.

Everyone looks to me expectantly. Though, it's not for direction. I'm suddenly aware that I've been in a daze and they're making sure I am ready to do this, because I'm the one who might screw it up.

Nya's daring Westward flight is all the boost I need. I harden my expression and nod for my party to proceed.

Marlok leads us into the open. Mora and Huxley are right behind him, with a few Ori in tow, then it's a Fori and myself, with a few Fori behind me.

As we string out in single file toward the river, not one of us can resist looking over our shoulders at the lookouts up top, even though we end up slamming into each other or stumbling over stones when we do.

Running across open ground leaves me feeling sorely exposed. My whole body tenses, for a spear launched from the apex could skewer a good few of us with a single shot. I'm inclined to suggest we spread into an extended line, but even my breathing sounds too loud, so I dare not risk a word.

Marlok reaches the riverbank first and drops to a knee. The waterline sits below, out of sight from me but visible to him, so when he lowers his head I'm not sure if it's in despair or relief, or to simply catch his breath.

I sprint across the remaining distance to see for myself. Though it was I who had claimed our boats are still here, I am beyond relieved when I see two mounds on the otherwise smooth riverbank.

A few hands pat my back and squeeze my shoulders in praise, and I manage a smile. But this credit belongs to our Ori paddlers, who'd had the foresight to bury our boats when we'd arrived for the epic battle however long ago.

The Ori dig up our boats and slide them into the river. I rush down into knee-deep water and grab the gunwale of my plastic vessel to steady it, then invite the Ori to board. Marlok does the same for his boat and passengers.

The faces of those who occupy our boats are a much different mix than those who'd arrived with us. Mora's gang makes up only half of my crew, with the rest lost in battle.

Sorrow grips my heart. *How many more will be lost before this war is done?*

"Come on," Mora hisses, her nervous gaze locked on the towering pyramid behind me. "Get in. Hurry."

I push the boat into waist-deep water and then jump in. I brace myself between both gunwales as the current pushes us into a northward spin.

The Ori get swiftly to work with the paddles to set us straight. Mora had made a claim back in the forest, just after my dear friend Mali's death, that her Ori are fair paddlers. I'd call them exceptional. Though they are small in stature, they are stubborn at heart. They'd fought the river current tirelessly to get us to the great battle here, and when we arrived, not a single one had stopped to shake her arms loose or catch her breath. They'd rushed straight toward their fallen cousins to render aid and fight off the scavengers while us humans began climbing the backside of the pyramid.

I sit back into the stern with the tiller on my lap and relax. The Ori in our boat are keen to paddle despite the powerful current pushing us toward the sea, and as Marlok's boat creeps up beside us, I notice his Ori paddlers giving Mora's gang challenging looks.

It's enough to make me smile. Even with all the darkness that battle has left in us, these wonderful creatures can still manage some lighthearted fun.

Floating down the Nile, unarmed and exposed, I find myself able to rest for the first time in weeks. Our fate here is out of my control, so I sink back and let the current sweep us away. My mind drifts elsewhere, toward a future beyond our boat's shifting bow. When we reach the forest I'll visit Mali's grave. We'll hold a proper funeral, and—

Wait. The forest, it's... it's all burned! How will we find Mali's burial place?

I take a deep breath to calm myself. Perhaps the Ori can distinguish geographic features without the trees. They are very in tune with the land, after all. But it's not the dead I should be worrying about.

My belly winds into knots as I think of our next destination. Have the Watchers traced the origins of their attackers at the pyramids back to our caverns? Did our interference in the battle stoke their fury and drive them in force to flush out every last one of us? My people may be fighting for their lives at this very moment.

I grab a paddle to add my strength to the race. The Ori speed up their strokes to match my pace, but it's not long before smoke scorches my lungs and my arms shake with fatigue.

My eyes itch, yet I dare not close them for longer than necessary. Instead I keep my stare locked on the river ahead. Every wide point in the bank has me sitting up straighter for a better view. The open sea seems as if it could be right out there beyond the veil. So close, yet ever moving away.

This seems to be a race without a finish line, so we ease off on the paddling to save our strength. Marlok's boat eventually overtakes us and assumes the lead. We cruise a long while in silence, until a peculiar noise rises from a distance.

Mora shoots to her feet and tries to see over the East bank. Us paddlers stop and listen intently. The noise grows steadily louder and is one I've heard before, back during the battle. They are the cries of wounded Fori.

My heart quivers. The fighting to the East is closer than I'd assumed. I was sure they were directly East of the Great Pyramid, and we've already come a good distance North on the Nile. But how had I been so sure of something I could not see?

Marlok points to a stand of trees on the East bank that somehow survived the burning. I nod and push the tiller left, which swings our bow rightward toward the bank. My Ori paddle us across the current until our keel hits sand.

I hop out and drag my boat up beside Marlok's. He's already crawling on his belly into the trees, and my passengers are quick to join him. I make sure our boat is clear of the waterline so it doesn't get swept away, and then scramble to join both crews. When I reach the crest of the bank, where everyone has gathered within the shrubs, I wish I'd have stayed with the boats.

All I see is smoky blue haze, but it carries a noise that sends a shiver through my soul. The screechy, desperate squeals tell us many Fori are suffering tremendously somewhere out there.

Mora trembles beside me. Her eyes are rife with terror, yet her jaw is clenched so tight I swear I hear her teeth crack.

"This is Hell," says Marlok. His breath shudders through his nose while his eyes rattle side to side.

"What are we gonna do?" asks an Ori.

"We gotta save 'em," Huxley says.

"It's a trap," I say. The words leave my mouth without thought, but I know they are true. Those wailing Fori are bait. "There are Watchers nearby."

"Just like the two lone guards back there?" says Huxley, clearly upset I've jeopardized Nya with my miscalculation.

"We move on," says Mora. I'm glad it's her who says it, for it's she who holds most sway over this group.

We slink back to the boats and are pushing them into the river when Marlok stops suddenly. Something farther down the bank has seized his attention. He sloshes from the water holding a paddle and stomps toward a cluster of shrubs a bit farther downriver from ours.

That's when I spot a few unfamiliar Fori. Unlike their unseen sisters crying through the smoke, these tree tenders are silent. They lie prone upon the hillcrest, cradling scavenged weapons of platinum and gold, waiting to pounce on the Watchers should they come check on their trap.

Of those four Fori, there is one I do recognize. In fact, I could never forget her. She is the one who murdered Mali.

The Fori ambushers are so distracted by the ghastly disturbance they fail to notice Marlok until he's within swinging distance.

Mali's killer turns just in time to take Marlok's paddle off the cheek. The smack is so loud it makes my own face burn in response. As she rolls down into the river, her three sisters tackle Marlok onto his back, and together they all roll down into the water in a ball of flailing limbs.

Despite the three Fori trying to restrain him, Marlok manages to wade over to his dazed target and forces her head under water. Her thrashing and splashing plucks at my nerves. So loud.

Mora and her Ori rush into the water to break up the fray. I pick up a dropped spear and scan the sky for Watchers, but I'm too late.

On the hillcrest above stands a dozen of those two-winged devils, their hair and skin smeared black with soot. Four of them aim bows at the wrestling match below while their comrades cradle their spears and watch the quarrel in amusement.

One of the Fori on Marlok notices our spectators and freezes. She slides off his back and sinks to her neck in shock.

"Marlok," I say.

He shoots me an angry glare, to scold me for not helping him drown Mali's killer, but when he notices the Watchers his hot rage freezes to fear.

"Drop your weapons," says the Watcher Lieutenant at center.

Whoever is armed among us exchange frazzled looks.

An archer to the Lieutenant's left opens her mouth to release the cries of a dozen wounded Fori.

My companions drop their weapons and cover their ears. I drop my spear to the ground.

"Walk up to us one at a time," orders the Lieutenant.

Marlok releases Mali's killer and raises his hands. She tries to stand clumsily in the river while choking and spitting up water, and Marlok's slight smirk suggests he enjoys this combination of noises. I can't deny that I take a measure of pleasure in it as well.

Marlok pushes past me to begin his climb up the bank, but then stumbles over the wet rocks. When he regains his footing and rises, it's with my dropped spear in hand.

I step aside as he stands tall and heaves it back to launch. He's mid-swing when an arrow punches through his wrist to stop his arm dead.

The platinum spear clatters off the rocks as Marlok keels over, holding his arm in pain. A low growl and heavy shiver suggest it takes all his strength to contain his scream.

"Anyone else want to try their luck?" the Lieutenant asks.

The archer who'd shot Marlok already has another arrow nocked and drawn, ready for another hero to reveal himself.

Mora instinctively raises her hands in surrender. Everyone else, myself included, are quick to follow.

"We give up," the Ori leader says.

CHAPTER 9
NYA

"They's catchin' up to us," Sheffa says from above me. "We gotta hurry."

We fly high above the ground, where the smoke is still thick enough to choke me. An orange glow ahead reveals where flames pump out black plumes of caustic clouds. Soot plasters my sweaty skin and coats my lungs, but I can't muster the energy to rise above it.

If the Watchers had ditched their armor they'd have caught us by now. I'm actually amazed they've not done so, which leads me to an empowering conclusion: They're afraid. They believe there are more dust maidens in the area.

My heart flutters with hope. If any of my sisters are around, then we'll have a good chance at taking the fight back to our enemy.

Sheffa drops to join me. "This all you got?"

The lightness in her voice tells me she's playing with me. When she sees my struggle is genuine, her playful expression turns to worry.

"You's hurted bad."

Instinctively I feel my rib for the wound. I jolt at the sting, which acts like a jumpstart to get my wings buzzing faster. But it's only a short burst and is wildly unpleasant.

Sheffa swallows hard and glances nervously over her shoulder. "I'll lead 'em south," she says. "You stay low and head north, to Deka's caves."

I'm quick to shake my head. Sheffa can't face three Watchers on her own. In my condition even I'd have a hard time squaring off with them. "We stay together," I say with a cough. "The wind is blowing from the West. We just have to reach the fires and break through this smoke." A good dose of sunlight will do me wonders.

Sheffa nods enthusiastically, clearly relieved I declined her offer to lure them away. She pats my shoulder and says, "Race ya."

We fly hard Westward. Sheffa rises occasionally to check on our pursuers, and each time she returns to join me, she brings worse news. They are slowly gaining on us. Their endurance will outlast my weakening state.

"We may have to fight again," I say, inviting more smoke down my throat. We're approaching the heart of the wildfire. I can no longer see the glow through the billowing black cloud, but I feel its heat on my face.

I cough furiously and try my hardest to rise above the suffocating smoke, and I do think I'm gaining altitude, but the smoke is too thick to be sure. Here I can't see the sky at all.

And before I know it I'm flying over an orange wall of flames. Hot wind blasts me from below and tousles my hair. When the source of this wind comes into view up ahead, my blood flashes to a boil.

Through the smoke screen, at the border between

burning forest and brown desert, three sets of feathered wings blast smoke Eastward, toward the pyramids. The Aeri hover close to the ground, a good distance below me, to catch a bulk of the smoke before it drifts over the desert behind them.

Blazing rage inflates my fists. As if turning against us at the battle for the pyramids wasn't bad enough, they now suffocate us with smoke and starve us of sunlight.

I angle my wings to dive at the right-most Aeri. She notices me at the last second, and her scream of terror sends a flicker of hesitation through me. But it's only a flicker.

We collide in an explosion of light and sizzling dust. Then my dive ends abruptly when I strike a dune with a muffled boom.

Wild rage springs me swiftly to my feet, where I find myself at the bottom of a crater. A curtain of sand whooshes up and out from the sloped bowl all around.

Sheffa bursts through the wall of black smoke.

"Dust maidens!" wails a remaining Aeri.

Her fear floods my heart with pride. The Aeri beating their wings frantically to escape like prey awakens the predator inside me. My kin are a force to be reckoned with, to the point that Watchers now burden themselves with armor, and the Aeri cry out in fear at our approach. And though Sheffa is no Entropath, the fury in her eyes matches the firestorm burning up the forest she'd helped raise, and I'd think she was one of my own if I didn't know her myself.

The two Aeri veer wide and fly up through the smoke. Sheffa glides between them and loops around to give chase, but a flash of armor emerging through the black curtain forces her down to the dunes.

Here the smoke works to our advantage. The Watchers spot the Aeri just as they disappear through the smoke, and the trio breaks their formation to give chase to our fleeing scumbag cousins.

Sheffa and I watch them vanish through the billowing black curtain. The Aeri are much faster flyers, and in that smoke it should be a good while before the Watchers get close enough to realize their mistake.

Sheffa scrambles up the outer face of the crater and stops on the crest. "We lost 'em," she says, keeping a close eye on the wall of flames pumping smoke Eastward.

My heartbeat drums a savage tune of revenge. Wouldn't I love to chase down those Watchers and make the Aeri watch me dust them.

I'm about to tell Sheffa my plan when I cough up a cloud of soot. It burns my throat and waters my eyes, so Sheffa slides down to pat my back. It actually helps.

"You gotta find a safe place to rest," she says.

"The *sapien* sanctuary should be due North of here." There'll be time to recover there. Right now those caverns seem like the safest place on Earth. The Watcher invasion fifteen years ago had started at the pyramids and spread West. Every wave to arrive since had passed that sanctuary, with Jexa herself leading an attack into its depths at one point, and yet Deka's tribe have endured. They are resilient; they are our nearest and greatest hope.

"You think they got away?" Sheffa asks, looking East as if she might actually glimpse the pyramids through the smoke. "Maybe them lookouts spotted 'em."

Part of me wants to smack her. Why even suggest that? You shouldn't speak unwanted possibilities into this mysterious Universe. That's what Mora had told us after we ended up in the Mistress's sanctuary within the pyramid, and right now I'd rather not risk sending bad luck Deka's way.

The thought of his plight tempers my rage. Fear rises in its place, and my surging muscles slacken. I wobble on my feet, so my wings lift me from them. I watch the smoke cloud anxiously, fearful of a Watcher return as reality slams me in the gut. I was going to chase them in anger. *What was I thinking?* That's something I'll have to keep in check, or I risk leading more cousins to their deaths.

"Let's go," I say. "We'll be exposed in the clear sky, so we'll have to keep a sharp lookout from here on."

Sheffa nods and flies upward. I rise with her, and she watches me warily as I cover the wound in my chest. Her concern for me is so great she doesn't notice a bird approach until it lands on her shoulder. If that ever happened to me I'd go Berserk. Sheffa simply looks left to meet the falcon's gaze, and finds its beak nearly touching her nose.

"Oh, hello," Sheffa says. "Where'd you come from?"

I watch this interaction curiously. It must be a Fori thing.

The brown falcon opens its beak to release a series of clicks and creaks. These noises mean something to Sheffa, because her eyes open wide in alarm. Her jaw goes slack and her bottom lip quivers.

"What is it?" I say.

Sheffa gives me a look of despair. "He says the *sapiens* got taken prisoner by the Watchers. They's takin' 'em back to the pyramids."

A lump swells in my throat. "Ask him how many Watchers are around."

The falcon clicks its beak a few times while cocking his head North.

"Ten thousand," Sheffa says in awe. This news drags her to the ground and drives her to her knees.

My heart grows so heavy I sink to the ground beside her and collapse onto my side. My face rests on hot sand, which invades my lungs with each inhale, so I roll onto my back.

Sheffa doesn't stay down for long. She paces around, rubbing her head in distress and muttering at the ground.

"Ten thousand?" Panic rises in her voice. "We gotta get to the *sapien* colony so we can hide!"

That's a terrible idea. The last time those *sapiens* heard from Deka and his tribesfolk, they'd left the safety of their home at my urging. If I return without them, they'll assume I led them to their deaths. And they'd be right. I'd really been counting on the Nixies to usher them there before our arrival.

"We can't go there without Deka," I say. It was a stupid plan to begin with.

"Then... where?"

The falcon squeaks and clicks, this time nodding Southward.

Sheffa translates for me. "He says South is the only way for us. He knows where to find them other humans, the ones the pyramid witch told us about—the civilized ones."

I sit up and give the falcon a scrutinizing look. "How does he know such things? For all we know he's a Watcher spy sent to lead us into a trap."

Sheffa joins me in giving him an interrogating look.

A few squeaks and squeals, accompanied by some hard side-to-side shaking of the falcon's head, has Sheffa nodding in understanding.

"His name is Horus," she says. Apparently knowing it has a name should make us feel better, and it seems to work for Sheffa. "When the Watchers caught Deka, the Mistress of the Pyramid sent him to guide us."

I don't like the sound of this. We're expected to fly South to the lands of this mighty civilization, to warn them of an attack from beings that look just like us. If the greeting I received from my first two contacts with Deka's tribe is any indication of how this species reacts to our appearance, then entering their domain will spell certain death for us. If they're capable of fending off the Watcher invasion for so long like the Mistress claimed, they'll find little trouble stopping Sheffa and me. If the Watchers have dared not trespass there, then we'd best rethink our mission there as well. After all, our gateway to recruiting them had been Deka's presence.

Oh, Deka! My heart feels like it's being ripped in half. I pray they don't kill him. Though, if what the falcon says is true, the Watchers had taken him alive. That means they have good use for him.

I look to the falcon. "Is there any way we can free them?"

Horus rocks his head side to side.

"No," Sheffa says. "They's in Watcher hands now. But don't you worry, the Watchers need 'em alive for something big."

I tuck my hands under my armpits to hide my trembling. Something big? No doubt it has something to do with flooding this planet with more Watcher legions from distant galaxies.

Horus squeaks and bobs his head up and down urgently.

"He says we gotta hurry," Sheffa says. "Ain't much time."

My wings buzz and lift me to my feet. Ashes have clotted my wound, but when I try to wipe them away the sticky clump smears across my skin.

Sheffa and Horus both examine my wound with unblinking eyes.

"Show us the way," I tell Horus. Then I step close and lean in to jab a threatening finger at him. "And if you even *think* about betraying us, I'll crush your bones to dust. *One. At. A. Time.*"

Horus screeches in my face. Then he flaps his brown feathered wings to take flight, rising high into the sky. Feathered wings like those of our Aeri cousins. Traitors' wings.

High into the open sky he rises. That sky which belongs to ten thousand Watchers or more. This Southern journey is already off to a bad start, I can feel it in my bones. But lacking a better plan, I dare not waste a second more.

CHAPTER 10
DEKA

When I was a child, my mother often told me about the Great Pyramid of Giza. With her words she painted a world where gods shaped our ancestors into intelligent beings, passing on the knowledge they used to build wonders that withstood the ages—even outlasting the industrial civilizations that followed.

Having lived my entire life within the confines of a cave, the belief in structures of such grand design made me question my mother's sanity. How could she trust in the existence of such an impossible monument without first seeing it?

When we arrived to join the battle at the pyramid, their majesty had been lost on me. There was so much killing happening on and around it. Fighters fell from the sky like giant clumps of rain, any one of whom could have been Nya. I was worried sick, and never had I moved so fast in my life as I did when charging up from the Nile.

My return to the pyramid on this day is much, much slower. Desert sand burns my feet as I shuffle through the midday heat. We've been walking through hot smoke for so long that my legs feel like sacks of rocks. Marlok walks before me, staggering side to side as if he may collapse either way. I'll probably beat him to it.

Despite the smoke screen blocking out the sun, its heat torments me. Each breath I take draws more ash than air. Soot sticks to my skin in clumps. Every time I wipe it off it sloughs away like burnt skin and unsettles me, so I resign myself to staying dirty.

With several dozen Watchers hovering overhead, and open ground in every direction, the thought of escape only crosses my mind in the context that it would offer a quick death. I'd not get five steps away from this line before they brought me down, so I'll exercise that option only when I've had enough of walking through this hellish wasteland. Besides, it could be worse.

Wails of despair rise behind me. They come from the Fori who'd had their wings clipped off by our captors. One of them is Hadria, the Fori who'd killed Mali to avenge the deer that Mali had killed. When they cleaved off her wings shortly after our capture, Hadria's screams of agony did not bring me the satisfaction I'd craved. Instead, I shed a tear for her. If an afterlife exists for my people, I'm sure Mali will have some words about that should we ever meet again.

When the three pyramids take shape through the smoky haze ahead, it's almost a relief. This was the place we'd been desperate to escape, but all I want now is to collapse, and it's clear our destination has come within reach.

The remainder of the walk gives me a new appreciation for the grandeur of the pyramid complex. Its size makes it appear so close, yet it's still another long while of trudging through the desert before we reach it.

It seems like forever ago that we watched Nya lead the Watchers on a chase. At the time I could not wait to escape the pyramid. The place seethes with dark energy, corrupted by Jexa's touch. It showed me things others could not see, things I wish to forget. But right now my body is more tired than my mind is worried, and so I plod along without fuss.

As we draw nearer, my physical ailments become overshadowed by a new discomfort. The noise that had cluttered my head while inside the pyramid has returned. The pyramid functions like a gigantic transmitter, filling my head with static that grows louder the closer I come to it, so that by the time I reach its base it's near deafening.

Our captors force us into the drained moat that circles the base of the Great Pyramid. A small section of the north side has been barricaded with two piles of pickets to form a holding pit. A small group of Fori await us inside. Our arrival crams the holding space so that most of us bigger folk are forced to stand, which makes for easier observation by the Watchers.

They force Mora and her Ori up the pyramid steps, to the fifth level. Whispers from the Fori around me explain this is because the Ori could tunnel out if they were on the ground. So now they're forced to sit on the stone levels, in full view of our cunning captors.

"What are they going to do with us?" asks Huxley.

I size up the pyramid, wondering the same thing. They kept us alive and brought us here for a reason. Perhaps to help set the Capstone. But Nya seemed to have destroyed it, for it is nowhere in sight. If it were near, there'd be a heavy presence of guards to indicate where. That doesn't seem to be the case.

Four guards watch over our pit—two from the pyramid's bottom level, and two from the moat's outer edge. Here they certainly earn their name. They watch us without breaking their stares or sparing even a blink. It's actually quite impressive how they can focus fully on us without losing interest, even as hours pass by.

I try not to look at them, because each time our gazes meet it's like a cold hand grips my spine and paralyzes me. These creatures have evolved to weaken their prey with a simple look.

Whispers rise around me.

"Our sisters will come for us," says one hopeful Fori.

"Mayhaps," agrees another, but I can tell she doesn't believe it.

More whispers reveal most warriors who survived the battle have gone East to fight over the Capstone. Apparently Nya didn't destroy it after all. Instead, she blew it way out into the desert. A company of free Ori have been creating obstacles, traps and entrenchments, while Fori rebels do dive runs to lead the Watchers away. Our enemy will need all hands on deck if they hope to get the Capstone back here and free their leader.

Many of the Fori end up crying themselves to sleep before nightfall. I'm glad they drift off early, because I've noticed how the Watchers enjoy their misery. Their appetite for despair leaves me to worry over my own fate.

The only Fori still crying when the dusk sky darkens is Hadria. She lies in the fetal position, facing the wall, weeping away with no sign of stopping. Clear fluid leaks from four cauterized slits in her back, where the Watchers had gouged out her wings. One of her sisters sits beside her and tries to console her, but the effort is wasted.

Marlok sits on his haunches, glaring at the crying Fori through a veil of locs. I see he's torn. He wants her to suffer, but her wailing brings none of the satisfaction one might expect of a brother starving for revenge.

When he shifts positions, I see it is more than fantasy that plays tug-of-war inside his heart. The knife concealed in his lap is of Watcher design—wavy inscriptions on the silver blade, and twisting runes around its golden handle. He must have picked it up from the sand during one of his stumbles on the march back. Perhaps his wavering gait had been a ploy all along.

Now he's debating about putting the instrument to use. He glances at the Watchers watching us, keeping an eye out for an opportunity. They don't seem to be losing interest in us anytime soon, so he needs a distraction.

I myself had begged for this opportunity in my darkest hours. I'd even been willing to offer my soul to see Mali's killer suffer. Now that it's here, I see I was a fool. Her misery offers me no comfort. Quite the opposite, really.

This realization brings me more peace than revenge ever could. I want her suffering to ease, and there's only one sure way to see it done.

I reach into Marlok's lap and pull the blade from his hand. He responds with a bewildered look. Something about my demeanor seems to put him at ease though, because he sits back and pulls his knees to his chest.

My fingers curl naturally around the handle, as if it were designed for my grip. I crawl through the cluster of sleeping

Fori toward Hadria, my stare locked between the two charred stumps where her upper wings had been. I envision where her heart should be to ensure a quick and silent end. That's *my* intent. The knife, however, has a mind of its own.

It guides my hand to her lower back. The point angles left of her spine and downward, and suddenly I remember Nya's heart beats from inside her belly. The Watcher blade knows exactly where it needs to go.

My heart pounds with dreadful hesitation. I'm about to cross a line. Sure, I've killed before, but only those who've tried to kill me. This... This is murder.

As if sensing my indecision, the knife edges forward, urging me on. The throb of Hadria's heart beckons the weapon like a magnet, seducing the steely point. My hand holds it with stalwart conviction as images of the ghastly deeds I can achieve with this blade flash bright in my mind.

Sweat trickles down my forehead and stings my eyes. My knife hand shakes, so I place my other hand on her shoulder to steady myself.

Hadria's sobbing stops. A long moment passes.

"Do it," she says.

I grip her shoulder in what is almost an apologetic squeeze. My right hand is at odds with the intentions of my left...

Wait—My *left* hand? Only now do I realize I'm holding the blade with my non-dominant hand.

I glance up at the Watchers watching us. Each holds her spear with her left hand, confirming my suspicion: I am channeling the skill of the weapon's previous owner... and all of her ill-intent that comes with it.

The blade trembles in my hand. It craves to smother itself

in flesh and blood. The energy of its previous owner lives on through it. The longer I hold on and maintain this connection, the more I become her in both thought and desire.

My heart quivers and grows heavy with dread. What will I become if I behave like my enemy? If I slay the defenseless in their weakest moments, how will I be judged? I'd managed to live a life of innocence until recent days, when Nya discovered me outside my home. She brought me to this pyramid like the Valkyries of whom my father had often spoke. I am bound to this ancient gateway. It is where my mortal story ends. If a creator does exist, and I am soon to meet him, I'll not stand in judgment with hands blood-soaked from revenge.

I reach across Hadria and place the knife to her belly. The handle rests side-long against her navel, and when her hand reaches over to cover mine, I slip free and leave the weapon in her grasp.

A stillness falls over the trench. Hadria's breathing changes. She breathes now not in despair, but with purpose. I have used a gift of mine to offer my enemy a gift of their own. I've renounced my revenge to offer another theirs.

The meaning is lost on Marlok. I can tell he wants to throttle me, but under the eyes of the Watchers it will never happen. Still, I don't return to his side. I remain at the far wall nearest Hadria.

I'm just settling down to rest when fear creeps into our trench. To my surprise, this fear does not come from us.

The Watchers on the pyramid stiffen and stand at attention. Something of great interest approaches. One Watcher across the moat notices the reaction of her peers and turns to see what the fuss is about. Whatever it is sends her stepping back toward the edge of our pit, where she barely catches herself from falling. She about-turns stiffly and stares ahead with eyes wide in fright.

Heavy footsteps announce the approach of a giant beast. Over the moat top it first appears as a fountain of black hair, below which comes the meanest face I've ever set eyes on. I've seen this four-armed monstrosity before, when it was squeezing the life out of Nya.

Cold sweat slicks my skin. I thought for sure Marlok's shot had killed the four-armed freak. I'd believe her to be a different creature if not for the arrow still sticking out from her right eye.

The sight makes my belly squirm, and it takes great effort to keep myself from retching.

A Fori notices her and gasps in fright, which sends a ripple of panic through our group. *Butcher*, they call her. And they're just as surprised to see her alive as I am.

The eight-foot Butcher looms over our pit, her lips twisted in revolt as her one good eye sizes us up.

"More," she croaks.

One of our moat guards bows and then races away. The speed at which she obeys her command is unsettling. If our captors fear her so much, then it will be wise for us to as well.

The ledge below the Butcher's feet sags under her weight. A crack stretches down the wall behind Marlok, who hugs his legs and rests his forehead on his knees, no doubt fearing she may recognize him for her assailant. Which may not matter in a second anyway. The outer moat wall will soon collapse and bury him.

A Watcher on the pyramid jolts and points to her right.

The Butcher's stare follows and, by the way she clenches her four fists, suggests some Ori are making a run for it.

Our hulk of a warden breaks into a sprint away from the pyramid.

I slump back and bury my face into my hands.

When the last light of dusk fades, shouts rise from beyond our pit. Many Fori sleep through it, but as the night darkens, the yelling grows louder. Closer.

The Fori stir, curiosity and fear luring them from their dream worlds. A few climb onto each others' shoulders and stack high enough to see over the ledge. Word travels down the wobbly column of heads. They describe a great workforce building a ramp, some two thousand Ori fashioning dirt into a slope. A force far greater than Mora's gang.

Fori whispers speculate they are Jexa's personal slaves. They've lived their entire lives underground, and it was they who tunneled the Capstone here before the great battle. They come out only at night, for darkness is all they know.

Darkness, like the energy venting from this pyramid.

Bile creeps up my throat. These Ori workers have come to help unleash eternal night upon Earth.

CHAPTER II
NYA

The Sun over the equatorial desert does me wonders. The farther South we fly, away from the haze of that caustic smoke, the higher I rise into the sky.

This isn't good.

I drop to glide close to the dunes. Best not to make easy targets for any Watchers to spot us. I've already had too many close calls and am lucky to still carry the message of warning to the Southern Sapiens. The way I'd just dove at those Aeri back there... *What was I thinking?*

I wasn't, clearly. My better sense seems to abandon me in a fight, and that usually ends with the death of my companions. If I'd given chase to those Watchers when they mistook the Aeri for us, I'd have gotten Sheffa killed, breaking my promise to lead not a single more of my kind to the Dark. I'll have to keep that in check, starting right now.

Sheffa flies high in the clear blue sky. Her shield reflects sunlight that's sure to attract attention.

"Hey!" I shout. "Get down here!"

She's too far up to hear me and carries on without noticing.

I'm forced to rise high, which is actually easy with the blazing sun uplifting me. I soar to Sheffa's altitude and fall in behind her, then stick two fingers in my mouth to whistle.

She turns and stops to await my approach.

"We have to stay low," I tell her.

Sheffa squints to scan the surrounding sky. "What for?"

"Watchers."

Sheffa frowns and gives me a quizzical appraisal. "Is you really a feared of a few Watchers, Nya? You saw them's armor. They's scared of us. They'd rather let us fly free than shed them steel shells." She raises a fist high and shouts, "We's dust maidens!"

I snatch her wrist and pull it down. "We ... Are ... *Messengers*. Got it?"

"Sure," Sheffa says, pulling me in close, "but won't our message sound a lot more convincin' with a swarm a Watchers chasin' us?"

I can't deny Sheffa's logic outright. But there's no guarantee the Watchers won't ditch their armor in frustration, especially if there's a good number of them. Even forty dust maidens wouldn't last long in a fight against a thousand Watchers.

If it were only my life on the line, then maybe I'd risk it. But Deka and the others need us to get word to his distant kin. They're counting on us. When the great Southern Sapiens attack, or when they receive the Watcher offensive, that will provide the distraction I need to help Deka escape.

"Let's just stay low," I say.

Sheffa raises her chin and looks down her nose at me. "You askin' me to do this, or you tellin' me?"

"If I asked you, would you listen?"

Sheffa appears on the verge of nodding, that she's wary to defy me, but I see the bloodlust in her eyes. She's tasted victory and hungers for more. It's the same boldness that drove Jinny to call out the Butcher. We all know how that ended.

I point to the wavy sea of dunes rippling below and say, "Get down there, *now*, message-bearer. That's an order."

All traces of defiance evaporate from Sheffa's eyes. She dives down toward the ground and hopefully from sight of Watcher patrols.

I rub my throat, which had tightened at the issuing of that command. I really don't like bossing people around, but at least it's to keep her from harm's way. That's what I'll do from here on—I'll use my authority to keep people safe. Except the humans, of course. This is their planet. Let them bleed for it.

A black speck catches my eye ahead. I squint and see it's racing toward us, growing with each beat of my heart. Its course locks onto me, so I ball my hands into fists.

I must be giving off a real threatening vibe, because the avian incomer swoops down well before reaching me. Two brown wings spread below to reveal it is Horus gliding down toward Sheffa.

A pang of jealousy heats my chest. *I'm* Rebel Marshal. All reports should come to me first.

Wait a second... *What am I saying?* I'm a messenger and nothing more. At best, I issue warnings; at worse, I lead escapes.

Horus falls in alongside Sheffa. Her body stiffens as she listens, then she looks up to me in alarm. When she flies up toward me, I slow my pace so she can catch up.

"Horus sees something," she says. Her voice is low and her eyes frazzled as she surveys the Southern horizon.

I scan the sky all around for danger.

Sheffa grabs my wrist and hauls me down. "Best we stay low so they don't see us first."

"Who? *Sapiens*? Where are they?"

Sheffa drags me low over the dunes. I wrench my arm free and fly higher into the sky. It doesn't take long before a Southern sunrise blinds me. Strange. This platinum glow arches over the dunes ahead, between us and the horizon. The light shines brighter the closer we fly. Before I can suggest a cautious approach we're already there, staring directly at the source of this light. It's certainly no star that casts this silver glow.

We glide gently to rest at the edge of a canyon. Below, in a shadowy valley surrounded by rock walls, sits a glowing ball of light. A small sliver of the rounded top sits above the valley's shadow, and it's this surface that casts the brilliant light that lured me here like a moth to flame. Seriously, I must have fallen into a trance upon spotting it.

When a cloud covers the Sun behind us, the light disappears to reveal the ball is made of steel. The polished silver is so smooth I see our convex reflections on its curved surface.

"What is it?" I say in wonder.

"An Amplifier."

"A what?"

"It reflects radiation from the Sun," Sheffa explains, "or

siphons energy from the planet's core. Or sometimes it draws power from both. We use 'em to bring light to dark places, like when there's a volcanic cloud covering a whole continent, or to grow plants at the poles in winter."

Sheffa casts a sweeping gaze all around us. Her brow furrows in confusion, as she sees what I see—endless desert. Even if the rebellion hadn't halted the Fori's work, it would have taken years for the forest to reach here. And even then, there is no shortage of sunlight to require a boost. Unless...

My mind draws some dark lines, and my hands go clammy with a dreadful realization.

"It's winter at the Southern Pole," I say.

Sheffa's face blanches. "The great *sapien* civilization... they's way down there!"

"That's why the Watchers haven't attacked them. It's six months of darkness."

"And even the six-month day don't give the same energy as up here. The Sun is too weak down there. But now The Watchers is gonna use the Amplifier to attack 'em in their night."

I look to the Sun in the sky over my shoulder. It's so high here, which means we're still close to the Equator despite a long flight.

"How much farther to the pole?" I ask, as if Sheffa would know.

Much to my surprise, she says, "Gimme a sec."

She flies straight up into the sky and extends both arms in front to form a diamond with her fingers. I watch curiously as she squints through her finger diamond and bites her tongue, almost as if she's surveying the horizon.

I fly up to join her, hovering nearby as she passes her

diamond sight over the Southern sky. Then she spreads her arms, her left hand pointing at the Sun overhead, her right hand toward the Southern horizon. This goes on for some time, more time than we have to waste, so I say, "What are you doing?"

"Tryin' to figure out how far the Southern Pole is."

"With your fingers?"

"Of course. How else?"

Sheffa must sense my skeptical stare, because she lowers her hands to address me. "Just like you feelin' the energy of things before you dust 'em, we feel the frequency of the Sun. We gotta know its energy when we start a forest, cos sunlight is the fountain of life. But this planet got a tilt, so the UV strength is always shiftin'. That's why Ko Mirah teached us how to calculate the tilt just by lookin' at the Sun."

"And you can tell how far the Southern Pole is too?"

"Yes!" she says with a bright smile.

"Well? How far is it?"

Her smile flattens. "If I told ya, you'd probably cry."

I don't like the sound of that.

"What do ya wanna do?" Sheffa says.

The fact she is asking me that says it all. The distance is so vast that Sheffa thinks continuing South isn't a good option. Though, right now it seems better than returning North, where certain death awaits us. At least by flying South we'll be moving toward the unknown. In the unknown there is at least hope, however slim. With any luck the Southern Sapiens will have a defense station nearby.

"If these humans are so great," I say, "then their borders will spread wide. We just have to reach their nearest outpost."

"Could be one real close."

"Let's hope so." At least there we'll have a chance, even if it takes me farther away from Deka.

My heart squeezes at the thought of him. All I can do is hope he's made himself useful to the Watchers.

CHAPTER 12
DEKA

The Ori slaves work all through the night without pause. They move about with not a single order shouted, but their feet stamping the ground and their grunts reveal their frantic pace. And, as predicted, they retreat at the first sign of dawn. But a single night is all they need to make incredible progress on their project.

From our pit, the first glimpse of the ramp had appeared after midnight, when it rose to half the height of the pyramid. So tireless did those stout Ori work, that the Watchers never once had to shout for them to pick up the pace. Not a single threat had been uttered, much to the astonishment of my co-captive Fori. Jexa has trained her private workforce well.

"They'll make good allies for a revolt," Marlok notes. He rocks back and forth on his haunches, nursing his wounded wrist, restless.

"You're wrong," says a Fori. "They see Jexa as their god. They'll not betray her for us. In their eyes, she protects them from their true enemy."

"Who's that?" Marlok asks.

"The light," I say.

The Fori nods gravely.

Marlok narrows his eyes, skeptical. His mind is like a book with no blank pages, and any new information must be squeezed in with his current understandings. I've seen many times how he struggles to work in such revelations.

With nothing better to do, the Fori watch the constellations pass over the sky. The three stars of Orion incite vague recollections of times past.

"The planet was called Praxa Niner, I think. All volcanoes and molten rivers."

"Was a moon, is what I thought."

"Yeah, you're right. Its parent planet was a lush paradise. I remember it. Having to look at it all the time made our assignment so much worse. Couldn't tell you how many Ori died trying to rework that soil."

"Exactly. See, we've been through worse. Out there we had an entire planet trying to kill us. Fear not, dear sisters. The others will come for us. I bet they're devising a plan to free us right now as we speak."

Their Fori sisters come at dawn. They join us as prisoners of war, bringing with them the coppery smell of blood and the stench acrid smoke. They're all young, and it's hard to tell who is their senior until the Fori here gather around her.

"How goes the battle?" asks Hadria.

The young elder ignores them, giving all her attention to a wounded Fori cradled on her lap. She appears to be my age, yet the ten black bands around each of her wrists tell me she's their senior by at least double. This resistance is now being led by younglings.

The elder strokes the dying Fori's sweaty hair as she sings a solemn tune. The cryptic words come defiantly despite Watcher threats, and everything about the soothing melody makes me long for Nya. My heart aches for her. I think of all the missed chances in our safe haven to hold her, how I regret them so. If she were here right now, everything would be okay. If she were here, we'd not be trapped in this ditch.

The song is the most beautiful thing I've ever heard, and, despite the suffering surrounding me, I am grateful for this moment. To still be alive is a miracle. Each breath a blessing. Here, in this moment, I live for those who cannot.

A heavy sense of security falls over me like a blanket, and the exotic words of her song manage to calm the chaos of my mind. Oddly enough, I'd take this over hiding away in our caves like a bunch of cowards. We weren't made to live like that. This, right here, is life. Living so close to death, experiencing what no other human has ever felt before, it's as legendary as it is terrifying.

As the tumultuous waters of my mind settle, the elder's foreign words reveal themselves clearly to me.

Tooooo weary to go on,
Here's to you this hero's song.
Death creeps in, steals our grace,
Eternal darkness taunts this place.

Healing hands shall work no more,
Far from here your Spark shall soar.

Noooo sunlight shows the way,
When darkness comes to steal the day.
Mortal hearts be still and done,
One trillion Sparks return to One.

Haaaaa-ah-ahhh-ah-ahh. Haaaaa-ah-ahhh-ah-ahh.

Darkness falls and steals the day,
Shadows rise to chase their prey.
Night forming in their hearts,
Light ends where darkness starts.

You'll shed a tear no more,
No longer live in fear and war.
Dawn rises from the night,
Welcome to eternal light.

Galaxies of swirling gems,
Welcome home the faithful dead.
Stars of races born then gone,
Night forever turns to dawn.

Haaaaa-ah-ahhh-ah-ahh. Haaaaa-ah-ahhh-ah-ahh.

Someone squeezes my shoulder. I must have dozed off, because I open my eyes to see it's mid-morning. The ramp has reached the apex of the pyramid, with Mora's Ori just putting the finishing touches to smooth out the top.

The Watchers toss a rope into our pit and order us to climb out.

Everyone stands and shuffles back into me, fearful of what awaits us up top.

I shove my way to the front and grab hold of the weaved vine.

"Deka!" hisses Marlok. He demands that I keep a low profile. But there is no such hope here, and our captors hold no respect for the weak.

I climb the rope hand over hand. Seven armed Watchers greet me at the top, but not even their intimidating stares can hold my attention.

To my right, sitting at the bottom of the ramp that starts half a mile East, is the Capstone. At a distance, the forty-foot pyramid of gold is minuscule compared to the stone mountain standing beside us. But it's to that smaller pyramid that we owe our lives.

Grunting rises from the moat as others clamber up to join me.

"You have until sunset to set the key," says a Watcher with purple hair. *Lucidia,* some call her. She wields a platinum sledgehammer. Swirling seams of gold decorate the handle and cap the hammer face, the sight of which gets the Fori hustling toward the Capstone.

A lingering Fori climbs from the trench and makes to follow her companions. Lucidia whacks her with the hammer and launches her fifty feet. She hits the ground and doesn't get up.

I race to join the others at the Capstone, where the Fori lay a dozen logs on the ramp before it. They've done this before, it seems.

A Fori grabs my wrist and drags me to the gate key's backside. In passing the Capstone, I notice the golden surface is wavy and its corners warped. When I round the back, I remember why.

Two handprints indent the gold at chest height.

My heart swells at the memory of Nya's attempt to destroy the gate key. She was going to kill herself for us, and her bravery had inspired me to do the same. I'd volunteered to follow her into the darkness of eternity without a second thought.

I look to the sky. Part of me wishes to see her come swooping in to save us, but another part of me would dread the sight. Here she'd be outnumbered. Even Ko Skadia would not stand a chance against such odds, especially with so many Watchers wearing gold-plated armor.

"Move!" shouts Lucidia.

A dozen Fori line up to either side of me. They lean in and give me an urgent look to do the same. Lucidia falls in behind and grips her hammer so tight it groans.

I press into Nya's handprints. Her fingers are smaller than mine, but not by much. Mother always said I had musician's fingers. My father said I'd been born into the wrong time, and to that my mother did not disagree.

"One…" says Mora, her voice a distant echo. "Two…" Her words pulsate inside my head, trailing off into eternity. "Three."

Silence.

I fall deaf to the world, and in doing so I see the static in my head for what it is—twisted cords weaving knots in my mind. Looking at them from outside, they unravel and straighten before me. A silver line connects two points in space-time. One is the Capstone against my palms, the other is its seat atop the Great Pyramid of Giza. In this moment they are the only two points in the universe that matter.

At the apex, a vine of silver cords disperses in every direction. Each of those squiggly strands reaches into a great beyond, to distant planets in far-flung galaxies.

My heart hammers with excitement. Those silver lines are portals.

Pressing my hands into Nya's handprints, I hear her voice call out words that soon become my mantra.

Summon the Magister, she says in my head, her voice a welcome intrusion. *Summon the Magister, and all will be well.*

Myself and everyone around me shove the Capstone with all our weight. Though Nya's folk lack the physical density of us humans, fear boosts their strength to match ours.

The golden pyramid moves about a foot.

"Switch!"

An Ori gang shoves in between us and pushes the golden pyramidion. Huxley joins their group to balance the load. They move it two feet and block it in place, then step back to give our team access.

Together we push, eager to gain our two feet of ground and earn our brief moment of rest. Huxley's team rushes in when we stop and make their two feet before I can catch my breath.

By our fifth round we are hardly off the surface of the ground, but my arms and shoulders burn like they're on fire. A glance to the pyramid peak at the top of the ramp makes me nauseous. So far to go. I see why the Watchers kept us alive for this.

"Is this how you usually set the key?" asks Marlok.

"Yes," says Mora, her voice tight. "But there are usually more of us."

When it's our turn again, my feet slide so hard the skin peels from my soles. I ignore the pain and curl my toes into the dirt for leverage as I push with all my might. The faster we set this key, the sooner I can call upon our savior.

Summon the Magister, whispers Nya's voice in my mind. These words repeat in my head until they come by way of my own inner voice.

Wooden logs crunch under the Capstone's weight. We grunt loud and manage to move the massive hunk of gold another two feet before we're forced to stop for a rest. An Ori rushes to set a stone near each back corner to chock it in place.

"Think they'll leave us here when they jump through the gate?" asks a hopeful Fori to my left.

"Maybe," says Mora from behind. "But where are they going?"

"They might not be going anywhere. Might be they're bringing more reinforcements."

"For what? They got us beat bloody enough. Look at us!"

Lucidia jabs that Fori's face with the butt of her hammer, splitting her cheek wide open. This puts a stop to the chatter, but the Fori takes the blow pretty well, with not so much as a whimper. Her rattled eyes suggest she's in shock.

When we step back to allow the Ori their turn, I venture to the edge of the ramp for a peek up at the apex, where a dark cloud now obscures the top of the pyramid. It grows darker with each push of the Capstone.

That black cloud reveals to me the real reason for setting

the gate key. The Watchers don't plan on leaving this planet, nor do they intend to summon help from other worlds. Their Marshal is trapped in an energetic confinement, a space similar to the sanctuary we'd spent our time recovering in. Only, her scenery is far less endearing. A steady white light has been driving Jexa mad, and every dark servant bound to her shares her suffering. They must free her at once.

As we reach the midpoint of the ramp, nervous whispers rise around me.

"What if we open the gate out of Alignment?" says a Fori. "Jexa did it."

"She studied the dark arts though. She musta knew what she was doing. What does the Butcher know? Even with a whole brain that freak was only half bright. Now with that arrow stuck in her head…"

The Fori around me ease back on their pushing. Those at the corners to my left and right look ominously up the ramp, presumably weighing their options. Would it be better to die in Watcher captivity? Or by the surprise of whatever comes through that gate if it's opened at the wrong time?

A frightened Fori backs away during our push, so Lucidia whacks her with her hammer to launch her off the ramp. She lands on the pyramid and tumbles down its many tiers.

My group rushes to resume pushing, while the other group shoves in between us to help.

I've heard the Fori speak many times about the importance of a gateway's alignment. After we'd arrived in our sanctuary, their speculations suggested Jexa had waited for the exact right time. But I've come to see the truth.

"We need to get this key in place," I tell Marlok under my breath.

He scoffs. "Well, at least you and the Watchers agree on something."

"So long as it's my hand that opens this gate," I say, "I can get us to safety."

If my plan works, we'll open a portal to the Magister and summon his legions of light. The prospect of that brings a smile to my face. As I push into the block, I whisper the beginnings of my plan to my work party.

CHAPTER 13
DEKA

By late afternoon we've conquered three-quarters of the ramp. A few hours ago I figured this venture would have killed me by now. Yet here I am, pushing harder than when I started.

The Fori are into it too, eager to hit back at our Watchers atop the pyramid. Hadria is so fired up she'd pushed too hard and popped out her shoulder. Even with one arm now in a sling fashioned by Mora, she offers an admirable effort with her free hand. The heat of her anger warms my heart. Our enemy won't know what hit them.

Marlok looks over his shoulder to size up the captor-to-captive ratio on the ramp. Six Watchers follow Lucidia in two columns. Our hearty effort has left them with little to do, so they chat idly and pay us little mind.

"We outnumber them ten-to-one up here," Marlok notes. "The element of surprise will give us—"

BROOM-BROOM-BROOOOOOOOOOOOM. Two quick horn blasts, followed by a long droll, stops us dead.

The nearby Watchers grip their spears tight and scan the sky warily.

My heart kicks into a hopeful dance. Did Nya and Sheffa recruit the human army on their own? Have they come to call the Watchers to battle and free us?

I join the Watchers in searching for signs of attack. The thick haze makes it hard to tell where even the Sun is, let alone human warriors creeping in. Only a faint red glow to the West tells me it's evening.

A Fori next to me gasps and clings to my side. She points north and screams, *"RIPPER!"*

Though I have no idea what she means, everyone's jolting panic tells me it's bad.

To the north, a black dot materializes through the haze and swoops toward the pyramid.

The panic around me flashes to terror. Everyone stampedes down the ramp—Fori and Ori and Watchers alike —racing in every direction while their terrified screams rattle my backbone.

At this distance the approaching *Ripper* appears similar in size to the Fori and Watchers, yet everyone runs as if it were Jexa's sky serpent making another attempt to cross into our dimension.

"Deka!"

Marlok waves to me from down the ramp. I'm suddenly aware I'm alone up here, and when I return my attention to the approaching predator I see its trajectory is lined with me.

I race down the dirt ramp toward the bottom, where everyone spills out toward the desert. Even the Watchers sprint away without looking back. Their eagerness to create distance between them and the ramp concerns me, so I pick up my pace to join them.

Two Watchers ahead of me stop at the bottom and turn back toward the pyramid. The anxiety in their reptilian eyes tugs at my curiosity, and I can't resist stealing a look over my shoulder. I do so in time to see the *Ripper* cross into the Anomaly.

She dips into a dive, falling into a crash course with the ramp. The lack of feathered wings assures me that packed slope will be her final resting place, as not even the Watchers can maintain flight so close to the pyramids.

I watch her approach in wonder. Her size is a marvel to behold, because, as she draws closer, I see she is indeed no bigger than Nya. Strange. Even if she were a dust maiden, the Watcher response to her approach seems grossly exaggerated. But I don't have to wait long to see why she's earned her reputation.

The air beneath her distorts like heatwaves over a midday horizon. It's soon followed by a sound like tearing fabric. As the creature falls closer to the ground, the heatwaves thicken and crystalize into a downward wedge that looks like warped glass. The point of this wedge cuts into the ground with a blast of sand and shredded earth that rips at my eardrums.

A fountain of dirt explodes to either side of her dive path to form a stretching *V* line. An upward rebounding force seems to level the Ripper's flight, though I can't see her through the line of erupting dirt.

Every instinct begs me to look away. Instead, I cover my ears to shield against the piercing ripping noise and watch the line of exploding dirt converge on the ramp, right up to when it hits the side with a deafening *BOOM!*

A shockwave blows me back off my feet. Yet even as I fly backward through the air, my attention remains locked on the violent upheaval before me.

The ramp explodes in a fountain of dirt, with chunks of stone flung well beyond the Anomaly's border. A suicide mission for the Ripper no doubt.

Or maybe not.

Among the eruption of debris flies the four-winged Ripper. The upward blast flings her out past the Anomaly's boundary, where her buzzing wings bring her back into controlled flight. She flies away unscathed.

Cheers rise from my Fori co-captives as rocks and pebbles rain down upon us.

Metal rattles and squeaks as two dozen Watchers race toward the southern boundary, past the toppled Capstone, to make chase. It quickly becomes clear they don't have a chance at catching their target at this rate. And by their swift end to the pursuit, with not a single one taking flight, they aren't too eager to catch up to the Ripper anyway.

The Fori cheers fade as the Watchers return their attention to us. Though the tree-tending folk welcome this destructive intruder, their Ori cousins slump in despair. Pushing the Capstone up the ramp once had been a grand feat. To do it a second time...

I kick a rock and join them in wallowing. We were so close to setting the key, so close to summoning the Magister to save us.

"Back to work!" shouts Lucidia.

Every Ori races to repair the smoking gap in the upper ramp. The Capstone sits upside down near the pyramid's South corner, which the remainder of us set off to retrieve. As we gather rolling logs and lashings, the Fori fall heavy into gossip.

"Bet it was Drusilla," says Hadria.

"No way! She died back in Klora's day."

"So did Klora. But who came to square off with Jexa during the battle here?"

"Yeah, well, it was Klora who killed her. And she killed her good. Remember?"

"I don't care what you say, I'd bet my right thumbnail it was Drusilla."

"She might've came through the portal right before the dragon blocked it up."

"*I* heard she shoved her way right past Jexa's sky serpent. That's what kept him from getting through the gate."

"Yeah right! With scales hard as iron, even a Ripper couldn't rough up a beast like that."

"Then who just blew up that ramp?"

"Had to be Ko Skadia."

"It wasn't," I say absently. Dozens of eyes fall on me, and they demand elaboration. "She's dead," I tell them. "Her body is inside the pyramid."

A long silence settles over us.

"Well," someone finally says, "if she comes back, be sure to get a better look next time."

CHAPTER 14

NYA

The south end of the continent isn't very welcoming to us.

Sheffa and I land on a flat-topped mountain that marks the bottom of this great land. It is where the desert heat clashes with the cold wind of a violent sea. White waves smash against the rugged coast, where sheer cliffs suggest assaulting storms are more than frequent.

I stand at the edge of a cliff to get my bearings. The wind whips my hair and blows dirt into my eyes, but it's not enough to distract me from what lies ahead.

Black clouds veil the sky to the southern horizon and beyond. Flashes of white light crack the black ceiling, splitting the sky in every direction before fading away. A steady, ominous rumble purges any hope that my eyes might be deceiving me. That is without a doubt lightning warning us against trespassing.

"How far you reckon it is till next land?" Sheffa asks.

"Does it matter? Look at that storm. We're stuck here for a while."

"But when it passes—"

"Deka doesn't have that much time! They've been under Watcher blades since the second they got caught. You think we have time to laze around waiting for bad weather to pass? We have to go back. There may be rebels in hiding. We can rally them, and..."

A lump balloons in my throat. Through tears blurring my eyes I can see Sheffa believes returning is not an option. Too bad. She's not in charge here.

Her gaze lowers to my chest, and I see her doubt comes from concern. "You ain't healin' proper."

She's right. My wound hasn't healed much at all, probably because I've been burning so much energy to travel swiftly and without rest. It's been a real race to get here, and without a wound I'd be doing fine right now.

I collapse to my knees and slump so low my forehead nearly touches my lap.

Sheffa places a hand on my shoulder. "You okay?"

"We've come all this way... for... for nothing. We've wasted all this time... It was all for naught."

As if on cue, Horus swoops down and circles us until Sheffa offers her arm for a perch. The tone of his clicks and creaks seizes my attention. Whatever he's telling Sheffa is causing him either great excitement or fierce distress.

Sheffa's stricken gaze shifts to the black clouds over the sea. Her bottom lip quivers.

"What is it?" I say.

"He says we gotta go now. That we'll find no better time."

I give the falcon a suspicious look. Only now do I realize I'd accepted his guidance with little thought, and that trust has brought us to this dead end. But now his insistence that we fly into the storm is proof enough that he's leading us to our deaths. He's not even trying to hide it any more.

Anger boils in my chest and steams down my arms to my hands, which burn as they squeeze into fists. I rise to my feet and jab an accusing finger at the bird. "You're trying to kill us!"

Horus shrieks at me, and the way he spreads his wings warns that he's about to peck off my face.

I raise both hands, ready to fight.

"Easy, Nya," says Sheffa. "He says he finded a safe way."

"Yeah? Where?" I cock back my fist, ready to slug the bird when Sheffa relays the wrong answer.

Sheffa looks to the sky directly above us.

My fists tighten until my knuckles crack. "He can't be serious."

"He says there's a strong airstream up high."

"He's saying that because he thinks we're idiots. Above those clouds is Aeri domain, and they can't be trusted any more than the Watchers."

"Horus says there's no Aeri up there. It's all clear."

Even Sheffa can't hide the doubt in her voice. She can't believe a storm like that brewed up out of nowhere without help from our rainmaking cousins.

"Why are you trying to kill us?" I ask the bird.

Horus shrieks in my face. Sheffa *shushes* him and strokes his feathers to soothe his nerves.

"Fine, Nya," she says, "you go back North. I'll go warn them Southern Sapiens. Better yet, just stay here and rest."

I give Sheffa the nastiest look I can muster. She knows she can't face an enemy attack by herself, and that I won't let her go South alone. In committing to Horus's plan, Sheffa has committed me with her.

My glare mustn't be very threatening, because Sheffa's expression remains neutral.

I turn and uppercut a boulder into dust. The release excites me and manages to brighten my mood briefly. But it's just a flash and fades as quickly as it came. I need a real good session to work up a lasting sense of satisfaction, but right now I can't spare the energy for that.

I lean in close to Horus. "If you're leading us into a trap," I say through clenched teeth, "I'll turn you to dust, feather... by... feather."

Sheffa shivers at my threat, but Horus meets my eyes with a cold black stare. This bird either doesn't understand what I'm capable of, or he knows I'll never get the chance to follow through. Either way, our choices are limited.

"Let's go," I say, and the bird launches into flight before I can finish.

It's hard for Sheffa and me to fly straight up with our wings, so we have to zigzag our way up high. Rising to such altitudes makes me feel woefully exposed in the open sky. But this soon becomes a minor concern.

The higher we climb, the more effort I must put into my ascent. The air up here is thinner, so my wings have less atmosphere to leverage. Adding to the strain is the lack of oxygen to fuel me. By the time we rise above the clouds, it takes twice the effort to gain half the upward distance. I'm about to ask Sheffa how much farther when my ascent suddenly reverses directions.

I fall at such frightening speed that I scream. My frantic wings catch nothing, like I'm tumbling through a void, and it's the worst feeling ever! The last time my heart dropped like this ended with me shattering my leg inside the Great Pyramid's Anomaly. But seeing how far the ground is from me right now, a broken bone will be the least of my concerns.

My scream fades until I run out of breath. I breathe in and am about to resume screaming when my wings catch air. My downward plummet angles forward and levels off, and soon I'm flying upward again, breathless. As my panic settles, Sheffa falls in beside me.

"Air pockets," she says. "They's caused by the storm, but they won't hurt us."

I have no choice but to take her word on that.

We continue our ascent, crossing air currents that toss us this way and that, until a mighty gust hits me like a tsunami and hurls me Southward.

My arms flail and legs kick in a desperate attempt to steady myself, and every instinct begs me to drop out while I can, but then I realize my wings aren't even moving. The air current sweeps me away like a great sky river, propelling me at unnatural speed. My wings spread out stiffly from my back, angling only occasionally to keep me level.

Sheffa cruises ahead, beyond yelling distance, but she looks over her shoulder with the biggest smile I've ever seen. Horus is a good distance ahead of her, rising and diving to test the current, showing Sheffa and I the boundaries of this particular airstream. Perhaps it's in warning. If there's a crosswind blowing at even a tenth the speed of this one, we might break our necks if we hit it the wrong way. But there seems to be more to it than that.

Horus flaps his wings steadily, which means he's trying to create distance between us. If he's leading us into a trap he'll likely do something suspicious right before we reach it. It's best we keep him in sight at all times, so I get my wings humming to pick up speed.

It works. I move so fast my eyelids blow back and it's hard to force them closed. Good, because with each blink I risk losing that small falcon in the darkening sky.

I whiz past Sheffa and startle her in my passing. She races to fall in beside me. The wind screams in my ears, so Sheffa must yell for me to hear her.

"You got to save your energy to heal!"

My hand goes instinctively to cover my wound.

"If you can't keep up," I say, "just say so and I'll set a more leisurely pace for you."

Sheffa frowns at me, almost hurt. "I can keep up just fine, Nya. You's gonna waste your energy is all I'm sayin'."

"Deka doesn't have time for us to be dallying along. Besides, Horus is setting the pace here. We need to keep up."

"You don't trust him."

"Someone has to have a healthy suspicion. You fell for his charm the second he showed up and started clicking in your ear. There's a better chance he's working for the Watchers than for us, and I don't plan on forgetting that anytime soon."

Sheffa opens her mouth to speak, but before she can say anything I shoot off in pursuit of Horus. There's something off about that bird, and I'll be damned if I'm going to let him lead me into a trap.

CHAPTER 15
NYA

"Nya! Wake up!"

My eyes snap open to find Sheffa has a death grip on my wrist as she drags me through a pitch-dark sky. Somehow I'd fallen asleep in my flight. Sheffa must have been watching closely and grabbed my arm to keep me within the airstream. At least my four wings had locked stiff to keep me in level flight.

I can't see the ocean, but I hear its violent roar beneath the black storm clouds below. This sea isn't just restless on this night. It's downright furious.

How could I have fallen asleep during such a storm?

I lightly prod my wound. It's healed only half of what it should be. Why is that? Stress, most likely. This race to warn Deka's people will end with a monumental task in its own right.

My belly twists into knots. I'm supposed to convince them I'm not their enemy, then tell them an enemy that looks just like me is coming to exterminate them. And that's not even my main worry right now.

"Where's Horus?" I say.

"He got hit by a lightning bolt!" Sheffa's distress assures me she'd witnessed it clearly. Her nails dig into my wrist, and I realize she's clinging to me for comfort instead of guiding me along.

I embrace her, and together we ride the airstream. We've passed the lightning, and without its illumination it feels as if we've entered the Darkness itself—just endless black all around and a constant wind to keep us from forgetting we're exposed in an unpredictable void with no land in sight.

I'm not sure how long it takes us to reach the edge of the storm, but when we do it's nothing to celebrate.

The black clouds retreat Northward behind us as clear night sky opens all around. But we've lost the airstream, and without its boost I sink.

"You got to put in a better effort than that," Sheffa says while hauling on my arm.

I shift my focus to my wings. They'd locked stiff in our airstream glide, twitching only enough for basic steering. When they get fluttering now over the sea, it takes considerable effort to stay aloft. And when Sheffa releases my arm I drop.

My wings flutter but do little to stop my plummet.

No! Panic sends me into a frantic search for land. I scan all around, where nothing but ocean horizon greets me in every visible direction.

My heart kicks into overdrive and burns like a smelter inside my belly, consuming precious energy. Terror floods my chest and throat, stifling my efforts to scream or breathe, much like I'm drowning.

One look at the sea below sends a violent shiver through

me. That cold, dark abyss will become my grave if I don't find a place to land in the next few seconds.

I cast my gaze left toward the Eastern horizon. It's dark for as far as I can tell, with no hint of dawn anywhere. A rightward search to the West yields much of the same, with no trace of a recent sunset.

The cold air blowing up from the sea tells me the Sun hasn't graced this place in some time.

My shivering intensifies.

I reach up toward Sheffa, desperate to cling to her for comfort, but she drifts away and keeps her distance. She watches me nervously as I dip lower toward the sea. I see she's debating whether or not to grab hold of me if the time comes, knowing the act would doom her too.

I should tell Sheffa to ignore whatever I say in the coming minutes, no matter what pleas they may be. That no matter how close to the water surface I drift, she is to keep her distance and allow me to fall. That's what I should tell her. But I can't. Besides, it doesn't matter.

Sheffa locks her gaze forward and sets an urgent pace ahead of me. I try my best to catch up but drift lower as she sustains level flight. She cruises on without looking back while I dip helplessly toward the sea.

A lump swells in my throat. Sheffa has made up her mind. I'm about to die and we both know it.

I'm about to shout out for help anyway, but ballooning panic chokes me. This helplessness stokes my terror even further.

I'm about to die!

Like a spawn learning to fly, my legs and arms flail to compensate for my faltering wings. It's an instinct we're born with, and this impulse returns at the approach of my death.

It's no use here. I'm falling! Falling! *FALLING!*

My heart slams against my navel like a fist trying to punch its way out my belly, but the extra energy each beat sends to my wings doesn't cut it. I angle into a nosedive toward the ocean surface, its merciless whitecaps now so close I swear their briny mist dampens my hair.

Last-ditch instincts kick in. It starts with narrowing vision, an effort by my mind to spare me the awareness of my impending doom. My heart rate slows to cut off blood flow to my brain. An easy peace falls over me.

Mist sprays my face from clashing whitecaps. I'm about to hit. I'm about to die.

I hit the water so hard I bounce back into the sky. At least... that's how it seems at first.

As I fall back down, an updraft curls upward from a colossal wave and hurls me back into the sky, which feels exactly like my first bounce. I seize the momentum to reclaim some altitude.

"Nya!" comes Sheffa's distant voice.

I scan all around and see she's higher up, over my left shoulder, cruising along effortlessly. Horus is just ahead of her...

Horus, the bird who supposedly got hit by lightning. Either Sheffa's rattled mind had imagined the falcon's demise, or he played a trick on her.

Neither one matters now. Their rigid wings tell me they've found a new airstream.

Fury burns inside me. This anger is toward myself, for not trusting that bird. For allowing my stubbornness to lead me toward my own death. I'd ignored Sheffa's advice to pace myself and instead burned precious energy pursuing Horus, and in doing so I've become a burden to our cause.

A wildfire rages inside my chest. Its heat blasts dark energy through my body, fueling my wings enough to get me rising again. A miraculous effort lifts me all the way to the air current, where I fall in behind Sheffa, and soon we're gliding effortlessly South again as if nothing happened.

Horus shrieks from ahead. The wind carries his message forward so that it's barely audible to me, but Sheffa is halfway between us and makes out his meaning.

She looks over her shoulder at me and screams, "Land!"

Tears blur my eyes. I almost can't believe it, and my inclination is to think that bird is playing a trick on us— whether malicious or to keep us in good spirits, I do not know.

I've never been so happy to be so wrong in my judgment as I am when a rocky point rises from the dark sea ahead. The barren island is high and narrow, but I wouldn't care if it were a scat-stained rock scarcely sticking out from the sea. It's a place to rest, and right now that's paradise to me.

I put my head down and ride this airwave toward safety. Toward hope itself.

CHAPTER 16

NYA

The land's initial presentation had misled me greatly. That mountain was not an island at all, but the tip of a great peninsula.

Faint starlight exposes a sprawl of jagged peaks that stretch South for as far as I can see. From the sky, these rocky mountains have the appearance of a petrified sea storm—like tidal waves hardened to rock.

As we fly closer, more land emerges from the distant darkness, spreading wide to occupy the entire Southern horizon.

Sheffa exchanges quick chatter with Horus and then slows for me to catch up.

"He says the humans used to call this place Antarctica. Now it's called Anterra."

The land of Anterra is both beautiful and frightening. Being so far removed from sunlight, any solid ground for me is most welcome. This may be why I think it's beautiful—for the simple fact that it is land—with quality having very little to do with it. Either way, I race toward it before my wings give out on me.

Horus crosses over the northern shoreline first. He circles around one of the nearest mountain peaks, and his spiraling descent guides me to where I hope is a safe place to stop.

Passing the first three peaks at the peninsula tip without landing for a rest requires extraordinary willpower on my part. I follow Horus into a sunken summit, where faint orange light glows from a crack in the great rock bowl.

This place reminds me of a volcano I'd recently visited, when Ko Tora convinced our rebel army to fall for Jexa's counterfeit Capstone trick. That fight ended the worst way possible. It almost cost us the war. But that memory and my resentment haunt me only briefly.

My body shivers with a sudden and fierce craving for thermal energy. It's no solar radiation by any stretch, but here I'll take what I can get.

Heat blasts me from the glowing crevice as I glide down the crusted-over volcano. This ashy air I welcome down my throat like cold water in a hot desert.

I drop outside the tall crack, where orange light reveals a short entryway. I waste no time crawling toward a bubbling red lake glowing inside. Gaia's core energy flows through this molten liquid and radiates to fill the cavernous space and, despite the sweltering air, breathing becomes easier for me here. The tightness in my chest instantly loosens.

Inside, on a ledge to my right, I encounter my first Southern Sapiens. Ash buries the two seated skeletons to their necks.

I nestle in between them and let the heat blast me. A whole week of this energy won't heal me half of what a few good hours of sunlight could do, but it should sustain me. That's better odds than I had a few minutes ago.

When I close my eyes, beautiful orange warmth glows through my eyelids. I could melt away right here with a smile on my face. Perhaps that's how the two *sapiens* beside me died.

Darkness falls before me as something comes between me and the lava. This interruption to my heat source sends a shiver through me.

"You don't look good, Nya," comes Sheffa's voice.

"I just need a quick rest. Get out of my way."

The warm glow graces my face again. But I sense something is wrong. When I open my eyes I see Sheffa crouched by the exit, whispering with Horus, who bounces restlessly on the ground. I can't tell if he's nervous or excited.

Sheffa returns to me. "Horus says there's a huge human Hive nearby."

"Where?"

Sheffa nods toward the entrance, beckoning me to come take a gander.

I feel like a jellyfish out of water trying to stand. My wobbling legs barely carry me to the exit, and I'd surely fall over if not for my fluttering wings propping me up. We emerge into the freezing night air and fly straight upward.

The continent flares wide for as far as I can see, from horizon to horizon. I dare not waste a look back at the dreadful sea. To the right ahead, a dome of yellow light glows up from the land and into the sky, advertising one massive *sapien* settlement.

My heart flutters with excitement. That glow is our first indication that our errand here has not been in vain. At this distance, the light's intensity suggests the people of Anterra are a mighty presence on this formidable land.

I breathe a sigh of relief. We're almost there. But... as my struggling wings remind me, almost is not enough.

I sink back to the ground and collapse to my knees. Though I've traveled a much greater distance in recent days, I'd started that journey not knowing how far we'd have to go. Had I known the distance before setting off, I might not have attempted it.

Sheffa kneels beside me and gives my shoulder a squeeze.

"It's okay, Nya. You rest here. I'll go give them our warning."

I give Sheffa a scrutinizing look over, and her frown must mirror my own.

"I can handle it," she says.

I must be showing some serious doubt, because she stands defensively and says, "Just because I can't speak the best doesn't mean they won't understand me. Maybe they'd even understand me better than you. You got no idea what these humans is like."

"It's not safe to go alone, is all I mean."

Sheffa steps back. "You think I'd be safer with you? Look at ya. You'd only slow me down."

My face burns hot with anger. *Slow her down?* How dare she talk to me like that!

I jump to my feet with my fists raised.

"What are ya gonna do," Sheffa says. "Hit me?"

"Say that again and you'll find out."

Sheffa shoves me with both hands. Her attack is so unexpected that it actually knocks me off balance and onto the ground.

Rage swirls like a firestorm inside my chest. I spring to my feet, but I don't stay up for long. The dark world spins like a tornado around me, and I quickly find myself returning to my back.

"See," Sheffa says, looming over me. "You need rest, and the humans don't got time for that."

"Sheffa, I order you to stay here with me!"

"You's a feared a bein' alone?"

"Of course not." Sheffa is a fool if she can't see what I'm doing here. This is for her sake.

Black spots bloom across my vision. Sheffa blurs into a shadow before me, so I rub my eyes to focus them. It doesn't help.

Sheffa crouches beside me. When she speaks, her voice is softer. "I just gotta spook 'em is all. They won't have seen the likes of us down here I bet. A quick flyby should put the fright in 'em good enough. I'll make all kinds a noise that'll put 'em right on edge. It'll actually be kinda fun."

The thought of stirring mayhem and leading *sapiens* on a chase right now sounds anything but fun to me. Which means Sheffa's assessment of me is right—I'm in no shape for this mission. And worse, Deka really doesn't have time for me to heal.

"Try talking to them first," I say. The intensity of those artificial lights in the distance suggests these folk are more developed than Deka's tribe, and may be more receptive to our arrival. "And hurry back. You're not done taking care of me yet."

Sheffa slides her heels together and raises her left arm in a flimsy salute. I return it with a two-finger salute of my own, and then she nods dutifully before bounding off and taking flight.

I use my remaining energy to crawl back into the cave. Gratitude swells in me for Sheffa's insistence. Humanity doesn't stand a fighting chance without this warning, and I am in no shape to deliver it. All I can do is hope I'm still alive when she returns. By the worry in her eyes, I'd say she's thinking the same thing.

CHAPTER 17
DEKA

The Great Pyramid has become a hornet's nest since the Ripper attack.

Sunlight glints off Watcher armor as their patrols fly a circle around the gateway's Anomaly. At first their numbers were so sparse and the patrol circumference too great that their lines stretched into thin strings, but more have since arrived from distant fighting. They now circle the pyramid in a cyclone of sharpened steel.

We march in two lines to the bottom of the repaired ramp under the afternoon Sun, where our burden awaits us. It's going to be a long day, but I'm ready for it.

It's been two days since the Ripper blew up our ramp. Two days since disappointment floored me. I'd fallen asleep the second I sat down in our captivity pit and not woken until the midday Sun passed overhead.

The arrival of the Sun that afternoon had indeed jarred me awake. The feather-winged Aeri had blown away all the smoke to give the Watchers clear view to the horizon in every direction, and suddenly the shaded patches in our pit had become precious ground to us humans. The Fori, however, soaked up as much of the rejuvenating light as they could.

We get straight to work. With us humans and the Fori well rested, we're able to manage three-foot gains with each push, but we do this for only a few rounds. Best to save our strength for the fight up top.

With so many Watchers around, there's no way they'll be expecting trouble from us. Their focus is cast outward, as evidenced by the many Ripper attack drills they've been practicing. They run them each time a new group arrives, to ensure everyone knows the response plan, all forces congealing to defend the side of attack.

Good. We don't need any more delays. We need to set the Capstone and send our distress signal to the Magister as soon as possible, so we push and push, and then push some more.

Hadria doesn't let her pinned up arm slow her. She stays at the block each time, her determined eyes staring down her own reflection in the gold surface. Her teeth remain clenched the whole time, forcing her breath through her nose, the whistling blows growing louder with each push. She ignores the occasional bubble that pops out. She's not fully here. She is a few beats in the future, shoving a blade through the Butcher's one good eye.

As we rise up the ramp, my enthusiasm for the coming fight wanes. But it's not fear for myself that gives me pause.

On the stone levels to either side of the ramp, chip marks and blood stains pay tribute to the many Fori and Ori slain during that deadly climb. It's also a grim reminder of how dangerous our enemy is. We only survived that fight because of our numbers and the fact we'd held the high ground. Here on this ramp, we are unarmed and hold only a slight numerical advantage. Our first move must be swift and accurate. And still, many who breathe and grunt beside me will die.

Mora's group finishes their turn, and I step in to take her place, but as I'm about to push she reappears to my left. "Ten feet," she whispers.

My heart drops. Really? Already? No, it can't be. It feels like we just started.

We gain another two feet with this push, then I creep to the edge of the ramp to confirm Mora's claim. She's right, and by the time the current group pushing the Capstone finishes their turn, it sits only six feet from the flat pyramid top.

I fall in beside Marlok for our turn to push. "It's time."

His eyes widen with worry and surprise. He's feeling what I'm feeling—severe panic. I thought we'd made it only halfway so far. I thought I'd have more time to work up the nerve to ignite this revolt.

I look to Hadria, who's been watching me expectantly, and she seems to misinterpret my expression. She takes it for a signal to kick our plan into action.

She staggers back from the Capstone and drops to her knees.

"Get up," threatens Lucidia, pulling her hammer back for a swing.

Hadria reaches her good arm out toward the Watcher. "Please," she says, weeping. "I can't go another step."

My heart races. She's actually going for it.

Marlok slips around the Capstone to retrieve a rolling log, and with that log it's agreed we're to plow our captors from the ramp. Then I'm to set the gate key and summon the

Magister. That's it. That's all I have to do. Easy enough, right?

I hear wood dragging over dirt from behind the Capstone. Marlok and Hadria are so far successful in their tasks. We can do this. Just breathe. Don't panic.

"Stop!" orders Lucidia.

My throat tightens and my muscles lock stiff. Right now Marlok is probably hoisting the log to come around for our attack. In front of me, Hadria reaches into her arm sling for the blade I'd given her a few nights ago.

"That's close enough," says Lucidia.

Hadria digs for the knife handle in her sling. She's about to stab it into Lucidia's leg when our Watcher steps back and points her hammer down the ramp. "The Capstone is close enough. Back to the ground."

I sneak to the side and see the Capstone's forward edge is still five feet from the pyramid top.

"Down the ramp," snaps Lucidia. "Now!"

Our Ori helpers are first to obey. They're not into the fight anyway, and have even tried to talk us out of it.

The six Watchers on the ramp below seem to sense something is up with the rest of us. They widen their stances and hold their spears at the ready.

Cold sweat slicks my skin. It's not a good time for us. Our plan relied on them being distracted by the gate opening.

A Watcher down the ramp leaps over the side and scrambles up the stone levels. At the top she stands upon the flat apex, where the Capstone should be sitting right now, and pulls out a horn.

Marlok must have dropped the log, because the Watcher pays him no mind. She blows into her horn, and though her effort is long and hard, no sound leaves the other end. She spins in a circle and, when she faces me, I see her cheeks puffed out as if she is indeed blowing.

The storm of Watchers swirling around the pyramid drop from the sky and land at the Anomaly border, then race to form ranks before the pyramid.

To Lucidia, I say, "What about the Ripper? She could knock the Capstone over again."

Lucidia responds with a smug smile. "She could try. Now, get out of here."

A Fori grabs my wrist and drags me down the ramp. When I realize it's Hadria, I rip free from her grip and stomp down to join Mora and her Ori.

Lucidia takes up the rear and holds her hammer threateningly to inspire a faster retreat down the ramp. I hurry along with the others.

"Think the Ripper will come?" I ask Mora.

She shakes her head. "The Ripper is an Entropath, like Nya. That means her wings can't fly into the Anomaly at this height. To reach the pyramid peak she'd have to come in at too great an angle, but then she'd end up crashing to the ground. No fancy upward blasting tricks will stop a plunge like that."

"Will she at least try to free us?" I say. "She can't keep fighting on her own like that. Not if she hopes to win."

Mora watches the sky warily. "If that Ripper is who I think it is, then she's a bigger threat to us than the Watchers. Next time she comes around, you run as fast as you can in the other direction."

The silent call of the Watcher horn must have traveled far, because by the time we're midway down the ramp there are black dots in the sky in every direction. They grow larger with each worried beat of my heart.

My spirit sinks. We've given up the high ground and allowed our enemy to double their numbers. If we'd made a move and at least killed that hornblower...

I can't even think about how bad we messed up right now. Our chances of seeing another sunset have just crashed and burned.

The newly-arrived Watchers gather before the bottom of the ramp in clusters of seven neat ranks, each forming a separate block of fighting units. I've seen similar arrangements in mother's books, in chapters devoted to war and military parades. The words that accompanied those passages often described terrible outcomes.

A quick tally suggests five thousand Watchers on the ground already, with about as many more rushing to join them. They are all plated in titanium armor, but the colors and designs imply different makers.

Ori whispers suggest the Watchers have been mining distant gold. They've put Ori crafts-folk to work, fashioning protection for their masters to defend against the surviving dust maidens, and of course now the Ripper.

"There she is!" screams Hadria, pointing North while bouncing excitedly on her feet. "The Ripper!"

Everyone halts to follow her indication North. Watchers must have far better sight than the rest of us, because Lucidia quickly concludes the black dot there is not the Ripper. "Just a bird, you idiot. Just a—*ARGHHH!*"

In the corner of my eye I see Hadria drive her knife into Lucidia's thigh.

Lucidia backhands Hadria and sends her spinning onto

her knees. The Watcher then stomps on the Fori's back to flatten her onto her belly, then raises her sledgehammer to smash in her assailant's skull.

Huxley tackles Lucidia onto her back before she can swing. I pounce on top, where we each grab a side of Lucidia's hammer, and together we push the bar down onto her chest. A bad move.

Lucidia slips both hands under the middle of her hammer handle, then springs us into the air, hammer and all. We land down the ramp between Lucidia and her six backup guards.

I'm quick to my feet with the platinum hammer in hand. The metal handle twirls smoothly in my twisting hands, which seem to know exactly where to grab to best turn the head's shifting momentum into fluid movements.

Lucidia watches with worry as I whirl her hammer gracefully around my back. It feels similar to when I connected with the knife I'd given Hadria, but not quite.

I become mesmerized by my own hands as they spin the blurred hammer. I'd call it elegance if not for the anger and hate channeling through me. My mouth waters and my jaw locks, eager to smash the heavy hammerhead into Lucidia's chest plate.

Lucidia raises her fists and backs away, and my companions should seize this opportunity to attack. Instead they watch me in amazement.

I myself wonder how this is possible. Is it some form of consciousness that radiates through me? Lucidia's energy? Where does it start? My head? My hands?

This overthinking causes me to fumble the hammer and drop it.

Lucidia bends her knees to lunge at me, providing Hadria

an opening to leap onto her back. Hadria covers our warden's eyes with both hands, revealing she'd been faking her shoulder injury. As Lucidia thrashes and reaches back to grab hold of her assailant, she stumbles off balance and steps over the ramp edge, with Hadria still latched to her back.

A crash onto the pyramid to my left sends a shiver through me. But I don't have time to investigate.

"RIPPER!"

My already-frayed nerves split even further. I join all eyes in looking East and up, to where a black dot approaches high in the clear blue sky. The absence of armor glare and the cacophony of clinking metal from a thousand Watchers racing to take flight leaves no doubt that it's the real Ripper this time.

The nearby Watchers race down the ramp. Whether it's to take flight or escape the coming carnage, I do not know. Only the hornblower remains. We servants must look mighty menacing sizing her up, because she jumps back around the Capstone and out of sight.

Lucidia's gang notice we've not retreated with them, and that we now control the gate key. They reverse course and charge up from the bottom of the ramp.

Marlok growls behind me as he tosses a log over my head. It bounces down the ramp toward the rushing Watchers, who leap to avoid it, which works for the first few, but those behind get tripped up. Huxley grunts as he flings a second log toward them.

I turn and shove past my companions toward the Capstone. "Let's go! Push!"

A wall of two dozen bodies slams into the sloped face of gold, but our hasty effort manages to slide the golden pyramidion only two fingers' width. A quick peek around the corner reveals we have nearly five feet to go, and a look back down the ramp tells me we don't have much time to get there.

Two dozen more Watchers sprint up from the bottom of the ramp.

Marlok jumps down over the side. A moment later he clambers back up carrying Lucidia's hammer, then squares off with the rush of Watchers. Huxley picks up a rolling log and falls in beside him.

I lean into the Capstone and shout, "Push!"

The ringing of steel and smacking of flesh gets us all shoving harder than ever before. The Capstone slides two feet.

Steel sings loud behind us.

"Push!"

We slide the Capstone another half foot.

A growl of pain rises behind me. I glance over my shoulder to see Huxley stumble toward us holding a belly wound, which leaves Marlok to face the main wave alone. Fifty more Watchers race up the ramp behind them.

I pick up a rolling log and hurry to join my war leader. With a lucky swing I may be able to sweep a good few off the side of the ramp. But I am no fool. I know that one swing is all I'll get.

The Watchers see me coming and skid to a halt. A quick trace of their line of sight, however, leads me back to a four-winged figure climbing onto the flat pyramid top.

The hornblower sees Ko Skadia coming from behind and jabs a spear at her belly. The Entropath Elder sidesteps and grabs the shaft, and immediately the Watcher begins convulsing so fiercely she's forced to release her weapon.

Ko Skadia swings her new-found spear into the Watcher's flank—*DING!* Her titanium armor rings like a bell as she flies from the pyramid and tumbles toward the ground.

Marlok breaks into riotous laughter. When the Entropath Elder steps around the Capstone and onto the ramp, he tosses Lucidia's hammer to Ko Skadia.

She snatches it from the air while keeping her glare locked on the Watchers congealing down the ramp, and the way she twirls it reminds me of my own movements during my brief handling of it. It seems Lucidia had kept Ko Skadia's hammer for a trophy.

She tosses Marlok her spear and stomps past him.

You'd think the Watchers in the rear to be the bravest, because that's where the push to attack comes from. Funny how that works with an army of bullies. Seeing they have no way back, the dozen Watchers who make up the front rank charge forward.

Ko Skadia skips into a side shuffle and swings wide into the nearest Watcher. The whack of metal rattles my teeth and launches three Watchers from the ramp.

The following ten Watchers rush up, seeking to get the jump on her before she can wind her hammer back for another blow.

Ko Skadia clears the whole line of them with a single backswing. The clatter of armored bodies raining onto the pyramid steps cautions the following Watchers. They back away, but Ko Skadia isn't letting them off so easily.

She marches toward the remaining forty Watchers, who form a tight group at her approach.

The clatter of Ko Skadia's hammer plowing through titanium armor is the most wretched noise I've ever heard.

"Deka!" shouts Mora.

I return to pushing the Capstone with everyone else, but we are not enough. Huxley lies on his back nearby, his face pale in shock.

"Marlok!" I shout. "We need you."

Marlok stands behind Ko Skadia, waiting for an opening to fall in at her side, but her wide swinging keeps him away. He's reluctant to leave her, but seeing we're all doomed if we don't set this Capstone, he rushes to join us.

His strength is just what we need. When the center of the Capstone crosses the top of the ramp, the block tips and lands flat onto its seat. No one has placed a rolling log there, yet the giant key slides forward with little effort.

Actually, *slide* is the wrong word. Right now, the Capstone *glides* to the far edge. It advances so easily the Ori and Fori jump back. Their uncertain eyes tell me they don't want to be touching the key when it unlocks the gate, with a few even leaping down to the pyramid steps.

Marlok backs away, leaving only my hands on the gold surface. Crashing steel and wails of agony fade. A warm breeze caresses my skin. Here I stand at the edge of death or some other form of transition beyond this life, the border between darkness and light.

Summon the Magister, whispers an ancient wind.

I slide my hands into Nya's indented handprints.

Call forth the Protector of Light and Life.

I lock my elbows and step forward to guide the Capstone to its seat. It does not resist. It glides with purpose, one that is born of light and love. The gate key wants to open this portal for me. This gate key has become the embodiment of my desire. It wants what I want.

We are in Alignment.

The golden edge hovering before my toes lines up with the edge of the pyramid top. With the corresponding corners to my left and right matched up perfectly, the Capstone drops onto its seat.

A blast of cold wind drives me back. The pyramid shakes violently and sends me stumbling back down the ramp, where I'm faced with a familiar sight.

A silver beam shoots up from the apex and explodes in the sky above. From the center of the blast blooms a bulbous portal, with a three-hundred-foot energy stream anchoring it to the Capstone. The balloon-shaped gateway is much smaller than the one Jexa had used to summon her intergalactic army to Earth. The pyramid also rumbles now with less intensity than at that great battle.

And then a realization hits me like a slap to the face: Nya's damage has reduced the gateway's capacity and diminished its functionality. Unlike the portal Jexa had opened, which shimmered with threads displaying scenery from distant planets, this portal reveals only darkness.

The clamor of battle behind me settles into silence. I turn to survey the danger and notice everyone, including Ko Skadia, staring at the black portal above in fright. Their alarm reminds me why.

Nya had once told me the Watchers punish their Servants by sending their souls to a place called the *Dark*. They access the edge of that black hole through a gateway like this, and I suspect many fear that's what I've opened here.

Is is true? Have I opened a portal to the dreaded Dark?

I look at the Capstone before me, to the two sunken

handprints marking its face, and my heart goes cold with a dreadful realization. In my mind I'd aligned myself with the Magister, but what if my heart had aligned with Nya? If I actually managed to open a gateway to her, and this is what I got, then that means...

Tears water my eyes and burn down my cheeks. Has she fallen into darkness, passed into her afterlife? Did the Watchers capture her and Sheffa and damn them to the Dark?

"Kill them!" screams a voice from down the ramp. It's that four-armed freak, the Butcher.

"Ripper!"

This alarm comes for Mora. She's right beside me, pointing at a swarm approaching from the South, where the Ripper has redirected course and led the Watchers on a chase. At this height I see feathered wings spreading wide from her back. I'd not noticed them before, and it changes everything.

I grab Mora's wrist and pull her toward the energy stream. "Let's go."

The Ori senior resists me with all her might. By her stricken stare, she'd sooner take her chances between the Ripper and the Butcher than risk entry to the Dark.

I turn my attention to Marlok down the ramp. He looks to Ko Skadia, who frowns at him in what seems an attempt at recognition. The warmth she once held for him did not accompany her back to this reality. But still, he plants his feet firmly by hers to join her in facing the growing flood of Watchers rising up the ramp.

"Do what you need to do, Deka," he says over his

shoulder, and I know they are the last words I'll ever hear from him.

An appraisal of everyone else reveals they'd sooner face the Watchers than jump through this gate. Fori and Ori split wooden stakes from a rolling log and fall in behind Ko Skadia and Marlok.

Ko Skadia leaps onto the pyramid steps three levels down from the Capstone, and then swings sideways into the ramp. Packed dirt and stone explode out the left side in a plume of dust. A few Ori and Fori fall through the smoking gap.

Screams and ringing steel rise from the pyramid steps below Ko Skadia. No Watcher is eager to challenge The Hammer from the low ground, a weakness the Fori and Ori quickly notice. They scramble up past her and gather on the level directly behind, while Marlok falls in beside her to confront the Watchers gathering on the steps below. Thousands more Watchers race up the ramp, and at the gap they leap onto the pyramid tiers.

The fight on the steps below no longer concerns me. Good thing, too, because when I return my attention to the portal, the gliding Ripper is within crossbow range.

I'd sooner risk an eternity in darkness with Nya than a lifetime in daylight with this rabble, so I clamber up the throbbing Capstone and jump into its energy stream. It's the ultimate leap of faith, and it swiftly reverses into a downward fall through to the other side.

I close my eyes and brace for impact. It comes quicker than expected. My feet hit stone and marks the beginning of a long tumble down the Great Pyramid's west face.

CHAPTER 18

NYA

You wouldn't think sleeping beside a lake of lava would be very comfortable, but I am pleasantly surprised by how rested I am when I wake.

I have no idea how long I'd been sleeping when I finally open my eyes, but the heaviness in my eyelids and weariness in my muscles differs from the fatigue that nearly drove me into the sea. It is the weight of oversleeping, of having become too relaxed that now afflicts me, and I welcome it with outstretched arms. I'd have slept even longer if not for an annoying bird pecking at my toes.

I prop up on my elbows to see Horus hopping around my feet. He looks to the cave exit nervously and spreads his wings in short bursts to get my attention. When I sit up all the way I feel pressure in my rib wound, and a look down reveals a brownish-gray mass bulging out.

I jump up in panic. I'm about to dig out the festering rot when I notice its cooling effect. Rather than burning painfully, my wound tingles.

Horus stops jumping and gives my wound a long and

knowing look. This bird I've given so much distrust must have flown far and wide to find the right ingredients for this healing poultice, so I offer him a nod of gratitude.

He responds with a shriek unlike anything I've heard from him so far. This cry of panic echoes off the rock walls in a frequency that rattles me to my Spark. I suddenly feel cornered in here, so when he hops toward the exit I'm quick to follow.

I crawl out into the cool night air. Wary of nearby danger, I stay low on my hands and knees. I've lost sight of Horus in the dark crater, but his claw prints lead me to a ledge facing inland, where I see a storm brewing to the South.

Blue lightning flashes across the Southern sky. It's bright enough to blind me, yet is far enough away that the thunder reaches here as a low rumble.

Horus hops onto my back and bounces between my shoulder blades. He screeches and jumps to either side of me in distress, declaring there is something unnatural about that storm.

"What is it?" I ask, fearing it may be a weapon or a trap. "Is it Sheffa? Is she in trouble?"

Horus stops before me and rocks his head side to side. I gather this isn't about her. It's something bigger. Horus, I am learning, does not fret over people. He becomes rattled by events, and I don't have to wait long to see what's got his feathers all ruffled.

A blast of blue light explodes in the distant sky. The powder-blue glow bathes the peninsula's mountain peaks for about five seconds, and its frequency differs from that of lightning.

Returning darkness steals my breath away. A shadow of

suspicion shrouds my heart, and I launch into flight so that I'm at the right altitude when the evidence reaches here. Though the shockwave hits me with little more force than a gust of wind, its energy leaves no doubt that it is indeed a shockwave.

My heavy heart drags me to the ground, where I collapse onto my belly and bury my face into my elbows. We're too late! This land hosts one of the planet's gateways, and someone just opened it! The Watchers are probably pouring through by the thousands right now, and... And...

Wait a second.

I spring into flight and rise back to my previous height, where I squint at the horizon. Even from this distance I should see a portal glow in this deep dark night. The only light I see is the yellow glow from the Human Hive, which casts a distinctly different energy than that of an open gateway.

Come to think of it, that shockwave did carry a familiar and non-threatening frequency with it. The short flash also suggests it was open only briefly. It could've been an accidental activation, or maybe gateways just randomly release a burp of energy like that sometimes. Either way, I have to investigate.

"Come on," I tell Horus. "Let's go check it out."

CHAPTER 19

DEKA

My tumble down the Great Pyramid begins just as expected, with my feet hitting stone and momentum flipping me forward onto my face. But that's where my expectations end.

Rather than crash down the two hundred steps toward the ground, I slide on my belly across loose rocks. I reach out and manage to snag a branch and jerk myself to a stop.

Wait— *A branch?* This is not something you'd find on a stone pyramid. My next guess might be the limb of a dead Ori or Fori if not for the fact it's rooted well and offers no give.

I open my eyes to confirm that I am definitely no longer on the Great Pyramid. Nor am I in Giza. The darkness and cold nip in the air tell me I'm not even on my home continent.

An assessment of the slope above ends at a flat mountaintop fifty feet above me.

I gasp in disbelief. This breath then leaves my mouth in a white puff that rises before my face. A fierce shiver shakes me to my soul. Yes, I am definitely a long way from the deserts of Africa.

A survey of the vast blackness below reveals little on this moonless night, but a yellow glow draws my attention to a distant cluster of lights. I squint to see they are a collection of... Domes? Yes, like a colony.

A colony!

I jump and yell in excitement, but cold air freezes my lungs and leaves me breathless. For a long while all I can do is stare in astonishment at those distant lights defying the darkness.

Maybe I'd gotten it wrong. Perhaps my heart had reached out to a savior and led me to the place of our true salvation—the great human civilization Nya had told us about.

Those distant lights shine like a beacon of strength and hope. This branch of humanity lives boldly in the open, displaying their existence proudly. True civilization. It radiates such power that not even the Watchers have dared attack them.

My hands tremble with excitement. We humans are more than just cave dwellers struggling to survive. My colony has fought the good fight alone on the front line for fifteen years, and it's high time I call the rest to arms. Time to reclaim our planet from the Watchers. When we evict them, the Fori and Ori will transform Earth into a lush paradise, where Nya and her race can all live in peace with us.

My heart flutters. *Nya.* I hope she received a warm welcome at our caverns. What did she do when we didn't show up? Hopefully she settled in to await our arrival. She wasn't up for a fight anyway, and our colony had lost most of our warriors at the pyramids, so her options would be limited to hoping we'd simply gotten held up.

Yes, she'll have stayed put to await our arrival. She is safe there.

I laugh in delight. It echoes down the mountain slope and sounds like madness.

Shouting interrupts my laughter.

I hold my breath and listen closely. Cocking my head to the side, I narrow the chatter's location to the other side of the mountain. The bickering sounds like Ori and Fori. A few captives must have changed their minds after seeing me jump through the gate, and now they're arguing over where we've ended up.

Shale rock slides under my feet as I trudge across the loose mountain, which seems to have four sloped sides. Like a pyramid. With each sliding step, the bickering grows louder and more discernible.

"I told you it was a bad idea," says one voice. "But *noooo*. You had to dive into that portal anyway."

"I told you *NOT* to go through the portal."

"Well, ex-*CUSE* me! The wind was blowing in my ears and I was pretty distracted by all those arrows flying at me."

"At *us*. We're a team, remember?"

"Hah! We're only a team when you need me!"

I round the corner, desperate to see some familiar faces, but the two arguing on the far mountain slope are far from familiar.

One is a young Aeri, the other an elder Fori. A coiled ponytail of hair as white as sea foam crowns the back of her head. She stands taller than her Aeri companion, and my understanding of these races tells me this is unusual.

The Aeri spots me and jumps back in fright. She spreads her wings threateningly as she scans the ground for a weapon.

The Fori spins on her heels with both hands raised. I don't recognize either of these figures on their own, but with the feathered wings of the Aeri spread out behind her partner in front, and the air rippling before the Fori's hands, I realize she is no Fori at all. She is the Ripper.

Starlight glosses The Ripper's tight white hair. Her black sunken eyes and pallid skin give her the look of death, and her fierce green stare holds no warmth for me.

Though we are a good stone's throw away, the Ripper jabs through the air as if to punch me.

Having seen her in action, I know to dive aside before a shockwave rips me apart.

BOOM—pebbles rain down around me.

I roll to a stop and throw up both hands. "Wait! I'm a friend of Nya. Don't kill me!"

The Ripper frowns and stands up straight to study me curiously. "Who?"

Her Aeri companion steps out from behind and says, "Evening Star."

The Ripper's frown deepens in confusion.

"The spawn of Klora," clarifies the short Aeri.

The Ripper's eyes flash wide with knowing. "Ah, Klora," she says, lowering her hands. "How is that little devil?"

I sigh and look to the stars in relief.

"Ha!" The Aeri points at me. "You should've seen yourself. You were all like, '*Oh, no, please don't kill me!*'" she says while waving her hands in mocking surrender. Then she clutches her belly and keels over in riotous laughter. Her right eye is bigger than the left, and when she laughs it bulges to about the size of my fist, flaunting a sapphire-colored iris.

The Ripper's tight lips curl into an amused grin.

"Have you seen her?" she asks. "Klora, I mean. It's been so long, and she has a youngling now?"

It seems the Ripper and Nya's mother were close, so I'm reluctant to deliver the news—that Jexa killed her at the pyramids. To avoid an explosive reaction, I offer a lie.

"I haven't seen Klora, but Nya is back at my colony in Africa."

"Why were you helping the Light Ones?" the Ripper says.

Light Ones. I've heard Nya's folk call the Watchers by that name. "We weren't. They used us to set the Capstone. They were trying to release Jexa, but I tried to summon the Magister and ended up here."

The Ripper narrows her eyes on me. "*You* opened the gate?"

A balloon swells in my throat. I swallow it down and nod.

The Ripper's hands tighten into fists. "Well, you flung us too far from the fight."

Although we've ended up far from where I'd expected, upon a gate I had no idea existed, I'm positive the glowing city in the distance is the alignment my heart had fallen in with. "We have great allies here," I say.

The Ripper raises her chin. "Back to Klora's daughter. What business do you have with her?"

"She's the Rebel Marshal, leader of your people."

The Ripper clutches her chest and recoils, offended. "When did this appointment happen?"

"When she led an attack on the Watchers. Every one of

your kind rallied to follow her. They still do." *What's left of them,* I almost say, but I keep that part to myself.

"What's *your* relation to her?" asks the Ripper, and her interest is oddly sincere.

My cheeks and the back of my neck burn. I'd not considered how to define our relationship.

"We're friends," I say, though that description doesn't sound right. Mali and I were the best of friends, but my heart never fluttered when someone mentioned her name.

The Ripper scoffs. "Don't lie to me. I've seen how you barbarians lust after us fair folk."

The stunted Aeri points at me and bursts out laughing. "You like her! Oh, man, that is so messed up. You're not even the same species! Could you imagine, Drusilla, the two of them... *together?!*"

The Ripper—whose name is apparently Drusilla—gives me an amused smile. Then she nods to her partner. "Let's go. We have a long journey North."

"The Watchers," I say, "they may come through the gate here."

'Drusilla the Ripper' glances over her shoulder toward the mountaintop.

"Sure, they could open a gate to here," she says, "but they can't take the Capstone through with them. They have to move it here across the physical plane. Only then can they activate this backup gate for an interplanetary jump."

"They may send a force through to hold the mountain. We must organize a defense."

Drusilla plants her hands on her hips and spins around, surveying the horizon in every direction. She nods faintly, contemplating. She seems to have come to share my concern, so it's a surprise when she says, "Unlikely." She looks to her partner and points up the slope. "Come on, now. We need to get moving."

"Wait," I say, rushing to block their path. "Why don't you think they'll come through the gate?"

"Not worth it. They'd have to await the Capstone's arrival, which could take weeks. There's no energy source for them here, so any defense force will weaken beyond worth. No, they'll travel from the northlands in force... *if* we give them the chance. Now, out of my way."

The Aeri races up the slope. Drusilla faces downslope and kneels with her back to her. She spreads both arms wide and wraps her four clear wings around her chest. The Aeri leaps forward and glides down into Drusilla's back, hooks her arms under the Ripper's armpits, and lifts her from the ground.

They glide down the mountain, then veer out and loop around to the side I'd fallen onto after crossing the gate.

The Ripper's dependence on that Aeri to fly near the gateway reminds me of Nya's struggle in Giza. If she could find an Aeri lackey to transport her around, the Watchers wouldn't stand a chance at taking this mountain. Too bad most Aeri are traitors.

Scumbag traitors, Nya calls them. Her voice says these words in my head, and my heart aches with longing. Even her most provoking rant would sound like music to me right now.

A cold breeze blasts me, and only now do I realize I'm naked. I gasp in surprise. The portal must have ripped my clothes clean off! I'll have to find new garments or shelter soon, but it could be worse. That portal could've dumped me into the Dark, or sent me tumbling down the pyramid steps like I'd thought. Or it could have closed before I jumped through.

My heart breaks for those I've left behind. They'd been holding the high ground, but they were poorly armed and sorely outnumbered. Our best hope relies solely on my shoulders, and I can only pray that Nya and Sheffa don't return to the pyramids when they realize we'd been captured.

Nya...

A hand smacks my face—my own. My mission is not Nya. It's to warn my people here of the coming attack. My best chance to accomplish that is by reaching that distant city, so I begin my long descent down this mystical mountain.

CHAPTER 20

DEKA

I don't think I have to worry about the Watcher invasion anymore. The cold will kill me long before that could ever happen.

My walk down the mountain consists of incessant shivering and teeth chattering so severely I'm sure they'll soon shatter. I'd not be surprised if the nearest settlement hears me coming. Hopefully they'll send a rescue party with blankets and hot soup. Wishful thinking, I know, but I can't help it as I hug myself tight and carry on.

I've never known such cold. My breath puffs before my face and I swear it freezes my eyelashes. Each blink is stiff and, if I'm not careful, may be my last.

Smoke rises from a cluster of trees at the mountain base. Smoke means fire, and fire means heat. Precious, precious heat.

Sure enough, as I continue my descent, I catch a flicker of orange light through a latticed canopy of bare tree branches. That fire is my new objective. It's all that matters, and it becomes my world, because my mission will fail if I do not survive this night.

I check the surrounding horizon for signs of daylight. It must have been midnight when I arrived, because there's no trace of dusk or dawn light in any direction. This gets me stomping faster downslope.

Get to that fire, commands a voice inside my head. It's more forceful than my mind's chatter, perhaps a desperate part of me that awakens to dispense obvious advice when death looms over me. But that fire is important in more ways than one. There I can at least pass on my warning to whoever tends it. With any luck, they'll have a way to get word to their leaders so I can rest. *Get to that fire, and all will be well.*

I'm two-thirds down the mountain when the smell of burning meat stops me dead.

Saliva floods my mouth as I'm reminded of the time Mali killed a seagull with her crossbow. We'd snuck to a cove and cooked it over a driftwood fire. I'd never tasted bird meat before then, and I'd soon come to regret it. That rare delicacy had developed in me a high standard for future meals, one which could never be satisfied by the grub we scrounged from the earth.

Here that smell weaves a spell in my mind. I cannot resist it. I dare not resist it. An invisible harpoon pierces my belly and hauls me toward the bonfire below. I rush down the rocky slope with complete abandon, my knees buckling every few paces, and it's a miracle I don't pop one in my reckless haste. The tantalizing smell grows stronger with each step and soon has me bounding down the mountain.

Somehow I reach the base without breaking anything. My legs feel like jelly, making it hard to walk in a straight line. I stagger side to side as I enter the winter forest, where the dark ground is hard to see, so I trip over roots and rocks every few steps. I catch myself on tree trunks and use them to steady my feverish walk toward the seductive smell.

This forest is nothing like Nya's gift to us—the one the Watchers had burned. Bare branches overhead and dead leaves crunching underfoot gives it a spooky, mystical vibe. Blue smoke wafts through the air to create an otherworldly haze. And who's to say it's not?

I turn and look back up through the canopy. That mountain gateway very well may have delivered me to a spirit realm of sorts, like the Dark. Or Hell. Or purgatory. The fire ahead may be some form of torture—a smell that grows thicker and more flavorful with each step, yet remains ever out of reach. A hunger that forever grows and shall never be relieved.

Shadows cross before the glow ahead. The fire has so far permitted my approach without retreating from me, so I slow my pace to lighten my steps. Despite starvation and looming hypothermia, I can't let my wits abandon me. I know nothing of the people who occupy this land. They could be cooking a fellow human for all I know, so it's best to learn more about them before I introduce myself.

There's three of them—two guys and a girl. The girl stands out most because of the sheen of her golden hair in the firelight. It actually takes me off guard. Though I've heard of this physical trait, I'd always taken it for the makings of fairytales.

Next to draw my attention is their clothes. Grey and black trousers blend in with the surrounding foliage so well it seems intentional, like patterns designed to conceal, which gives rise to a realization.

They're warriors! Just the people I need to pass on my message to.

I step out with my hands raised to appear non-threatening.

One of the boys notices me first and reaches behind the log he's sitting on to produce a long black firearm. This sudden movement alerts the others to my presence, and soon I'm staring down the speaking ends of three rifles.

"Who are you?" says the other guy, who sports a black mohawk.

Though they're armed and outnumber me three-fold, these warriors appear more fearful of me than I am of them. Their hands shake and their eyes dart side to side as they search the forest behind me.

"My name is Deka," I say, thrilled to hear we speak the same language. It's a promising start.

"What are you doing out here?" asks the war leader. He appears to be Marlok's age, early twenties or maybe younger, and his soft face contrasts his macho hairdo.

"I just arrived," I say, pointing back toward the mountain.

All three glance up at the sky nervously.

"That flash," the blond girl says.

"What was it?" the leader asks me. "Did your balloon crash?"

"Balloon?"

"How did you get way out here on bare feet?" Mohawk asks. "And where are your clothes?"

I nod back toward the mountain. "I came through the gateway. Are you its guardians?"

An exchange of confused looks tells me 'no'.

"Where are you from?" the girl asks.

"North Africa."

Her eyes flare wide in wonder. She lowers her weapon, but her two comrades maintain frowns of suspicion and keep their weapons level with my chest. A tense silence settles over us, with only the crackling fire to be heard.

Then, as if coordinated, all three of them burst into laughter. They laugh so hard that they drop their guard completely, with each setting their weapon aside.

The girl waves for me to join them by the fire. "I'm Clarian," she says. She points to her mohawk leader. "This is Darius, and the fella there with the glasses is Max."

Max gives me a faint nod while Darius tends the fire.

"You're lucky," says Clarian. "We were just about to have lunch. You hungry?"

The drool dripping from my chin is all the answer she needs. But...

Lunch? In my culture that's our midday meal. *If* there's food to be had, of course. Perhaps these warriors must remain well fed with midnight feasts.

"It's duck," adds Max.

I don't care if it's a half-rotted Watcher foot. If it tastes anything like it smells, I'll eat it with a smile.

"You need some clothes," says Clarian. "Darius, he looks about your size. Grab him your spare uniform. We won't be needing them where we're going anyway."

The mohawk leader offers me a black short-sleeve shirt, a pair of trousers, and a matching over-shirt of grey-and-black stripes.

I accept these offerings but hold them warily. "What do you want in return?"

"Just don't die of hypothermia, okay? I'm in no mood to go digging graves tonight."

The caring type. This is good, and I'm inclined to believe his sincerity. If they meant me any harm they'd have shot me a few seconds ago.

I don the uniform and kneel close to the fire. Clarian tears a leg from the duck and, when she offers it to me, my hand becomes a beast with a mind of its own. It snatches the cooked meat and stuffs it straight into my mouth.

The other three watch me devour my portion with bewilderment, but I don't care. It is the best thing any human has ever tasted. No one will ever convince me otherwise.

Any effort to savor the meal fails quickly, and I soon find myself gnawing on the bone. Allowing guests to eat first must be a custom among these people, because they watch me with great angst until I'm left licking the grease from my fingers.

Clarian exchanges an uneasy look with Darius, then holds her portion of golden bird above the fire.

"*For this gift we give thanks to the Mother,*" she says. "*And for your sacrifice we give thanks to you, our brother.*" Darius, Max, and Clarian each bows to the chunk of meat in their hands, as if in salute. All three of them then peel small strips of meat and chew them slowly, and suddenly I realize how feral I must have looked eating mine.

Shame burns in me, but it's only faint. At least my behavior should bolster my claim about not being from around here.

I sit back with a satisfied belly and appreciate the comforts of this moment.

"So, where are you really from?" asks Darius. His tone is lighter, more casual, but I can tell he insists on an answer.

I hate to spoil the good mood, but I do have a mission to fulfill, so I sit up to address my hosts. "I come from a land far away... to warn of an attack."

All three sit on edge.

"Who's going to attack?" Darius asks. "The Coast Patrol? The Dregs?"

"An invasion of killer fae," I say. "They're headed this way, so you must spread word to your war chiefs at once. All of them. Everyone needs to rally here to defend this mountain."

I receive the same surprised stares as my previous claim, except now, the ridicule comes faster. Clarian leans back, howling with such laughter that she nearly falls from her log.

Darius cuts his laughter short. "Seriously, though, where are you from?"

The laughter from Clarian and Max dies. Noticing Darius's intensity, his companions tense up.

"Just tell him the truth," Clarian says. "Then we can pass around the wine flask and have a few more laughs. No troubles."

"Yes," comes a new voice from the dark forest behind, "tell us where the attack is coming from."

My three dinner-mates reach for their weapons, but they freeze when a dozen warriors emerge from the surrounding darkness. These new arrivals wear the same clothing as us, but they train their weapons on my group as if we were all enemies. My new friends take it a step further by raising their hands in surrender.

The armed soldiers sweep in and check us for weapons, then lash our wrists behind our backs with plastic bindings.

"He's not one of us," Clarian says with a nod toward me. "He lost his clothes, so we gave him a uniform."

"Where's your I.D. bracelet?" the new leader asks me. A name tag over his left chest reads 'Sarx'. His gray hair and gruff voice differs greatly from Darius's, who now stares at his boots.

I have no idea what Sarx is talking about, so he orders his soldiers to continue binding me like the others.

They gather up our gear and march us in single file through the woods. Two warriors watch us from each side, their weapons always at the ready.

I slow my pace to allow Clarian to catch up.

"Where are they taking us?"

"Port Abersali," she says, her voice trembling. "They'll try us for desertion, then hang us."

My blood goes cold. "Hang you? For what?"

"I just told you—*Desertion*."

"What's that?"

She slows and gives me a truly curious look. "You really aren't from around here, are you. Well, our King forced us into military service to defend the border. But us three are pacifists, so we abandoned our posts."

"Pacifists?"

"Yeah, we don't believe in fighting. There's a rumor of an island where deserters go to live in peace. That's where we were headed."

I breathe easier knowing their king is preparing for the attack. He must have gotten word already, or learned of the

Watcher threat on his own. Though, I am a bit disappointed in Clarian's near-sightedness.

"The Watchers," I say, "they can still find you on an island."

Clarian gives me a blank look. It's like I'm speaking another language to her. "Who are the Watchers?"

"The creatures you're defending your border against. You know, the aliens trying to exterminate us."

Clarian stricken stare suggests I just blew her mind. "Trust me," she says, "our enemies are very human. If you really aren't from around here, then here's a quick history lesson for you: Anterra is home to two countries, but it's only got room for one."

There's a lot of information for me to unpack, so I start with the basics. "So your people are ruled by kings?"

"Ours is, yes. That much I know well enough. I'm not sure what you'd call the beast that lurks across our border. *The Wolf*, some call him. They say his research involves all sorts of horrible experiments. But our cause is no better. At the border, there are no good sides. That's why we were going to Arokya—that island I told you about." Clarian swallows hard and says, "Guess now it's the gallows for us."

"That's enough chit-chat," says the soldier to my right. "Next one who speaks gets strung up from the next oak tree."

A shiver rattles through me. I'd survived Watcher captivity because they had use for my strength. These folk seem to think my body would best serve as a warning, so I seal my lips tight and shuffle along in silence.

CHAPTER 21
NYA

I'm about to kill my first humans.

From my perch halfway down a maple tree, I see at least twelve of them escorting Deka. They keep a close watch on him and three others. Though they're all dressed the same, those with weapons point them at their unarmed captives. They utter threats that heat my blood so bad I want to dust them. But it's not them I'm worried about. It's the group watching their approach that concerns me.

I'd noticed them after Deka's capture around the fire. I was about to reveal myself to him and his new friends when those captors took them, so I flew ahead in search of a spot from where I could swoop in to pull him away. That's when I spotted this other group waiting along the path.

They are hyper-aware to the point they'd heard my fluttering wings approach from above. I'd clung to this tree for cover and dared not move since.

The sight of their weapons sends a quiver through my heart. I've seen them before, in Deka's books about seafaring. He called the silver barbs 'harpoons'.

The harpoonists lie to either side of the path, awaiting Deka's group with great anticipation.

I take shallow breaths to keep my puffing breath from giving me away. Sweat slicks my palms despite the chill as the distance between both parties narrows.

The tree I cling to leans over a bend in the path and offers me full view of both groups. Deka will be harder to free once these two armed forces unite, and every heartbeat I sit idle tightens their grip on him. I should act now, before they round the bend, but... I can't.

Even at my best I'd risk too much by attacking with both groups so near. The harpooners are spread out and on high alert, and one of their steel barbs to my heart will be the end of me. But where are the others? I'm assuming Deka had crossed through that brief gate opening I saw, but who did he come here with? Mora's gang? Watchers? Or have we both fallen into the dark lands of a shared afterlife? I have so many questions that only he can answer.

I'm equally curious about the behavior of his waiting compatriots. The harpoonists sink low to conceal themselves from the approach of Deka's captors.

The branch supporting my left hand jolts as something lands on it. My heart almost explodes with fright until I notice it's Horus. He hops down onto my lap and nestles against my belly, where he shivers fiercely, whether from cold or fear I cannot tell. Do birds of prey shiver when they're afraid?

THWAP!

That sound nearly sends me launching into flight, and it takes everything in me to remain planted on my branch.

A wheezy gasp rises from below. I look down to see the

lead captor lumber forward onto his face. When he hits the ground, a steel barb impaling his belly punches out through his back.

A captor watching the flanks shouts, "Squids!"

Silver darts whiz in crisscrossing patterns from the surrounding brush to skewer half of Deka's escort.

I cover my mouth to stifle a scream. In half a blink, six guards and one of Deka's co-captives fall dead to the ground.

The captors respond by blasting thunderous sparks out the ends of their weapons. Their arms rattle as they sweep side to side, spraying the surrounding forest with invisible projectiles. It's so loud I can hardly think.

We need to get out of here!

I push away from the trunk and slide back on my branch for a better look at Deka, but the flashing weapons ruin my night vision. Of the bodies curled and lying on the ground, I can't tell which is Deka. I can't even tell which are dead or alive.

The chaos has Horus in an awful state. He sits hard like a rock on my lap.

The rattling thunder tapers to a stop, and clicking metal reveals Deka's captors reloading their weapons. It's time to make my move.

I swing my left leg over the branch so that I'm no longer straddling it. I'm about to glide down when—*THWAP!*

A punch to the gut knocks me back off my branch. I hit the ground before I know what's happening, with both impacts knocking the wind clear out of me. I've landed within reach behind one of the captors, but all I can do is gulp for air as he resumes his firing. Flashes from his outward blasting gleam off a steel pole sticking up from my heart.

Terror locks my muscles, paralyzing my efforts to breathe. They got me!

I manage to raise my right arm and grab the harpoon with a clammy hand. I brace myself for the shot of pain that's sure to accompany the extraction of this cold steel barb. If not for my panic I'd hesitate with this move, but it needs to come out for my heart to continue beating, so I haul it up with one good yank.

To my surprise and dismay, my breathing doesn't get any easier. Even the tightness in my belly remains the same. When I lift my head to examine the harpoon, I see why.

Horus lies on my belly, the steel barb pinning both wings to his body. The bloody harpoon tip has barely broken through the feathers of his left wing and only nicked my navel.

Somehow my heart squeezes a little tighter. Horus's fear just saved my life by making his body denser. Or...

I gasp with a realization that rips my heart in half. Horus had foreseen my fate and landed on my lap to protect me!

I clutch him to my chest and roll onto my side, where I sob and caress his feathers.

"What the..." A nearby captor stares at me in shock.

I try sitting up, but my stiff body resists.

He finishes reloading his weapon, pulls back on a springy lever, and aims its open end at my face. Whatever is meant to explode out the round opening is sure to ruin my night if it hits me in the eye, yet all I can do is stare unblinkingly at his finger curling around the release mechanism.

I can't look away, which allows me to witness the instant a silver pole punches through his neck. His weapon lowers as he goes limp and falls onto his side.

I scramble to the nearest tree trunk and burrow under its giant roots. No feathered guardian remains to stop another harpoon for me, so I...

Oh no! I left Horus's body out there!

I smack my face three times at my carelessness. I'm about to crawl out to retrieve him, but silence keeps me back.

Underbrush swishes as the human *Squids* close in. From my hiding spot I see they wear long coats and knee-high boots.

The blond captive rises to her knees.

"We claim amnesty from the Lord of the Sea," she says, her voice shaking in terror. "We cast away our crown patches and bow to the trident."

The Squids wrench their impaled harpoons from the bodies scattered about. Anyone with signs of life are forced up onto their knees, and I see only Deka and the blond girl have survived the ambush.

I bow my head and let out a huge sigh of relief.

A Squid rushes to retrieve a harpoon sticking up from the ground near me. He holds it up to show Horus to his mates. "Who wasted a good shot on a bird?"

Another Squid stomps over for a closer appraisal. "I was aiming for the sniper. You didn't see him?"

"Sniper? Looks like lunch to me. Nice shot, though. Been a while since I had falcon."

His partner points up at the tree branch I'd fallen from. "Sniper was right there, I swear."

He searches the ground and perks up when he catches a trail of matted grass leading toward my hiding place. His grip tightens around his harpoon launcher as he follows the track with careful steps.

I try to retreat deeper under the roots, but there's no room.

"Move out!" shouts a man's voice. "That gunfire will have every patrol here within the hour."

My hunter stops and looks up the path. His fellow Squids must already be on the move, because he rushes to join them without looking back.

All I want is to curl up under this tree and hide away from this cold dark world, but I risk losing Deka if I do.

My close brush with death warns that these folk have better night eyes than me, so I rub soil over my skin and through my hair before crawling out from my hiding place. Hopefully this will conceal me better the next time I'm about to swoop in for Deka. But that's assuming I get another chance.

DEKA

This is turning out to be the longest night of my life.

I look frequently through the tree branches for signs of dawn, and for the life of me I find none. Deep darkness taunts me from every direction.

The Squids unbind our hands but keep their harpoons directed toward Clarian and me. Two lead us through the forest of swaying trunks under creaking branches, while the other four take up the rear. They wear long black coats, stocking caps and knee-high leather boots. Their faces are weathered above scruffy beards, and I'm surprised Sarx's warriors hadn't smelled the stink of fish from them a mile off. Instead, the Squids managed to slaughter their foe without taking a single casualty.

Clarian sobs over the deaths of her fellow pacifists, so I take her hand. She squeezes tight and leans against me in our walk through the forest.

"Was a harpoon that killed Max," she whispers.

Clarian's fear of the Squids should put me on edge as well. We wear the same uniform, one very different from our captors, which marks us for enemies. But I fear not. Together we've survived being ensnared twice—one of those times under extremely violent circumstances—which fortifies a theory I've been developing.

I've been captured three times under this same moon. Each change of hands brings me closer to reporting the coming attack to someone of high authority. The Squids have kept us alive for a reason. Surely they now escort us to a tribunal for judgment or questioning, and that's where I'll offload the burden of my message.

Go with the flow, urges my guiding voice, *and you'll end up where you need to be.*

A breeze blows cold air and shakes me to my bones. It rocks the trees, their bare branches creaking overhead, ancient wood that's lived through who knows how many winters. What wisdom could they impart upon us?

The wind grows stronger the longer we walk, and eventually carries with it the salty smell of sea.

My heart weeps. I can't help but think of my home on Africa, of Marlok and the others. Did the Watchers kill them? Did they secure the high ground and hold it? Maybe they reset the gate key and escaped to a safe haven. Or the pyramid goddess remained in Ko Skadia and led them inside the pyramid. Yes, I bet that's what happened.

The sound of lapping waves tells me when we're near the coast. Soon black water appears through the forest edge ahead, when both Squids in front pick up the pace.

We emerge from the woodland onto a stony shore. A brisk sea breeze nips at my face, and it's the most refreshing thing I've ever felt. Though the salty coastal air reminds me of home, it is distinctly different. It's cleaner, unpolluted. The water here is so pristine that a fishing boat trawls the seabed a short distance out, telling me these people feed on their sea offerings without worry of illness.

One of the Squids drags a black boat out from the tree line. Its bottom squeaks over rocks until he slides it into the water, where he wades knee deep to guide the whole vessel over slapping waves. He snaps his fingers at us and says, "Get in."

Clarian swiftly obeys. She's eager to leave this land behind, even if it's for a flimsy boat crammed with hostile captors.

I'm quick to join her. I check the soft deck for oars, to prepare them for our guards, but I find none. This is most unusual considering the absence of a mast and sail. Just a bulky machine mounted astern.

Two Squids jump into the boat—one in front, the other at the helm. The helm Squid presses a button on the stern machine to bring it to life. Its loud rattling puts me on edge, but the pilot is unfazed by it. To his companions on shore he says, "Hang tight. I'll be right back."

The machine roars and launches us forward. Cold wind blasts my face as we skip over waves toward the fishing trawler, forcing me and Clarian to huddle low in the center. We don't have to stay like this for long, though, because we reach the fishing boat in little time.

A spotlight shines from a rectangular wheelhouse that stands a third back from the front of the boat, blinding me.

My helmsman orders us to climb up a net hanging from the trawler, where sailors greet us with firearms. They size me up with hardened eyes.

"Take them below," orders a man from behind the

blinding light. "Commander Centaurus will see them at once."

The trawler's Squids escort us below decks. They lead us to a room surrounded by steel walls and a matching gray ceiling, then direct me to a chair beside Clarian.

When I sit I notice a man seated in the corner, left of the doorway. His long coat is like those of the other sailors, except for three yellow bars around each sleeve. I'm assuming these represent his status or experience, much like Nya's armbands, so I take him for Commander Centaurus.

If I had to guess the Commander's age just by his eyes, I'd say he's older than any human I've ever met—G-Ma included. But his coal-black hair slicked back into a ponytail and his patchy beard bear not a single strand of gray. On these features I must put him in his thirties, but his eyes tell me those years have been long and wrought with much sorrow.

Clarian sits with her eyes closed and her hands clasped on her lap. She shivers uncontrollably, muttering passages that sound like a prayer, the words of which appeal to a great Mother unfamiliar to me.

One of our escorts slams the steel door shut and pulls a lever down to lock it. He sports a ponytail similar to his commander's, but with hair of fiery orange. He ignores the Commander and devotes all his attention to us.

"Who is your commanding officer? Where did you serve? Does the name Jayda Onero mean anything to you? Why did you flinch when I said that name?"

Clarian responds with a stern expression and a mechanical tone. "Service Number R99042-01. Private Clar —" Her eyes flare wide as she catches herself. "I mean, I... I ripped off my crown patch. I no longer serve the King, nor his causes."

Our interrogator cocks his head curiously. "King?"

Clarian sits straighter with a frightful realization. "The *Imposter*," she corrects. "I've abandoned my post to come seek asylum from the Lord of the Sea."

The interrogator looks to me. "And you?"

"My commander is Marlok of Westerly. I know of no kings, and serve only my tribal interests. The name Jayda Onero means nothing to me, nor would the name of anyone else from this land."

Commander Centaurus's chair creaks as he leans forward, intrigue sparking life in his weary eyes. Our interrogator turns his head slightly to acknowledge this sudden interest. He returns his focus to me.

"You're from where, exactly?"

"Africa."

"You got here how?"

"A portal over the mountain, near where you found me."

The fire in the Commander's eyes fades. He leans back in his chair and folds his arms, disinterested.

He thinks me a liar.

"Right," says the interrogator. He stands back to address both me and Clarian. "You'll be returned to your King in a prisoner exchange. We'll offer you quarter on board until the arrangements are made."

Clarian shifts nervously.

"Don't worry," the interrogator says, "we won't tell Regulus you deserted. You killed a good few of our sailors, and it pains us greatly to turn you over. He'll give you both medals and commendations."

"He'll send us back to the border!" cries Clarian.

"All the same, we don't need more defectors. And we certainly don't need more crown spies joining our ranks."

"We're not spies!" Clarian shouts. Her voice is heated, her anger fueled by fear.

"Why have you come to us?" says the interrogator, heat rising in his voice also. "To participate in a rebellion against the King? No. You're looking for a ride to Arokya, where you hope to live out your days in gardens of sunshine and bliss. Well, we already have enough of your kind leeching off our goodwill."

"I don't care where you send me," I tell them, "so long as my message reaches the right ears."

The interrogator raises an eyebrow. "Assume I have the right ears. What message would you have for me?"

"There's an attack coming."

He nods in understanding. "Ah, yes. I suppose they'll be coming through a magical light in the sky as well?"

My cheeks burn with frustrated anger. "They're coming from the north. Right now they're gathering their army in the deserts of Africa, but it won't take them long to reach here."

The interrogator smiles sarcastically. "Right, and—"

"Lieutenant," says the Commander. "That's enough."

He rises from his chair, and the interrogator dutifully pulls open the door for him. Commander Centaurus steps out into the passageway, where he stops and gestures for me to join him.

Clarian gives me a frightened look. It's a silent plea that begs me to stay with her, but I dare not defy the Lord of the Sea while in his element. Instead, I give Clarian an assuring shoulder squeeze and step outside.

The Commander leads me up to the main deck and then ahead, to the starboard bow, where we watch the forested shore slip by as the ship cruises along the coast. I have no idea in which direction we travel. There's no trace of dawn anywhere. I can't even tell which way is east, and a look to the sky reveals an unfamiliar pattern of stars.

A wave of panic hits me. Did that gate actually deposit me into a dark afterlife, where its inhabitants are ever at war and live in constant fear? Where small bands of opposing forces spend eternity hunting each other down?

"Is the attack coming so soon?" the Commander says, noting my apprehension.

"When is sunrise?"

Commander Centaurus turns side on with the rail to square off with me. "You really are from there," he says, and his decisive tone suggests he's decided he believes me. "My helmsman reported a flash in the sky a few hours ago, over Mount Tuck. You're saying that was you?"

"It was the gateway. I came through it."

"From Africa."

"Yes."

"Will the attack come through there as well?"

His interest seems genuine. I feel like I'm getting somewhere with this man.

"I'm told they won't," I say. "They'll travel from the north in force."

"How many?"

"Ten thousand at least."

"Why have you turned on them?"

It takes me a few seconds to work out his meaning. "They're not my people," I say. "They are winged devils from another galaxy. They've been hunting us since they arrived, fifteen years ago. You've been lucky down here so far, but your time has now come."

The Commander gives me a skeptical look. Though, it's only brief before his face returns to neutral. I sense he's a man who's learned not to dismiss such claims until investigation warrants it.

He stares back at the ocean horizon. His gaze is far, reaching somewhere beyond the range of human eyes.

"I sailed out there once," he says, his voice faint in reverie. "In those northlands we trespassed against a great enemy, and upon my return home I vowed to defend Anterra from their retaliation." He rests his elbows on the rail. "Years went by. Then a decade. When half a decade more passed I finally started to believe we'd made a clean escape. But now it seems I was wrong."

"You fought the sky demons?"

"One sky demon, yes. But I think we're referring to a different manner of beast. Mine came in the form of a steel ship that flew through the air, breathing streams of hot bullets."

This description sounds a lot like a helicopter. The generation before mine had used a fleet of them to enforce peace across their empire, my warlord grandfather included. If Commander Centaurus has traveled to Africa and returned, then he is a worldly person. An adventurer of influence and renown. Exactly the champion I've come to see.

"The light that took you here..." he says in a hushed voice, as if fearing someone might overhear. "I've seen something similar before. We were following the African coast home when a blue sunrise lit up the eastern horizon. The night was blazing hot, but that light sent a shiver through me, deep down to my soul. That chill has been there ever since."

My heart flutters with this breakthrough. "You must spread word to all your tribes. The enemy is coming for that mountain. Every one of your warriors must come together to fight them."

The Commander raises his eyebrows in amusement and allows a laugh. "*Come together*. Well, that seals it right there. You truly aren't from around here. That mountain there," he says, pointing to the distant pyramidal silhouette, "it's on crown land, and you'll get no help from Regulus."

"Then who do you serve? How many warriors can you muster?"

He squints at the dark ocean horizon. "I oversee a small island territory. Our battleships give us command of the sea, but we hold no ground on the mainland here. We can make up the first line of defense, but it is a wide area to watch. It won't be hard for an airborne enemy to spread us thin or slip by unnoticed."

Frustration burns in my chest and heats my words when I say, "There must be *someone* we can appeal to."

The Commander's expression hardens. His cheeks glow red, and I can't tell if it's from anger or shame.

"There is the Wolf," he says. "But if the rumors are true, she'll be no more help than Regulus."

I'm really having trouble understanding the players who run the affairs around here.

Seeing my confusion, the Commander says, "Come, I'll show you."

Inside the wheelhouse, an elderly bald man stands

behind the ship's steering wheel. A chart sits across a table to his left, and I recognize the enlarged rounded outline from my mother's maps. It is a map of Antarctica.

I suppress a laugh of relief. So I really didn't end up on another planet or in some supernatural realm.

Commander Centaurus slides a finger across the continent. "Anterra is split into two countries—Polaria and Ortaria."

He taps the left half. "This is Polaria, where we picked you up. That's Regulus's domain, but you'd be wasting your breath appealing to him. Not to mention risking your life. He is ill-tempered and unwelcoming to outsiders."

The Commander slides his finger to the right side of the border. "This is Ortaria. Both countries have been at war for over four hundred years, and no foreign enemy will distract them from that."

"And the Wolf, she rules Ort... Ort-Air..." I struggle to recall the name.

"*Ortaria*, yes. But she is just one of many warlords ruling the wildlands on that side of the border. Ortaria is large and fractured—politically and geographically—but their hatred of Polaria binds them in common cause. The Wolf's grudge against Regulus runs deeper than all others combined, which has attracted a formidable following to her banner. At least that's what I've heard, anyway."

Commander Centaurus swallows hard and shifts awkwardly. I sense he's appeared in a chapter or two of the Wolf's history book.

"You know her," I say.

He shakes his head. "I *knew* her, many years ago. If what they say about her is true, she is not the person I once loved."

"You don't believe in her cause."

The Commander's ears and neck glow red. "It doesn't matter what I believe. When I donned this Coast Patrol uniform, I swore to protect both countries from the dangers of the north."

He's clearly heated, so he steps outside and makes his way down to the main deck. There is still no light of dawn lining any horizon, but I have other matters to pursue.

"You can't stop this foe with ships, even ones like this. We need warriors on that mountain defending the gate."

The Commander sizes up his wheelhouse with a sly grin. "This ship isn't used for battle. It's a disguise to slip into Polarian waters unnoticed. But yes, you are right. Even a fleet twice what I command won't do much against an aerial enemy. That's why I'm sending you on a special mission."

Commander Centaurus squeezes the steel rail and narrows his eyes on the forested shoreline. "I need you to deliver a message to the Wolf. Tell her our old friend Khalid has come for revenge. Don't say anything about winged devils, she'll not believe you. Khalid, though, he's a threat she's seen."

Khalid. An invisible hand grips my throat at that name, the same name that hung over my head all my life, casting an aura of expectation, a bar set so high that few men could ever reach. All my behaviors, words, choices... everything compared and scrutinized next to the man who ruled an empire until my birth, when the Watchers arrived through the Giza Gateway to end his reign. Is it possible the Sea Lord and Wolf made enemies of my grandfather in their youth?

Alliances and conflicts are already complicated around

here, so it's best I remain neutral and not inquire too much on the matter. Instead, I say, "What if she doesn't believe me?"

"I'll give you a letter. Show it to her and she'll know I sent you."

I stare at the shoreline shifting past. This boat moves faster than my sailing skiff even with the strongest gale behind it.

"We'll drop you off near the border," Centaurus tells me. "From there, it's a several-day hike to her stronghold."

"Several days? I don't even know where I'm going."

"The South Pole."

That may as well be on the moon for all the good it does me. "I don't know where that is."

Commander Centaurus reaches into his coat and pulls out a round instrument of gold. "This compass will show you the way. Follow it South and you won't miss your mark."

I accept the golden disk. It sits heavy on my palm and is the most beautiful object I've ever touched. And this man is just going to let me walk off into the wild with it?

"What if I lose it?" I say. "Or it malfunctions?"

"If you insist, I can send a guide with you."

"I'll go!" says an unseen girl.

The intruding voice infuses my heart with joy. No other could match the sweet, bratty tone of my beloved dust maiden.

I turn to see Nya standing on top of the wheelhouse. She waves excitedly, her eyes bright with a warmth unlike anything I've seen in all my fifteen years.

The Commander flinches and gasps, then reaches to his hip. When he raises his arm toward Nya, I see he's drawn a pistol. I slap his arm down, but not before he pops off two shots.

Both bullets punch through Nya's chest and send her stumbling backward off the wheelhouse. I hear her hit the rear deck with a thud.

"No!" I dash around the wheelhouse to the rear deck, where Nya lies coughing. Her frazzled eyes flare wide in shock as they assess the two smoking holes in her chest. Then her gaze lifts to Commander Centaurus at my side.

"Why did you do that?" she screams.

Commander Centaurus gives me a rattled look. "Winged devil?"

"Friend!" I shout.

He raises his hands defensively. "You warn me about an invasion of winged devils, then one shows up on my ship. What was I supposed to do?"

I kneel beside Nya and lift her head onto my lap.

She reaches up to feel my face with her hand. "It's really you," she says, tears glazing her eyes. These are tears not of pain, but of relief. "I couldn't believe it when I saw you in the forest. I thought I'd been dragged into a forever dreamworld, where my heart is forced to play tricks on my mind. Or the other way around. Or..." She sobs with laughter. "But it's you. It's really you."

Commander Centaurus returns with a red bag stuffed with medical supplies. Nya waves him away.

"It's only a few bullet holes," she says, as if a gunshot wound is little more than a stubbed toe. She sits up with a groan, then I help her to her feet.

Other than moving stiffly, Nya is otherwise unaffected. I

check her for other injuries and notice a half-healed wound in her right rib.

"It was a knife," she tells me.

Commander Centaurus gapes at Nya's recovery. "Sage's Grace, you're invincible."

"No," Nya says with a dark and threatening glare. "More like... *resilient*. To kill our enemy you'll need to do better than that."

"Cutting off the head works best," I tell him, "or driving something into their heart to stem the healing."

Commander Centaurus stares at his pistol with great caution. "So our guns are useless."

"Well, I wouldn't go that far," Nya says with an exaggerated gesture to her wounds. "Do you have any idea how hard it is to sleep with fresh bullet holes in you?"

"Blades and arrows are your best bet," I say, recalling the success of our primitive weapons on the pyramid during the Battle of Giza.

"Or harpoons," adds Nya, her voice laced with venom.

Commander Centaurus turns to look at the inland mountains cloaked in shadow.

"Then you really need to talk to the Wolf," he says. He then returns his attention to me, to my borrowed uniform. "But first, let's get you into something a little less conspicuous."

CHAPTER 23
NYA

I am never, under any circumstances, leaving Deka again. *Ever.*

When the *sapien* boat men drop us off on shore, leaving us alone to carry out our mission, I make a vow: *From here on, only death shall come between us.* We are meant to stay together. The impossibility of our reunion on this dark and distant land is proof enough of that, and I'll not provoke fate by parting ways again.

Deka stands by the waterline, rummaging through a pack provided for our journey. A deerskin cloak hangs to his feet. This garment of dead animal parts sickens me, especially its bushy fur collar, but it appears to provide Deka good warmth, so I swallow down my disgust.

I hug the leather bag containing Horus's body to my chest. It had taken some threats to convince the Squids to hand over their next meal, but I wasn't leaving him to that fate. This falcon saved my life. The least I can do is keep his carcass safe until I reunite with Sheffa, who'll know how to perform a proper send-off ceremony.

I wonder where that Fori friend of mine is. If she returned to that volcano and found me missing, she could ask the local birds about my whereabouts, so I'm not worried about her not finding me. It's that psycho Regulus who concerns me. Though, from what I've seen so far of these people, their defenses bear little consideration for skyward attacks.

A rumble echoes across the water from the ship's belly as its nose swings toward the open sea.

"Hey!" shouts Deka to the boat men, his voice booming across the cove's still water.

The Lord of the Sea steps to the rear rail to face us.

"You never answered my question," Deka says. "When is sunrise?"

From here I can make out the Sea Lord's mischievous smile. "Three months, my African friend."

Deka's face turns a shade lighter as his eyes flash wide in disbelief. His expression must mimic my own, because I feel my eyelids stretching unnaturally high in surprise.

Three months?! My knees buckle, and it takes everything in me to not shrivel to the ground in despair. The crescent moon won't provide me much energy under the best of circumstances, let alone heal my ever-growing number of wounds.

I prod the two fresh holes in my chest.

"Does it hurt?" Deka asks. The sting in his eyes at my pain hurts me more than any physical injury ever could.

"It's fine," I say. "Let's go."

Deka gives me a doubtful look over as he loops the pack straps around his shoulders and adjusts them for a better fit. By the amount of food the Sea Lord packed into that green bag for him, our trek must be a long one, so we waste no time setting off.

The rocky terrain is steep and hard going for Deka. He's not in the habit of hiking long distances, and the colossal mountains ahead promise greater trials yet. Here, he can grab the smooth bendy trunks of nearby arbutus trees to help him zigzag up the steep inclines. The shadowy mountains of rock farther up our path, however, will offer no such supports.

Me, on the other hand... I have it easy. My wings carry me over this landscape no problem, with my feet only brushing the ground occasionally.

We move along in silence for a good long while. I have so many questions, but Deka's labored breathing suggests he's in no state to talk, and a barrage of queries will only frustrate him in his struggle.

"I really, *really* wish I had wings right now," he huffs.

"They're pretty great," I can't deny.

As we rise higher from the sea, making our way closer to the monstrous shadow mountains, I hover closer to Deka. He probably thinks I'm watching over him, but the truth is that it takes great effort for my wings to lift me here. By the time we reach the first plateau, my feet are barely skimming the ground.

Deka struts across the open plain quickly. The Sea Lord had warned us about the King's men watching the border. He also warned us about the Wolf's. We're to avoid detection all the way to our destination, because either side will be quick to kill us without a proper password.

The far end of the plateau slopes up into mountains of jagged rock. They stretch to the right as far as I can see, with a swath of coniferous trees skirting the bottom. This great mountain range reaches from sea to sea, splitting the continent in two and serving as a natural border between both rival nations.

Deka cranes his neck back to take in their grandeur. Even his frequent stumbles over stones can't break his stare, nor can they wipe the wonder from his eyes.

Soft needles brushing my skin welcome me into the evergreen forest. It's a fine place to rest out of sight, but Deka insists we carry on. He also insists on checking his compass every few paces, so I meander ahead to scout for the clearest pathways. I hate leaving him, so I make sure to always stay within earshot.

My search brings me to a sheer rock wall at the far edge of the coniferous forest. A fauna trail leads to a crevice that I must squeeze sideways through, but it quickly widens after a short distance. I whistle a birdsong to summon Deka here. When he joins me, he takes a moment to admire the sky-scraping chasm walls.

"Seems like a good place for an ambush," I say.

Deka gives me a sly grin and draws a pistol. "They could try."

He marches forward, twirling the handgun around his finger in a blur as he whistles a cheerful tune.

My hands cover my fresh wounds as I watch the spinning gun warily. "Do you mind not doing that?"

"Don't worry. It won't go off."

"You some kind of gun expert now?"

He stops twirling the pistol and gives it a ponderous look. When Commander Centaurus had given him this to protect against carnivorous animals, Deka required no instruction at all. Not only did his fingers know how to pop open the cylinder to load and reload, they did so with smooth confidence.

He lowers the gun so it points at the ground and continues on, whistling.

"That, too," I say. "You'll give us away."

"There's no one around."

"Just like there were only two Watchers guarding the pyramids?"

He stops dead and gives me a wide-eyed, apologetic look. He shoves the gun into his waistband and carries on with his head lowered.

I shouldn't have said that. Even the smallest crack in our bond threatens our mission. A rift between us will doom all life on Earth, so I cling to his back, where I wrap my arms around his neck and my legs around his waist. He grabs hold under my thighs and carries me along.

We move between walls of sheer vertical rock for a long while in silence.

"What happened to the others?" I finally say. It's a topic we've both been avoiding, and I'm sure I'll not like his answer, but I have to know.

"They fought the good fight on the pyramid."

"Did any make it?"

"I didn't see, but they couldn't have lasted long after I left."

My heart sinks. I rest my chin on Deka's shoulder. "Why didn't they come with you?"

"Chaos... Fear of the unknown... The Ripper... Who knows?"

My spine stiffens straight as an arrow, and my heart grows so heavy I slide from Deka's back. I plant my feet firmly on the ground, unable to go another step. Deka turns to face me, curious.

"You saw the Ripper?" I say.

"She crossed the portal with me. I told her to guard the gateway here, but she flew north instead. We could really use that power of hers here."

I sit and pull my knees to my chest. This is bad. Really bad.

Deka crouches beside me and rubs my back. "We can defeat the Watchers without her."

I shake my head. "It's not that. It's better that she's gone, because when she finds out who I am, she'll fight against whatever side I'm on."

"Why?"

Mora and I had spoken of this a lot lately. Since the battle on the Great Pyramid, I had many questions to ask the Ori senior, and our days on the beach in the Mistress's sanctuary offered plenty of time to recount the tale of my mother's rise and fall. "It's a long story."

"It's a long walk," Deka notes.

He offers his hand and helps me stand. I cross my arms and grip my elbows as we walk the chasm floor. Where should I begin?

"The Ripper's days go way back," I say, "back to when us Servants had it pretty good. The Watchers hardly dealt out any punishments because Drusilla took responsibility for everyone. It got to the point no Fori or Ori got punished without her approval—like the time the Watchers sentenced a Fori to death. Drusilla, being her leader and all, claimed responsibility. She insisted the Fori's shortcomings were a failure on her part as a leader, and that she be executed in her place. That put Jexa in a tight spot."

"How?"

"It would make Drusilla a martyr. Besides, that's assuming they'd even go through with it. The Ripper was dangerous and every Watcher knew it. Rumors say Jexa even offered a reward to whoever could bring her the Ripper alive, but no one even considered it. Not even the Butcher."

Deka pulls his cloak tighter around his shoulders and shivers.

"Years went by," I say, "and the longer Drusilla thwarted Watcher justice, the weaker their hold on the Servants became. When my mother's fighting skills started to give her a good name, Jexa saw a use for her. Most think Klora rose to become Jexa's right hand for her skill in battle, but I think the Marshal had other plans for her. Jexa lied and told her Drusilla was organizing a rebellion. As a test of loyalty and to save her people from war, she ordered my mother to kill The Ripper."

Deka walks shoulder to shoulder with me.

"My mother didn't believe the story about the rebellion," I say. "Most of our kind didn't even know what the word meant. She was just going to force Drusilla into hiding, and then leave her on the planet when they finished and moved on.

"But it turns out The Ripper really was organizing a rebellion. My mother ordered her to stand down, but Drusilla refused. She had it all planned out, how they'd overthrow the Watchers, destroy their planet's gate, and live forever in paradise. *Drusilla's Dream*, they called it. She wanted to recruit Klora because of her close ties to the Watcher Marshal. But then..."

The next words ball up in my throat and form a lump.

"What did Klora do?"

"She became a spy against the rebellion. The story goes that she fed Drusilla information about the Watchers to build her trust. But I think my mother did this to show Drusilla the odds against them, or at least inspire doubt in her followers—that doing good work for the Watchers was the only way to freedom."

A wolf howls in the distance, long and solemn.

Deka draws his pistol, but he keeps it aimed away from me.

"Anyway," I say, "as the time to rise approached, my mother saw Drusilla wasn't backing down, so she killed her. And that was that."

Deka does not appear surprised by this. His face remains neutral, though I can tell he now sees what Drusilla is to me. A revenge plot in the making.

"The assassination didn't earn Mother much love from the Servants," I say, "but Jexa was mad too. Klora was supposed to bring Drusilla in alive, so the Marshal could claim her Spark for the Dark."

"Instead, your mother set her spark free," Deka says. His wary appraisal of the sheer rock face to either side of us suggests he's seen what The Ripper can do. "And when Jexa summoned Klora here to this timeline, The Ripper jumped through with her. She mustn't remember the betrayal though. She seemed pleased to hear Klora's name."

"Probably. Mother killed her before the whole sky serpent massacre went down. With Drusilla gone, Jexa thought she could do whatever she wanted to the Servants. But the Fori and Ori still had some fight in them. When Jexa told them she'd extended their Penance by thirty planets, the whispers of rebellion rose to screams. They declared themselves absolved of their debt and built a fortress in the forest."

My head slumps with the weight of my next words. "Then Jexa did the unthinkable: she unleashed her sky serpent upon them. That night, as the forest burned, my mother realized she'd done wrong by killing The Ripper. That's when she took *Drusilla's Dream* and made it her own.

"Jexa was expecting this, of course. So killing her wasn't going to be a matter of stabbing her in the back. But Mother knew where the sky serpent slept. She slayed the beast and brought its smoldering heart to the surviving Servants for each to hold, and that won her the love of a good many."

"And so began the real rebellion," Deka says.

I nod slightly. At least this part doesn't fill me with shame. "When her sister dust maidens joined the cause, *Klora's Dream* gained unstoppable momentum. Many believed in her more than Drusilla, because Drusilla was rash and knew nothing of the Watcher ways. As a Consul guard serving alongside Jexa and Jaleera, my mother learned more about Watcher tactics than most Watchers would ever know. But Klora's end came the same way as Drusilla's, when Jaleera stabbed her in the back. That won't matter to Drusilla though. Whatever cause I fight for, The Ripper will fight against it. To her, I am where my bloodline spoiled."

Deka twists his lips and furrows his brow, deep in thought. His perplexed stare reveals he is unraveling my words in his head. "The Ripper was willing to die for your people. Doesn't seem like she'd turn against them just to get back at Klora."

"So you'd think. But word is that, right before she died, with all her followers watching, Drusilla cursed them all for not rising to defend her. She damned each of them to the Dark, and promised to be waiting for them there."

"She has no memory of this yet," Deka says as he plods along, "that much is clear from our encounter. But we should expect the Watchers to use this story to turn her against us."

"Yes, we should. Drusilla will have less love for a traitor than an enemy, and that's what this comes down to. With the right choice of words, they can drive her Berserk."

"Berserk?"

"It's a spell that afflicts us Entropaths. Blind, inconsolable rage that can only be broken by the death of whatever triggers it. Since Klora is no longer on the scene, she'll have to settle for me."

Deka lowers his head, taking in the implications of my words. If he's seen the Ripper's power at work, he's no doubt picturing her mighty wrath devoted to my demise. If he is wise, he will begin to distance himself from me in the coming days. I'd not blame him for that. So I tighten my hold around his neck while I still have the chance.

At the end of the chasm, a trail zigzags up a series of steep cliffs for hundreds of feet. Deka's breathing becomes heavier just looking at it. I urge him to rest, but he gets straight to climbing. It's mostly shadow here, and his placements are sometimes limited and often unsure, so I carry his pack as I fly overhead, guiding him toward safe handholds.

Watching Deka struggle up this terrain fills me with urgency. Moving the Wolf's army in the other direction to the

Southern Gateway will be a grand task, so I am grateful for his haste.

The view from up top is worth the effort. Over the cliff that Deka now climbs, the ground slopes down to a massive bowl valley ringed by a crown of serrated mountain peaks. A forest occupies the center to give the appearance of hair inside the jagged crown. The curved slice of moon to my left casts enough light over the treetops to grant me a peculiar observation, but I'll need a closer look to confirm this irregularity.

Deka clambers over the upper cliff and rolls onto his back. I open his pack to offer him a packet of food, but he pulls the bag from my hands and carries on down toward the forest.

"You should eat soon," I say. Not only will this sustain his energy, it will lighten his load.

"I'm fine," he says, shifting the pack on his shoulders. "Can't give up the momentum."

Though it's not the answer I was looking for, his motivation pleases me. My two new wounds are starting to burn, which means I don't have much time. We need to rouse the Wolf before the fester stops me dead.

I fly ahead to scout under the canopy of oak and maple leaves. White birch trunks stand in staggered ranks, each of their branches flaunting loads of spade leaves. Strange.

I'm no tree-tender, but I'm pretty sure foliage needs frequent light to flourish. This place is in the middle of a six-month winter, yet not a single tree has shed its leaves. The altitude alone should leave this forest sparse, but sparse it is not. There is something unnatural about this place.

Or maybe it's me. Perhaps my wounds are causing

delirium, messing with my head to make me see things that aren't there.

One look at Deka when he arrives squashes this theory. His stare is full of wonder as he watches glowing green mushrooms bloom in spiral patterns around tree trunks.

I sit on a log and take his hand to pull him down to join me. Together we admire the midwinter magic until Deka's chattering teeth becomes too much.

"Best we keep moving," he says. "Unless you need to rest."

I do need rest, but only once we've delivered our message to the Wolf. Further delays risk my wounds disabling me, so I fly off to scout ahead. I don't get far before I encounter our first formidable obstacle.

The gorge is narrow enough to shoot a crossbow bolt across, but way too far for Deka to jump over. A river gushes below, and when I drop a rock it takes twenty heartbeats to hit the water.

I fly upstream and then down in search of a crossing. It's steep canyon for as far as I can see, with no place narrower than where Deka emerges from the forest.

"There's nowhere to cross," I say.

Deka drops his pack and sits cross-legged on the grass. He rests his hands on his knees and closes his eyes.

I watch him curiously. He stays like this, unmoving, for a long while.

"What are you doing?"

Deka keeps his eyes closed and says, "Waiting."

"Waiting for what?"

"The way to reveal itself."

I crouch before him and glare at his eyelids. He smirks as if sensing my stare.

"You think you can just meditate your way across?" I say.

"If I'm patient and in alignment with my destiny, the right path will reveal itself to me."

"That's insane."

"It brought me this far."

This is unacceptable. We can't afford to waste any time, so it's on me to keep us going.

I clench my fists and size up the trees across the gorge. The tallest redwood might do, but it'll be a stretch.

I fly across the canyon to the rust-colored sentinel. Her trunk is thick, but I sense she is young. This will not be easy for me.

I press my hand to her bark and whisper a prayer of forgiveness. Her energy throbs in response, pleading for its life, but my heart is deaf to it. I get a measure of her frequency and, with the bottom of my open hand, I chop a notch into the trunk nearest the gorge.

The tree leans forward with a long groan and then a sickening crack. I fly back as she topples across the gorge, and thankfully her sacrifice is not in vain as her leafy crown lands on the other side with a rustling thud.

Deka wastes no time climbing through the branches to make his way onto the make-shift bridge. His face beams with a smile.

"See," he says. "The way has been revealed."

Anger heats my chest. If Deka weren't making such a dangerous crossing I'd smack him off this log for his insolence. Instead, I hover nearby to catch him should he fall.

He holds his arms out for balance, his bare feet stepping

surely across the curved bark surface, but I notice he hasn't stolen a single look down.

The ruffle of wings glide through the air above me. Their familiar *whoosh* kicks my heart into a fright. I look up and raise my fists, ready to fight. It's for less than a blink, but that's all it takes.

"Whoa!" Deka's hand clamps my ankle as he falls sideways from the log, dragging me down with him. We fall with sickening speed. My wings buzz furiously, but for the life of us I cannot slow our plummet. It all happens so fast.

We hit the frigid river before I can scream.

CHAPTER 24
DEKA

When I was five years old, I fell into our sanctuary's rushing water supply. The last thing I remember about it was slamming into a steel grate. Thankfully someone had seen me fall and summoned help, and luckily the first to respond was a strong swimmer who knew the 'kiss of life'. Most kids teased me over the intimate revival technique the old man had performed on me, but I didn't care. I was grateful to be alive.

Death by drowning now seems a luxury compared to what awaits me in this war. If it were only me here, I'd be inclined to submit to it. But that is not the case.

I should have released Nya before hitting the water. I should have done a lot of things differently. Instead we plunge into the river, where the violent current sweeps us away. My head pops above water only long enough to draw half breaths as the rapids ravage us, so I can't see where we're going, and it's only a matter of time before we hit something.

With the river tossing me side to side, it's a miracle Nya

doesn't twist free from my grip. Though, I'm pretty sure I'd snap my wrist before ever letting her go.

We glide into a calm stretch, where I'm able to keep my head above water. I look to where Nya's head should be but see no sign of her. In fact, her leg is limp in my grip and drags me down!

I haul her close with all my might and wrap an arm around her torso. Her body sags in my hold, her head drooped forward with her mouth submerged.

My free hand claws through the water to drag us toward the left bank. I manage four strokes before more rapids ensnare us, and suddenly my efforts switch to steering clear of boulders in the river. We narrowly avoid two before slipping into another calm spot, where a vicious effort by my left arm lines us up with an outcrop from the riverbank. The current pushes me into waist-deep water, where I stand with Nya cradled in my arms and slosh up to the bank.

Nya remains limp in my arms. Her head touches the ground at the same time as her feet when I set her down.

Urgency electrifies every nerve in my body.

"Nya." I give her a shake, but her blue lips tell me she needs more than this.

I pinch her nose and seal my mouth over hers. Not a whisper of air slips out through her cold stiff lips, so I blow a breath into her lungs. Her chest rises and then falls, but then remains still as stone. I offer another breath that again raises her chest, but then it falls still once again.

Hot tears burn my eyes. I stack my hands on her chest and press down. Her bones resist and spring me back up, so I push down again and repeat the bouncing motion over and over, with each downward push squeezing more tears up into my eyes. Exerting such great force to help someone seems most unnatural, and for Nya's sake I push through my reluctance.

My persistence begins to pay off when Nya's chest warms. It's a strange feeling. The heating accelerates with each downward pump, so that by the fifteenth compression her skin burns my palms. It's so bad I'm forced to pull my hands away, and I use the opportunity to give her another few breaths with the 'kiss of life'. Her chest is near scalding when I resume my compressions, so I place my wet shirt over her skin and push through it. By my fifth cycle, my tears fall freely.

"Come on, Nya. Wake up. Please wake up." These whimpered words come from my mouth while my heart screams, *Don't leave me! Don't you dare leave me. Not now. Not ever.*

My pleading thoughts must hold some magic to them, because water erupts from Nya's mouth like a geyser. She coughs and sputters until I roll her onto her side. Water drains from her mouth and thickens to drool, but her eyes remain closed. Steam rises from the water on the ground around her, almost as if her lungs had boiled it. But not only that.

My hands had gone instinctively to do chest compressions, but her heart I now recall is inside her belly. In my panic I'd forgotten this, and I'm only now reminded by its fierce pounding against my knee.

This phenomenon holds my attention only briefly. With Nya now breathing, I need to dry her. My clothes are soaked through, so I need to make a fire.

I carry her away from the river mist and set her on a patch of soft grass sheltered by trees, where she curls instinctively into the fetal position. She's lost so much weight since Africa. The bumps of her spine bulge high between her wings, while shadows darken the hollows between her ribs. She has given more than she had to give. To get this far, her mighty spirit has destroyed her body.

I fight the urge to snuggle into her to share my warmth, for I am in no good state myself.

I'm loath to leave her, but I need not go far to find what I need. A cracked stone by Nya's feet offers good flint, and there's plenty of dry branches lying nearby. I peel paper-like skin from a narrow white tree, which, along with green-looking hair from living branches above, makes an easy start for a fire.

Once the first wood gets crackling, I rush to gather bigger pieces to add. It's not long before I have waist-high flames casting the most glorious heat imaginable, but this fire brings with it something horrid.

The smoke here smells different than Clarian's cooking fire. The wood itself is different. This tinder burns with a vibrancy unnatural to this world, and yet not unfamiliar to me. I've smelled this smoke before, on my last birthday. Smoke like this hung in the air when my dear friend Mali took her final breath, and the memory of that gruesome moment stirs my belly.

I crawl to the edge of the glade and retch. I've not eaten in so long that nothing comes up, and when I'm finished I am utterly gutted. This hunger swells to form a sickness of its own. Only now do I realize I'd lost my pack in the river.

The loss hits me like a punch to the gut and sends me retching again. *Why didn't I eat when I had the chance?*

Losing my pack is not something I regret for long. It was either those supplies or Nya. Easy choice.

My belly settles enough for me to strip and spread my wet clothes beside the fire. In doing so I notice yellow blisters bubbling over my palms. I don't recall touching the fire, so where could they have come from?

Nya. Her skin was hot enough to burn me.

I rush to her side and feel her forehead for a fever. Mildly warm skin tells me she's doing better than me, which inspires a sigh of relief. But I don't like the look of the yellow pus oozing from her wounds.

I give her a shake, but her eyelids remains still. Not even a flicker.

I lift her head onto my lap and feel her hot breath on my hand. I've only felt this helpless once before, not long ago. I'd give anything to hear Mali's voice again, and the thought of losing Nya here fills my chest with all the pressure of an atomic blast. I can't just sit here and watch her fade away. And I am not without help.

I set Nya's head gently on the ground and make my way down to the river, bearing a heavy heart. It seems destiny has betrayed me. Men are doomed to early death or lifelong heartache, nothing more. I've seen it all my life. Hope is the great deceiver. An illusion. My belief in some grand plan has ushered Nya to the gates of oblivion. I should let her fade away here in peace. It's the kindest fate anyone on Earth can now expect. But... I can't just let her go without a fight.

For the first time in my life, I'm inspired to turn to my

father's ways. And I'm not talking about the way of the warrior.

A large block of stone reaches like a wharf into the river, its top dry due to its height. This is where I fall to my knees, clasp both hands before my heart, and whisper a prayer for salvation. I pray to my forefathers for strength, to the moon for Nya's recovery, and to this land for a rare measure of mercy.

Luckily, I need not rely solely on the supernatural to answer my prayers. These woods are tended by forces alien to this world, confirmed by my own eyes when a feather-winged Aeri had swooped overhead during my log crossing and startled me into falling.

"I know you're out there," I yell. "My friend needs your help. She's one of you, and she's dying of wounds I cannot heal." I describe her injuries, hoping that the ears of the eyes following our journey take note.

"If Nya dies," I say, "this forest will die with her. Everything on Earth will fall into darkness. There'll be no dawn if the Evening Star sets on this night."

With that, I return to Nya with a sliver of hope in my heart. And a painful hunger scourging my belly.

I scavenge the forest floor for grub. Rotted logs provide me a few mouthfuls, but it's not enough. This starvation requires something substantial, which leads me back to Nya.

I stand over her, my mouth watering as I eye the leather bag clutched to her chest. She'd managed to hold onto it through the same raging current that ripped the pack from my back. Her grip remains tight when I give it a tug, but she doesn't stir when I pry it loose.

It's a long shot, but desperation has me checking anyway.

I open the bag and am elated to see the bird unspoiled—no maggots or rot. This falcon is still in season. Perhaps some grace of Nya's has helped preserve it, or a supernatural force, which gives rise to hesitance in me.

Do it, urges my guiding voice in response. *You must. Our mission and Nya will die if you don't.* These words are all the persuasion I need.

Saliva floods my mouth as I pluck the falcon's brown feathers. I'm feverish in my work, drooling and desperate to cook this bird and fill my belly with it. The task of preparing my meal takes forever it seems, and when I've pulled the last feather, I battle the urge to eat it raw.

The time it takes to cook is agonizing. Grease drips and sizzles on the fire, and the smell torments my wringing belly. But the agonizing wait is worth it. To my surprise and delight, the bird cooks evenly on the spit, with not a single charred spot tainting my golden meal.

Drool strings from my mouth as I set the bird on my lap. My eagerness to rip this meal apart, however, is tamed by the memory of Clarian's tribute to her duck. This falcon deserves a similar honor.

I bow my head and say, "Thank you for your sacrifice, brother. Thank you for your speed, your courage, and most-importantly for saving Nya's life. I ask you to continue your fight by blessing me with the strength of your ancestors. In return, I will honor your spirit with every move I make. You shall live on through my deeds and sustain me through the darkness ahead."

With that out of the way, I dig in. It's a real massacre. I can hardly breathe as I fill my mouth with juicy white meat, which surpasses Clarian's duck a million times over. My plan to save some for later becomes a laughable memory when I find myself licking the bones.

Well done, applauds my guiding voice.

I sit back, but satisfaction fails to find me here. A feeling in my gut tells me I'm about to learn why you shouldn't feast on the remains of mystical birds.

CHAPTER 25

DEKA

I'm not sure how I'll satisfy my hunger after a meal such as that falcon, but now that I have the taste, I know I'll want more. There's plenty of wood around to fashion a bow and arrows, I'll just need to find something to use for a bowstring. If only I'd held onto my pistol.

"Where's Horus?" says Nya's drowsy voice.

I launch upright to see her sitting up beside me. "You're awake!"

I try to hug her, but she shoves me back and checks the empty leather sack. Her gaping eyes go then to our fire, where my greasy wooden spit leans against the stone ring. She clutches her belly and recoils with a loud gasp, looking at me in disbelief with a hint of pleading. Her eyes scream, *Tell me you didn't!*

"It's okay," I tell her. "I said a respectful prayer, and—"

She shoots to her feet and looms over me with both fists clenched. "You *ATE* him?"

You'd never know she just woke from a coma by the ferocity in her tone. Her intense stare warns she might murder me in her rage, and I find myself lying onto my back with both hands raised.

My defensive position gives Nya pause. She takes stock of her posture and appears to scold herself for overreacting, but it's only brief. She turns to storm off into the forest.

A lump swells in my throat. I've seen that look before, in Hadria's eyes after Mali killed the deer that led to her death. It seems I've committed a great taboo by eating that dead bird.

I don't have to wonder where she's going for long. A sheer gray mountain face that overshadows the trees trembles, from which large rock chunks crash to the ground like thunder. This goes on for some time.

When Nya returns, she sits on the other side of the fire, but not directly across from me. She doesn't want to look at my face. She just crouches there, hugging her knees to her chest, muttering words of anger as she glares at the flickering flames.

The tension is suffocating. If my clothes weren't still damp, we'd be on our way again. Even the fire seems cautious of Nya's fury. Its flames lean toward me to escape her glare, and with it comes smoke that chokes me and stings my eyes. Tears stream down my cheeks as my chest burns and heaves.

I break into a coughing fit. I shift positions around the fire, but the smoke follows. It's as if my lungs are luring it in. I have to actually stand and walk away, which leaves me breathless. Coughs turn to wheezes that sound hauntingly similar to Mali's final fight for air. Her face appears in my darkened vision, wide-eyed and panicked.

I wander back to the fire in a daze. The world around me spins and my eyes hurt as if there's a glare coming off everything. I squint and shield my eyes from this harassing light, and then I sense its source directly above, with swaths of green light slithering through the sky like a river weaving from a parallel universe.

My jaw goes slack as I take in this wonder. Its meandering current dazes me, which flares my nausea, so I crouch by the fire and hug my belly with my head down.

"Is Horus ailing you?" Nya says, her voice surging with venom. "Do you feel sick?"

I shake my head, positive the queasiness comes not from my recent meal.

"Well, you will," she says. "Just give it time."

I nod and stare absently at the fire. She wishes a death illness on me, and it seems this sentiment will reside in her for some time. Hopefully my cloak dries soon so we can get moving again. Sitting around this fire with a hostile alien terraformer is not something the human psyche has evolved to deal with.

"It's the smoke, isn't it?" she says after a while.

I wince and nod. A hurricane brews in my belly, and I expect Nya will soon get her wish.

"You think of her often?" Nya says. Her voice is softer, but it's still far from friendly.

"All the time." I crack a stick and toss it into the fire. "Do you think about your mother?"

Nya rests her chin on her knees and stares longingly into the fire. "I never used to. Now that I know for sure she's in a bad place, I can't help it. But she's my mother. What was Mali to you?"

"She was my friend."

Nya's lips twist and her brow wrinkles with a perplexed look. I've heard dust maidens are typically solitary creatures.

"If I died," she says, "would you still think of me?"

I wince at the idea of losing Nya. "Of course."

Her eyes widen in surprise.

"Because we're friends," she says with a frown. She seems genuinely interested in trying to understand this concept.

Honestly, I don't know how to describe what Nya is to me. How many human teenagers have befriended an intergalactic pixie? There are no relationship books or psychology texts that cover this bond I share with Nya.

"You're not a friend like Mali was," I say.

Nya watches me with more curiosity in her eyes than I've ever seen before. "Then what am I?"

My heart flutters and gives rise to goosebumps on my skin. A fine question. What *is* Nya to me?

A firefly drifts over her head and casts a green glow over her brown hair. Another drifts between our faces, turning Nya's eyes the brightest shade of green I've ever seen. Her brilliance blinds me to all else. Even the grit of travel and the three wounds marring her body fail to dull her radiance. Her silky skin is a vessel that carries the most beautiful life to have ever sprung into existence.

"You're everything," I say.

Nya's eyes flash wide, and my words shock me as well. I do not know where they came from.

Actually, no. That is a lie. I know exactly where they came from, I'm simply not accustomed to speaking from my heart to recognize its language at first.

A shiver shakes my body as my eyes see Nya in a new light. I've seen her strength move mountains, and her stare is enough to undo any man. With Nya I've felt things I'd never thought possible. With her I feel hopeful, inspired, safe. But most of all, I feel that wherever she is, I am living my destiny. From the moment she drew her first breath on a planet one hundred million light-years away, and the second my cries announced my arrival into this world, a force somewhere decided we were meant to meet.

I crawl around the fire and kneel before her. She watches curiously as I lean forward and press my lips to hers.

She goes stiff, her lips tight and rigid. Her obvious unease warns I should back off, so I do and prepare myself to look upon her horrified expression.

But no. Before I can open my eyes, she grabs the back of my neck and pulls my face firmly into hers. This time her soft lips invite me to stay. They melt against mine, and suddenly my whole body tingles with a heat no flame could ever bestow.

She lays back and pulls me to the ground with her, and here time loses all meaning. We lie on our sides in each other's arms, our noses touching. We rest like this for hours, drifting in and out of sleep, taking a break from the world and all its woes. In Nya I have found a paradise like no other.

The world is still. Only the occasional creaking branch dares interrupt our rest, for these two heroes are on a quest to save their existence. We shall save all worlds and the life they hold. *Give them their rest*, the trees whisper to each to other, and not even a breath of wind slips into our sanctuary.

We lie like this for days, weeks, for months... For how long I do not know. I do not care. With sunrise three months away, we have plenty of time to warn the Wolf.

Eventually our fire dies from neglect. I pull my dry cloak

over us, and under this cover the whole world fades away. I end up on my back with a mat of soft moss below me and Nya's head nestled into my neck. I'd stay like this forever, her warm breath caressing my chest, if not for the ache growing in my back and hips. The ground seems to harden as the tiger's eye of stars spins around the black sky, so I shift onto my side. Nya doesn't stir.

Odd.

I give her a shake. Her eyelids don't even flicker.

"Nya."

She moans faintly.

I give her a harder shake but her muscles remain lax. When I sit up in panic, her head flops back lazily.

"Nya? Nya!"

"What?" she says, irritated, her eyes still closed.

I look to the sky. The moon is nowhere in sight, so I can't guess the last time she had a source of energy. Her temper tantrum appeared to have given her a burst of life at the time, but maybe that had come at a cost.

The stiffness in my body suggests we really have been lying here for a while. My knees crack when I stand, and away from Nya's warmth the cold air hits me violently.

I rush down to the river, hoping those who tend this forest have fulfilled my request.

I find the rock altar as empty as I'd left it. No medicine. Though, something strange occurs to me. A nearby plant summons me so urgently that I find myself kneeling beside it without knowing why. This weed with saw-like leaves appears unremarkable compared to the plants around it, but I sense its energy radiate with a faint pulse. I don't know how I know this, but this weed will help Nya.

I chew it into a wad as I scour the ground for something else. White moss beckons me from midway up a tree. I have to climb to retrieve it, then I return to the fire with both ingredients.

I pull the ball of wet weed from my mouth and stuff a bit into each of Nya's wounds. This act comes naturally to me. Though my handling borders on rough and must cause Nya a great deal of pain, I'm oddly unapologetic. It is something that must be done for the greater good.

I seal off each wound with sticky white moss and hope for the best. Even if I'm wrong, it's better than nothing. But if I'm right, this alone will not bring her back. For that task we'll require light.

I pull Nya's arms up around my neck and sit up with her. She stirs at the disruption and obeys my directions when I stand and lift her onto my back. She wraps both hands around my neck while I hold under her thighs to carry her like a backpack.

We follow a game trail between sheer rock faces. The movement up the zigzagging track loosens my body and gets easier the farther I walk. It's good for Nya, too.

Her cheek rests on my shoulder. "This is way easier," she mumbles from her sleep world. "Should've done this from the start."

"Enjoy it while it lasts," I say. "Soon it'll be *you* carrying *me*."

She laughs faintly, spreading energy into me that makes my whole body feel lighter. My feet practically bounce with each step so that I'm nearly hopping up the slope.

The path veers left and wraps around a mountainside. A goat trail traces the face of a black cliff, where any misstep might send us tumbling down the steep mountain slope to our left. Around any corner may wait a several-hundred-foot plummet, yet I stride forward with confidence.

As we follow this trail, the crescent moon rises to our left. Something is off about it. I swear the silver curve had faced the opposite way when Nya and I had fallen into the river. If that's true, then we really were resting in that glade for a long while. At least four days by my reckoning, maybe even eight. But that can't be. I must be remembering its phase wrong.

In this deep winter night, the curved sliver of moon is bright enough to ruin my night vision, which I desperately need to ensure my feet find good ground before me, so I do my best to avoid looking at it. This gets harder as the night goes on, when the moon skims the horizon to our left, making its way ahead yet remaining ever low, never higher than eye height.

Nya's recovery progresses with the moon's movement as it creeps ahead to our left. Her hold around my neck tightens, her body tensing as she fusses more at my jouncing steps.

Her resurgent strength brings the biggest smile to my face. By the time that moon disappears again, Nya really will be able to carry me.

Your time with her is done, says my guiding voice.

These words stop me dead. Did I just hear my time with Nya is near done? I intuitively reject the idea of that. So from where does this voice speak?

As the moon makes its pass before us, Nya becomes restless in a slumber. Her hold around my neck tightens as she murmurs names and hisses orders, no doubt reliving moments of battles past. We're just entering a cluster of trees when Nya screams, *"No!"*

She coils her elbow under my chin and cranks my neck into a headlock. I grab her wrists to loosen her grip, but I don't have a chance.

"No!" she screams. "No, *NO!*"

She lifts me from the ground and then screams a word that chills my blood: *"Charge!"*

You don't have to be a mastermind to guess what happens next.

She barrels forward with me held like a battering ram. I bet her eyes are either still closed, or she's seeing something else, because the last thing *I* see is a column of gray tree bark rushing to meet my face.

CHAPTER 26

NYA

Everything about the battle is so real... From the ringing steel and the smack of flesh, to the screams of agony and wails of rage.

Jexa hovers in a whirlwind of ash a short distance from me. She calls up for reinforcements, but her Watchers are all too immersed in their own fights to respond.

Jinny and Kassini fly up to join me. Thick scars circle their joints to fuse their limbs back to their bodies, and when their all-black eyes lock onto Jexa, they somehow blacken further. They speak through deep voices that thunder inside my head: *"Finish her!"*

My thumping heart pumps hot rage through my entire body. I clutch my battering ram and scream, "Charge!"

Jinny flies alongside my left side, with Kassini to my right. Jexa spots our approach and turns to square off with me. I pick up speed to pummel her good. The distance between us disappears swiftly, and when my battering ram slams into her belly with all the force of a meteor, it's like hitting a titanium wall.

The impact rips my weapon from my arms and sends me spinning into a tree. My backside hits first, bending me backwards in half so my toes touch my hair before I flop to the ground.

A ghastly sight nearby swiftly eclipses my physical pain. Lying face-down on the roots of a neighboring tree, is Deka.

I scramble over and give him a shake. "Deka. Deka, wake up. Deka. Can you hear me?"

His eyes remain shut. A large bump swells on his forehead.

"Please, Deka. Wake up!"

Still, nothing.

What have I done?

Tears bulge behind my eyelids. Why must I break everything I touch?

I scream loud at the sky. My cries echo off steep rock faces and travel to distant lands, adding more bite to the mountain breeze. I continue to scream until I am breathless.

I roll Deka onto his back and rest my head on his chest. His heart beats faintly in my ear.

Tears warm my cheeks and pool on his chest under my face. What if he doesn't wake up? He may need help, but where do I find it?

My gaze rises to track green embers drifting through the air. The trees here radiate with a vitality much greater than those of the lowlands, where the Squids stalk their prey. Something unnatural breathes life into this forest.

"Help me," I say, sobbing like a pathetic little spawn. "I know you're out there. Come here and help me, please. I need you!"

I know I'm being watched. My skin prickles at the

sensation, but it's different than a Watcher's stare. These are the worried eyes of quarry—frightened creatures in hiding. They take me for a threat, and may see this for a trap. If they witnessed me ramming Deka into this tree, they may think I'm up to no good, trying to lure them back to battle.

"I bring no quarrels to you," I say. "I just need some healing hands. I'm not a healer."

I am a destroyer.

Faint swishing graces the air. I know this sound as the flutter of Fori wings. They are around and no doubt nearby. Perhaps they fled to this place after the battle. Or maybe they came here long before that fateful fight.

"Where are you? Show yourselves!"

Nothing but a bitter mountain breeze answers me.

I sit over Deka a long while, waiting. Another shake gets only a wince of pain from him. The lump on his head is growing and will soon slide down into his left eye. He doesn't have much time.

I gather some kindling and spark a fire, hoping it will stir bad memories in his dreamworld and bring him back to this one. When I blow the smoke at his face, his nostrils flare and he instinctively tilts his head away to escape it, but that's all I get. He coughs and chokes, and I see my tactic is doing more harm than good.

I'm about to kill the fire when an orange flash beckons me around the tree. I scramble to snatch Deka's compass from the ground, and accidentally squeeze a knob protruding from the instrument's side. It flips open like a clamshell to reveal its inner workings. A red needle points back the way we came from; its opposing silver tip points along the path in our direction of travel — South. But it's what's on the outside that interests me most.

A silver octagram decorates its golden cover like an evening star.

I snap it shut and hold it close to my belly, over my heart. It's clear what I must do now, and I mustn't waste more time.

I pile moss under Deka's head for comfort and ensure his cloak is snug, then feed more wood to the fire.

The compass needle points steady between two black mountain peaks. They stand higher than anything in sight, with many smaller peaks and valleys between us. My wings will conquer the terrain, but I'm uncertain about the wind up there, not to mention my withered state. But I have no choice.

I kneel beside Deka and kiss his forehead. Every part of me yearns to lay beside him and keep him warm until he wakes, but my strength right now is peaking. If he fails to wake on his own, I'll have wasted all that time and energy here for nothing.

"I'm sorry, Deka. I never meant to hurt you." My eyes swell with hot tears, and my voice cracks when I say, "You're the last person I'd ever hurt."

I have one last message before I leave. Looking to the surrounding trees, I say, "Curse you all. You hear me? I curse every last one of you! If he dies, there'll be no safe place for you to hide. I'll burn every tree and smash every rock. I'll be the greatest enemy you've ever known, that much I swear to you."

The rage boiling inside my chest simmers. Damn, did that feel good to say. Those words were all truth, too, and they stir an energy in me that gets my wings buzzing excitedly.

And then I'm off.

Having a loved one's life in your hands is the worst feeling ever.

My innards twist into a ball like a nest of lecherous snakes as I race South. Our plan when reaching the Wolf had been to send Deka in first, because they'd be less likely to shoot him on sight. Now, I'll need to slip into their midst unnoticed and find an opportunity to reveal myself without startling them.

The approach to the colossal twin peaks is easy going. Updrafts from the many valleys below provide a gentle boost until I near the pass, where several wind streams funnel between the two vast opposing slopes. The swirling air sucks me into the gap like a whirlpool, which, with all my spinning and side to side tossing, doesn't seem so wide. My wings alone aren't enough to master this current, so my flailing arms join the fight. But these efforts count for little.

At midway between peaks, the tugging force reverses to a violent thrust that spits me out the other side. I tumble heels over head in uncontrolled flight. Thankfully I'm well above any other mountains, which means I have less of a chance at crashing. As my arms swipe futilely through the air, I notice both of my hands are now empty.

No! I lost Deka's compass!

I manage to steady my flight and scan the dark ground below, until something catches my eye up ahead.

A fire burns in the sky between me and the horizon. The blue flame screams unnatural origin, something I confirm with a closer look that reveals a giant ball hanging in the sky above the flame. It appears to be a fabric encasement shaped like an upside down teardrop suspended in the air.

Oddities in the sky are a greater concern to me than lost instruments on the ground, so I venture forward for a closer look.

A basket dangles from the suspended bulb, from which the blue flame no doubt provides the hot air needed to keep the hovering assembly afloat.

I gasp in wonder. These *sapiens* possess far better mobility than Deka's folk, which makes my heart beat lighter with hope.

Whoever occupies the basket could probably see my approach on this clear night. At this distance they might mistake me for a bird, so I dive low to make sure they do. Keeping my bearing on the floating balloon, I glide down toward the mountain peaks, where I'm soon rewarded for following this lead.

Amber light pulsates from the backside of a rocky mountain ahead. It comes out fragmented, like a glowing golden nugget embedded in rock. I squint and spot walls crafted of stone protruding from the mountainside. I've destroyed enough similar structures on previous planets to know that golden nugget is a fortress.

A string of smaller lights stretches diagonally from the stronghold down the mountainside at even intervals, revealing a trail. It appears to be the only access route by foot and, as I fly closer, I am glad Deka is not with me.

Defensive nests overlook the trail from stone archways that stand between each orange lantern. I'm unable to make out the guards' armaments, but their positioning and alertness lends great credit to the Wolf's mastery of defense.

I glide close to the sheer rock face below the trail. Directly ahead, a dam extends from the mountain under the fort's outer wall, holding back a lake that reaches around the backside of the mountain. Water gushes over a steel cylinder below and reminds me of the power drum in Deka's sanctuary. Down river to my left sits numerous wooden boats atop a hill.

I halt my flight to behold this peculiar sight. It would take a good many *sapiens* to haul those long narrow boats up that steep slope, which makes little sense considering all the flat riverbank to accommodate them below.

My belly squirms with an unnerving thought. What if these *sapiens* are a different breed than the others? Each of those long boats might be for a single occupant, and that high riverbank only a few steps up for a race of giants.

I force myself to carry on, my nerves fraying further with each strange observation. Do I venture now into the domain of titans?

The fortress itself is beautiful in a frightening sort of way. Sitting precariously on a ledge, its windows glow with orange light but does not feel warm in any way. A wall of stacked stones reaches from the mountain toward the edge, where two cylindrical towers form the corners of the outward wall that lines the outer ledge.

I really don't want to get shot in the chest by a frightened guard, but I also think it might look bad to get caught snooping around this place. The Wolf takes security very seriously, and that's unlikely to change within those walls, where there's probably traps and snares waiting to maim me. Better to present myself as an emissary than an intruder.

The last archway at the trailhead is an imposing structure. A round turret with a cone roof stands to either side of the track, each boasting a purple banner streaming from its apex. A walkway arches over the trail to connect both watch houses.

I stay close to the cliff as I flutter below and come up to land in a yard between the grand archway and the fort's front wall. A bright red gate reinforced by steel flat bars forbids entry.

With all these threatening defense measures, the lime green grass tickling my feet is a touch out of place. I can tell by the feel that it's unnatural, that its taken considerable effort to produce and maintain. Perhaps the Wolf keeps Fori slave hands at work.

My breath catches. What if that's true? Maybe their patrols snagged a few Fori from their nearby domain.

I force my feet to remain planted. I've come too far to back away now. The image of Deka shivering alone on the ground, breathing what might be his final breaths, is enough to get me marching toward the gate.

I bang on the high red door with the bottom of my fist. A boom echoes deep through cavernous passages beyond, with the mountain to my right seeming to rumble with the echo. The door's dramatic response leaves me holding my breath.

"Hey!" shouts a man from behind.

I whirl around to see two men in long coats approaching from the trailhead archway. They level crossbows at me and cock their heads to aim while creeping forward.

"Hi!" I wave both hands to show them I'm unarmed.

My friendly demeanor scarcely veils my terror. Those crossbow bolts pose more danger to me than the Sea Lord's bullets, but to show fear might portray me as an enemy. Then they'll treat me like one. Best I be acting like a friend.

"How did you get up here?" the left man says. He sports an indigo longcoat that's seen better days, but I must say he looks pretty sharp despite its rips and uneven fade. Even in disrepair their uniforms exude more class than the King's army, or even the Squids.

They stop at center field, between the archway and fortress. Their eyes flare wide as they take in the sight of me, and my wings wrap instinctively around my body, but it's not to guard against the chill.

The mesmerized stares of these men make me woefully conscious of my body. Their eyes swell with lust and ill intent. They've not seen my kind around here before. We are not devils to them, but instead something to be desired.

"I'm here to see the Wolf," I say.

My voice snaps them from their trance. They pull their weapons tightly to their shoulders and lock eyes with me, their suspicion soaring.

"What business do you have with our lord?" the left guard says.

"I bring a message."

"From who?"

"From the Lord of the Sea."

"Who?"

Right, I remember Deka calling him by another name. "The Commander," I say.

"What commander?"

My mind goes blank. What did Deka say the Sea Lord's name was?

The bowmen exchange a hissing of words. At my silence, they shake their weapons at me. "On your knees, hands up high."

This is not good. What was that name? Taurus? No… Centaur? No, not that…

"On the ground, now! Or I'll shoot!"

My heart quivers. I bounce on the balls of my feet, my body desperate to spring into flight to flee this place. Then, with my life literally depending on it, my subconscious blurts out the name: "Centaurus! Commander Centaurus sent me!"

The guards lower their weapons slightly to exchange confused looks. This name means nothing to them.

"Why did he send you?"

"To warn of an attack."

The guards tense even further. I cringe at the way their fingers curl around their crossbow triggers.

"Maybe *you're* the attack," one says. "You've got the makings of an assassin. A pretty, innocent-looking thing who can slip past our defenses."

"I say we take her to the dark cells below for some intensive *questioning*."

His partner's eyes light up with excitement.

"Don't worry," the rightward guard says, "we'll send what's left of you back to your *commander*."

"Smithe, Parker," snaps a girl's voice from above.

Their gazes jolt upward, to above the gate as they lower their crossbows.

"Did she say Commander Centaurus?" asks the girl's voice.

"Yes!" I shout.

I can't see the window from under this gate covering, but I dare not step out with those armed men so jumpy.

"She's got two bullet holes in her chest," says the left guard, "but she's acting like she doesn't. She's something unnatural."

"Let her in," says the unseen girl's voice.

The guards swallow hard and give me an uncertain look.

I return it with a victorious smile and stick my tongue out at them. *Not today, boys.*

They're more lucky than they'll ever know. That girl above the gate just saved their lives.

NYA

You could call the Wolf a fearsome beast. Frankly, I'm a bit disappointed. I'd been expecting a lot more fur.

The girl seated in the leather chair beside a stone fireplace has a head of brown stubble, over which a narrow strip of purple fabric wraps to cover her left eye. She sips from a glass as she analyzes scripture from a book. She appears the same age as the Sea Lord, double Deka's years, so early to mid-thirties.

"You're not from around here," the Wolf says, keeping her one eye on the book in her lap. She absently takes another sip while reading something that must be of great interest. "From where do you hail?"

I'm unsure how to explain my origins to someone of a race that knows so little about their place in the universe. These Earthlings have grown so big, yet they have fallen so far behind in matters of high consequence. It's no wonder my masters believe them to be of unintelligent design. The squabbles fracturing this continent provide strong evidence that I am the one who's been misjudging Deka's people, giving them more credit than they deserve.

"Do you have a name?" the Wolf asks.

"Nya."

"*Nya.*" Her tone suggests the sound of my name intrigues her.

She slams her book shut and looks upon me for the first time. Her one uncovered eye flares wide with surprise, but she quickly composes herself. "I've not heard this name before."

"It means Evening Star."

"Well, Evening Star, my enemies call me Alexandra. My friends... they call me *Lex.*" She sets her book aside and stands to approach me. "By which name would you call me?"

I'm eager to demand she send help to Deka, but she might use him as leverage over me. I need to establish some ground here.

"I'd call you Lex, because you've not yet crossed me. But there are many of my kind who'd not call you by any name at all, because they're not coming to talk. They're coming to kill off every last one of you, and if you're not prepared for their arrival, it won't take them long. Killing off races is what they do, and they're very good at it."

Lex's menacing smirk suggests she believes me, and that my ominous message comes as good news to her.

"Accomplished invaders would first send scouts to appraise our strength," she says. "Perhaps they are already here. Perhaps you are one of them."

Her icy blue eye locks me in a stare. It's long and awkward, and I'm not sure how to end it, so I'm glad when her attention shifts to the wall behind me.

I follow her gaze to a map. It's of a continent that looks like a fat tadpole with a short tail. A jagged red line divides the land into unequal halves. Whoever drew that border was angry when they did it, because chunks of marker had broken off and smeared the page.

Lex brushes by me to the map. She points to an upside down crown seated in the half containing the peninsula where Sheffa and I had parted ways.

"If this enemy does their research," she says, "they'll see my rival for the greater threat. They'll attack him first, but he will not go down without a fight. He'll put a good dent in their ranks, perhaps enough to give me a chance against whatever remains. I'll have better odds then than I do now." She shoots me a devious grin. "So, tell your people to come on down. Tell them to do their worst."

My fists tighten, and so does my jaw, so I take a deep breath and relax myself with a calming exhale. Good diplomacy will prevail here, so it's time to put the fists away.

Stepping toward the Wolf—I mean, *Lex*—I spread my wings to their full extent.

Lex cannot hide her astonishment. Her icy blue eye traces my wings and takes in my body that so much resembles her own.

"My race has a shadow side," I say. "They fly faster than me, heal almost instantaneously, can see one second into the future, and—"

Lex raises a hand to silence me. "Wait, what?"

"They fly faster than I—"

"Not that part." Lex steps closer. She glances at her guard near the chamber door, suddenly wary of his presence, and waves him away. The spearman bows and backs out of the room. Lex waits for the door to clunk shut, then looks to me urgently. "You know of time travel? Tell me about it."

Her fascination with this topic sets off alarms in me. And from what I've so far gathered, I suspect her intent is less than benevolent. I must tread carefully, to avoid making an enemy of her, while steering the conversation to more pressing matters.

"There is time travel, yes," I say, "and I am a master of it."

Lex abandons her boundaries and grabs my shoulders. "Tell me how. You have a machine? Where is it?"

"Well..." I say, turning from her hold. I walk to her bookshelf and pretend to read the texts. "You need a gate, and you need a key to unlock it."

The hair on my neck rises as I feel the Wolf's stare intensify. She desires this knowledge greatly, and in that I've gained some sway.

"The enemy I speak of now holds both. My people..." A lump hardens in my throat at the memory surfacing. "My people took the gate from them and managed to remove the key. We were not warriors, and we were few, yet we succeeded in that... if only briefly." I turn to meet Lex's stare. "If you combine forces with us, we could do it again."

Lex turns away and rubs her chin, contemplating.

"How many are they?" she asks.

"One thousand." That's a lie. They are at least ten times that.

"They're all airborne, like you?"

"Yes."

When she turns back to me, I see she's all in. "How do we kill them?"

It takes serious effort to contain my excitement. "Bullets

are no good," I say, pointing at my newest wounds. "Our cells regenerate too fast. You need something that'll hinder the regrowth—something jammed into the heart to keep it from pumping."

"An arrow through the heart," Lex muses, almost as if such a death could be poetic.

"That, or chop off their heads," I add. "We can grow a few limbs back eventually, but no one's ever sprouted a new head."

Lex smiles at me warmly. She gives me a good look over, and the gleam in her eye suggests she's developed a greater appreciation for me. "Tell me, Nya, do you think we'd benefit from having all of us humans fighting on the same side against this enemy?"

"Oh, yes!" I say, truly glad the Wolf has changed her stance on this. Whoever said a wolf couldn't be reasoned with hasn't met Lex! "If we have every human fighting with us, then we'll beat the Watchers for sure."

Lex nods as if she likes the sound of this.

"Perfect," she says, her eye flashing bright with enthusiasm. But then, her brow crinkles and she rubs her forehead with the back of her hand. "Oh, no, how could I be so foolish? I'm afraid it's not going to be that easy."

She hugs herself and turns away while hanging her head in shame.

I step up to take her arm. "Why not?"

She keeps her head lowered and gives it an ominous shake. "Well, there's something you have to understand about Anterrans. We have a long and complicated history that's left a lot of sour blood between us, and... Well, let's just say tensions have been a bit high lately."

"Forget about your past and cast aside your differences," I say firmly. "Make peace with Regulus. It's the only way."

"He can't be reasoned with!" Lex says, almost in despair. "He's forced all his able citizens into military service and treats them like dogs, starving them to madness before unleashing them on our border. He feeds them all sorts of disgusting lies about me, things like..."

Lex hangs her head and grips her elbows, too worked up to finish. When I step up beside her, I see tears glazing her one good eye.

"He is a king of fear and war," she says. "So long as he's alive, Anterra will never know peace."

Her head lifts suddenly, her eye wide with epiphany. She looks to me with a hopeful stare. "But there is a way."

"What is it?"

"Fly to his capital with the same warning you brought me. Tell him to open his border to my army so we can unite our forces. When he denies your request, you kill him."

I clutch my chest and step back in disbelief. She wants me to assassinate her rival? She's crazy!

The Wolf holds her hands out in front, pleading. "You'll be freeing his people of tyranny. They'll worship you as their mighty liberator, the champion they've spent their whole lives praying for. In the chaos that follows, I'll ride in to restore order, then we'll all vote to elect a council of leaders. That's all I want, Nya—for my people to be free. And when the airborne invasion begins, it will unite us even further."

She takes my hands and holds them against her chest. Her heart pounds against her ribs. "It's the only way, Nya. So long as Regulus sits on his throne, we'll remain divided. Remove him, and you'll have your army."

I pull my hands from her hold and turn away, my head swirling. Kill an enemy of a friend to gain an ally? This really sends my moral compass into a spin. On one side, I don't have any quarrel with King Regulus. But on the other, we cannot defeat the Watchers without Lex's help. If I leave here without granting her wish, I'll be leaving empty handed.

But we'd not be without hope. The Watcher attack might force both countries to throw aside their differences and join forces anyway. My heart beats a little lighter at this possibility.

I turn back to Lex and say, "I'm sorry, but I'll not be your manslayer."

To my surprise, Lex places a hand on her belly and offers me a deep nod of respect. "Of course. You must accept my apology. It was wrong of me to pressure you into fighting our battles." Her face twitches with a cunning smirk. *"Guards!"*

The door to my side swings open, through which six soldiers armed with black shields and spears enter.

Cold sweat trickles down my spine. I've come to recruit an ally and instead gained an enemy.

"I hope you understand the position you've put me in," says Lex from the side. "You've seen my defenses, perhaps identified weaknesses I've not considered. If I allow you to leave with that information, well, that would be very reckless of me."

Says the girl trying to send an assassin to kill her only hope! I grit my teeth and raise my fists, ready to fight.

"Take her alive," Lex tells her guards, "if you can. I'd like to study this creature while it still has a pulse."

The six guards join their rectangular shields to form a wall. This wall covers them from foot to nose when standing fully erect, and when they crouch they disappear entirely. At each joint between shields is a round hole through which they shove their spears, though it is not sharp tips that threaten me now. The forked butt ends crackle with blue lightning.

My hair jumps at the threat of electric shock, and my heart quivers as they begin their coordinated shuffle toward me.

I back up to the wall and perform a quick assessment of its wooden supports. A well-placed strike could bring the whole roof down, which will hurt me too, but I risk more by squaring off with six jabbing spears.

"Looks like we're about to get some practice on our new enemy," Lex says as she watches with folded arms. This is entertainment to her.

Anger boils and steams inside my chest, which seeps up my throat in a growl. And then something strange happens.

The soldiers behind the approaching shield wall slow their pace in the strangest manner. It's like they're walking through water or an unseen aether that resists their advance. To their left, Lex breathes slowly in anticipation, and a quick glance at the lazy flames in the fireplace tells me it's actually time that has slowed.

This is not the first instance I've experienced this phenomenon. Back at the pyramid battle, when Jexa led that massive arrowhead across the sky toward us, time had slowed for me then as well. Then it happened again, after the Butcher killed Jinny, when I went Berserk and destroyed all those pyramid blocks.

Jinny. The memory of her death adds fuel to the fire blazing inside my chest.

The first spear jabs at me with laughable speed. I meet it with an upward kick to the shaft, and the rising spear provides me enough opening to slide in and punch the center shield with all my might.

The guard flies back out through the open doorway and slams into a wall. His shield clatters to the floor as he topples down the stairs to his left.

I stare at the shield with alarm, the shield that remained perfectly in tact rather than exploding into a cloud of atomic particles. From what I felt, it actually absorbed most of my impact.

The guards around the punched-out gap listen with widening eyes to the clamor of their companion tumbling down the spiral stairway. When the commotion stops, their surprised stares harden. They shuffle sideways to close the gap and continue their advance at normal speed.

I spin on my heels and wind back my fist to punch the nearest wooden beam. I'm about to swing when—

"Halt!"

The wall of five shields stops at Lex's command. She steps in front to address me, her eye wide in appraisal that sees me in a new light. "This enemy you've warned me about, they are strong like you?"

"That was just a taste," I warn, despite my head swirling with a dizziness that often follows these fits of rage. "Try me again."

Lex raises a hand stiffly. Her guards break up their shield wall and retract their crackling spear tips, then shuffle back to give us space. They remain before the doorway on alert, watching me with distrustful eyes while one exits to tend to his fallen comrade.

Alexandra clasps her hands behind her back and holds her chin high.

"If you surrender yourself peacefully, I will offer you quarter," she says. "You shall remain here as a guest and an adviser to me, so that we can make preparations to face our approaching enemy."

"And your rival?" I say, my fists half-raised. The room spins, so I widen my stance to steady myself.

Lex tilts her head back and huffs in frustration. Then she shakes her head as if she can't believe what she's about to say. "I will dispatch a messenger to his capital, Amyria. For the sake of my people, I shall pursue peace with the Imposter King. Happy? Good. Now, come, there are other arrangements to be made."

"There's one more thing I need you to do," I say.

Lex's stunned expression tells me she's not accustomed to taking requests. I don't care. There's a lot she needs to change if she's to defeat the Watchers.

"My friend is hurt," I say. "Send a healer with me to go help him."

Lex wags a finger at me. "I told you before, Evening Star, I can't allow you to leave. You shall remain within these walls until I'm sure I can trust you."

My teeth grind. The room stops spinning, everything sharpening as time slows once more.

"But fear not..." Lex says, her voice slow and groggy. "I'll dispatch a balloon to locate his position, then send a physician on horseback to retrieve him. You just point out the direction."

"He's in the deep forest. He'll be too hard to see. They'll need my help out there."

Lex walks to a four-legged piece of furniture. From a drawer she pulls out a pair of goggles and offers them to me. "These will pick up any heat signatures within sight. If your friend is out there, as you say, then the balloon crew will spot him with these. Assuming he's still alive, of course."

I accept the goggles and hold them to my eyes. An orange flash blinds me, so I lower them and see the glow comes from the fireplace. I raise the contraption again to look upon Lex, who appears through the lenses as an orange blob of heat.

I lower the goggles and stare at them in wonder.

"Satisfied?" asks Lex.

I nod. This is actually good, because as my anger and caution fade, I find myself wobbling on my feet. These bursts of rage give me a boost when I need it, but they take their toll on me.

"Good." Lex's lips twitch with a smile. She must see this retrieval will provide her leverage over me.

I don't care. I just want Deka under the same roof as me.

"I'll send the balloon at once," she says.

CHAPTER 28
NYA

'*Make yourself at home.*'

That's what Lex told me before leaving to dispatch her balloon to retrieve Deka. Her fortress must be laced with traps. Why else would she leave me to roam freely about unwatched?

The guards who patrolled her corridors upon my arrival are nowhere in sight, but I get the feeling I'm being watched. The Wolf allows me to explore her den to test my trustworthiness. It's like she wants to see where I'll end up, what will interest me, or perhaps catch me up to no good. But I only care about one thing.

I pray Deka is okay and that he makes a good impression on Lex. After we steer her toward victory, she can thank us with a big swath of land, which we'll make into our paradise. As a human, Deka will have better bartering rights with that.

Oh, Deka... Though I'd have gone to him if I could, I'm glad Lex forbid me. All this action and no clean energy source has left me withered. I need only to look out the opposite window of this tower to see evidence of my depleted strength.

In the courtyard below, a black-clad warrior tests his sword swing on a sapien-shaped mannequin. His companions watch on, offering suggestions or insults on his technique until he's had enough. When he sheaths his sword and looks up to my window, I recognize his eyes. He is the guard I blasted down the stairs.

My heart drops like a meteor. The fact that he is still alive unsettles me greatly. I'd hit his shield with all my might, and not only did that fail to dust it, but I didn't even break his arm.

I hold up my hands and flex my fingers, disappointment and panic swelling in me. I'm trapped on this dark continent with only faint energy trickling in short bursts to feed me until sunrise. Here I waste away in a slow death with no way out, growing weaker by the hour with no means to bounce back.

At least they still fear me. I need to keep it that way by hiding my weakness until I'm forced to fight again.

The warrior draws his sword and hacks the head off the dummy. His threatening glare makes clear he wishes it was me, so I cross the library to sit in the opposite window.

I've lost sight of Lex's hot air balloon, but last I checked it was halfway to the twin peaks.

Chains rattle and the gate edges squeal up their tracks as the door rises below me. Twelve humans thunder through the gatehouse upon horses in two columns of six, boys and girls with shaved heads riding side by side in violet cloaks. A horse-drawn wagon rolls out behind them, its deck covered by an arched canvas tarp. They gallop across the grass square and through the upper archway to make their way down the trail.

I release an audible sigh of relief. Now that I know the retrieval crew is on their way, I can turn my attention elsewhere.

Lex's fortress consists of two walls in an L shape to box in a courtyard against the mountain. The front wall houses the gate, while the outer wall stands over a sheer cliff that overlooks a dammed lake. Each stone wall is hollow with three levels inside.

I tiptoe from Lex's study in the outer turret and follow the passage over the gatehouse. Purple carpet runs the length of the stone floor, with matching banners draped from the walls at even intervals. Golden embroidery depicts scenes of epic battles and seafaring adventures that captivate me so much that I reach the end without noticing.

Warm air blows through an arch doorway carved into the mountain. The chill of the stone passage behind me gives the heat on my face an even greater radiance. This warmth invites me into the mountain, where I step from a cold dark world and into paradise.

I'd never know I was underground by the violet light fluorescing from the ceiling. This glow breathes life into rows upon rows of plants that stretch across the enormous cavern for as far as I can see. Ultraviolet radiation, harnessed to provide food during the long winter months...

It's genius!

My skin tingles under the light, and the tightness around my wounds loosens to ease my breathing. As I wander between crisscrossing rows of plants—fruits and vegetables of every kind imaginable—my strength swells with each step.

The fog in my mind clears, and I realize how much of a daze I'd been in these past few days. My cells had been suffocating, starved of nutrients that left me nearly brain-dead.

I stroll between violet rows of elongated fruit to the end of the cavern, where a blast door bars access to something of obvious importance. Pressing my hand to the steel, I feel the frequency range and determine the barrier to be four feet thick. Whatever lies beyond either requires heavy protection from us, or we need such protection from it. I've recently learned that some things are better left to sleep in the abyss, so I dare not pursue entry.

By the time I return to the fortress's cold corridors, I'm soaring with energy. Not only that, but three white blotches mark where each of my wounds had been. I give them a poke to ensure the healing is more than just superficial, and I feel no pain.

I look back and marvel at the glowing violet entryway. Having such a powerful energy source nearby relieves me beyond words. I just want to fly around and explore, for this mysterious land contains secrets and wonders these people have yet to discover. But I must secure Lex's trust until Deka is safe by my side once more.

Ringing and whacking lure me to the gatehouse. A small side door opens into the inner courtyard, where Lex swings a sword at a shifting wall of shields. Three guards hold their black shields to cover their torsos, while another three hold theirs above to form a slanted roof.

Lex swings her curved blade down upon the upper left shield with such force that it parts its edge from the center shields. The bearer swiftly seals the gap before Lex can capitalize on the separation with a follow-up blow.

The Wolf presses her attack with a flurry of violent strikes. She grunts louder with each swing, her exertion drawing beads of sweat that slide down her scalp and drip from her chin. The shuffling shield wall stays tight, shifting to remain facing her attempts to circle them. A few kicks and punches succeed in knocking the lower left shield aside, and a well-aimed punch breaks the bearer from the line.

Lex viciously attacks the isolated guard. He holds up his shield to block her strikes, steel hacking from every angle, each blow gashing the shield as if she's actually trying to hurt him.

He flings his shield aside and drops onto his back with both hands raised. "Yield! I yield!"

Lex raises her sword high, her arm vibrating with enough restrained energy to split him in half with a single swing. The other shield-bearers watch nervously.

Lex must sense my stare, because she looks over her shoulder at me standing in the doorway. She smiles wide and slides her sword into its sheath, then cocks her head to address the defeated guard. "Target. Now."

The guard's face turns pallid. He scrambles to retrieve a dented shield that bears three pockmarked bullseyes in vertical alignment. It's a pitiful sight watching him try to shrink behind it.

Lex walks backward toward me and stops a few paces away. The dented shield across the courtyard rattles as Lex adopts a strange stance, with her hands hanging as if she's holding an invisible ball against each hip, her fingers twitching slowly.

"Attack!" she yells, and the shield-bearer charges toward her.

Lex throws the right flap of her long coat back to expose a handgun fastened to her belt, the same style the Sea Lord had given Deka. She pulls it from its carrier and shoots from the hip in one smooth motion—*POP-POP-POP*.

The first bullet smacks the bottom bullseye and tilts the shield-top forward; the second hits the upper shield and slams it against the poor fellow's forehead. He shudders to a stop as the third bullet slaps the center and knocks him onto his back, where he cowers under the shield to guard against further attack.

Lex twirls the smoking gun around her finger and then slides it back into its holder. When she turns to face me, the delight in her eye reveals the great pleasure she derives from punishing her followers.

The remaining guards rush to help up their companion. He groans loud and nurses his arm in a way that suggests it's broken.

Lex's cruelty toward her own should be concerning. Instead, it gives me confidence in their chances against the Watchers. If she treats her own warriors this way, she'll be ruthless against our enemy. Plus, she's bound to have bred some hardened fighters with these tactics.

My heart beats a little lighter. These people will hold their own against Jexa's army, and they won't require Deka or me to help them. I'll map out our escape as soon as he gets here. Our mission is complete. All of our sacrifices are behind us.

"Nya," she says, "I've been thinking—"

A horn echoes from a distance.

"Open the gate!" shouts a watchman from outside the walls.

Chains rattle beside me as the red gate rises. When it reaches half its height, hooves from a dozen horses pound over wooden planks. Riders gallop into the courtyard ahead of the covered wagon, the back of which carries Deka, who sits with his feet dangling over the edge. He clutches a blanket around his shoulders, his teeth chattering so loud they might shatter.

My heart bursts with joy. "Deka!"

He slides off the wagon and gives me a curious look.

I skip over to him with such enthusiasm that, when we embrace, I tackle him to the ground.

He growls and thrashes, pushing me away while scratching my skin in the process.

I jump up and give him a kick for his rudeness, but his crazed eyes tell me he's serious.

A healer hops down from the wagon with a leather bag over his shoulder. He helps Deka to his feet and pulls the blanket tightly around him.

"Deka, what's gotten into you?" I say.

"You mean what has gotten *out* of him?" says the lead horseman from his mount. He pulls up his sleeve to reveal a fresh bite mark on his wrist. "He'd have chewed off my arm if my other fist hadn't rocked him."

I look to Deka in disbelief. He returns my stare with a look that shall haunt me until my dying breath. This look I know too well. I've seen it on the faces of my cousins when they arrive onto a new planet, right after the portal temporarily wipes them of their memories.

Pointing to my chest, I say, "It's Nya, remember? You

know me."

He hugs his blanket close and looks to his feet, his jaw quivering fiercely.

The lead rider dismounts and offers Lex something. "This was the only object in his possession."

He opens his hand to reveal Deka's compass.

I gasp in wonder. Deka must have woken and went wandering, then somehow found it in the wilderness. But the odds of him covering that much ground and actually finding such a tiny instrument are so enormous I actually can't believe it.

Lex snatches the device and holds it in both hands. She stares at the silver star with great longing, and it's clear there is a deep history between her and the Sea Lord.

Everyone watches her fascination with fascinations of their own. Lex must sense this. Her eye flicks up to take note of her audience, then she straightens and clears her throat.

"Run our guest a bath," she tells the rider, "and bring him whatever food he can bear to eat." She returns her attention to Deka and grabs above his elbow to usher him away. "You're safe now. As my guest, you have my hospitality and protection."

It aches my heart to watch Lex lead Deka away. When she looks over her shoulder at me, her conniving smirk makes my face burn and fists clench so tight my knuckles crack.

Suddenly the word 'guest' sounds more like 'esteemed prisoner'. She will use him to control me. The Wolf thinks she has seen the extent of my strength. What she doesn't know is that a few more laps around her ultraviolet garden will give me all the power I need to pound down her entire fortress with a single punch.

CHAPTER 29

NYA

The Wolf of Amyria must never sleep. With so many projects, how could she? She's got projects here, projects there, projects everywhere!

I stand at a giant round table while she signs an important order. She said she wanted to pick my brain for information, and at first that sounded pretty gruesome. I imagined a trip to the dungeon where questions are asked with pointy weapons. Instead she invited me to her war planning room, where beeswax candles light walls covered by territorial maps. I guess life under the Watchers raised me to expect the worst. This manner is much more civil, except for one thing.

I pull on the twisted robe Lex 'gifted' me. She says I'm a distraction and that I need to keep the sunken hood down far enough to cover my eyes and ears. I could tell she dreaded handing over the purple silk garment, but I refused to wear the wool poncho she first gave me. That shabby thing was possessed by all sorts of miserable energy, not to mention fleas.

She hands the signed order to the messenger who

brought it and turns to rejoin me. The messenger leaves, but it's only a matter of time before we're interrupted again. This must have been the tenth intrusion since we arrived in this strategy room.

Lex's preoccupation actually gives me peace of mind. With so much on the go, there's no way she has time to check in on Deka when he's having a bath, or dine with him in candlelight, or...

A hand smacks my face—my own. *Just listen to me!* I sound ridiculous, and if anyone could hear my thoughts right now I'd die of shame. Lex has taken us in and given us more than we could ever ask for. She doesn't deserve my petty jealousy. Besides, it's clear she has better things to do.

She sets two glasses on the table and pours a splash of red liquid from a bottle into each. She offers me one. "Drink?"

From a distance, the fruity smell reminds me of the fermented berries my cousins swill to get their jolly on. I need to keep my wits in straight order here, so I shake my head.

Lex shrugs and spills the contents of one glass into the other. She takes a sip, then walks around the table. The way she holds her free arm behind her back gives her an air of sophistication that makes me evaluate my own posture.

She points her glass toward a crown carved into the wooden map. "This is Amyria — Polaria's capital and Regulus's center of power. It was entrusted to my father, back before the days of kings and crowns."

"What happened?"

Lex grinds her teeth as she glares at the crown staining her map. "Murder."

"They killed your father?"

"Yes. In one fell swoop, they sucker-punched democracy clean out of my home country."

She presses both hands on the table and leans forward. The wooden legs groan under her weight, and by the heat in her glare it's a wonder that wooden crown hasn't burst into flames by now. "One day I will stand over that King's corpse, I don't care if it costs me all that I own, including my life. I will see that man dead if it's the last thing I do."

"You want revenge."

She stands straight, almost defensively, and says, "I want *justice*. Justice for my family, and democracy for my people."

"These things will have to wait. You'll need the strength of your entire race when you face the Watchers."

"It seems my best strategy would be to hole up here and let my enemy, the *great King Regulus*, deal with the first wave."

I slap the table with my palm. The smack sends Lex into a rigid stance, from which she sizes me up warily.

Satisfaction swells in me. *That's right. You've seen what these fists of mine can do.*

"What would you have us do?" Lex says. "Meet them in the open? We don't even know where they'll attack."

"I do."

Lex gives me a suspicious look.

"There's a gateway here," I explain, pointing to a wooden bump on her map, "at this pyramid."

"Pyramid? There are no pyramids on Anterra."

"There are!" I say, and I nearly punch a hole through her table.

"Those are mountains."

"Funny-looking mountains." Besides, who's to say a

natural formation couldn't be used to channel the planet's power? If a landmark of the right size and shape happened to form over an energy node, then the gate masters might have developed it to conduct portal openings. This gateway was designed only as a backup anyway. It didn't need to be perfect.

"What do these Watchers want with this gate, then? You said they controlled the main one in Africa."

"It's damaged," says Deka from the doorway, where he stands with his arm in a sling.

"Deka!" I say. "Are you hurt bad?"

He ignores my question, sparing me not even a glance. The table map commands all of his attention from the doorway.

Lex steps aside and gestures toward the table. "Please, join us."

Rather than come join me on my side of the table, Deka falls in beside Lex. He stares at the wooden map without offering me any form of acknowledgment, and suddenly I remember my hood and flip it back to reveal my face.

My unveiling gains me not the slightest look. "Deka, it's me."

"I know," he says, and his caustic tone stings me deeply. Though, I see what he's doing. He must have sensed Lex would use us against each other, so he's pretending that we're nothing more than travel companions who've grown weary of each other. I must say, his brilliant performance even had me fooled for a bit there.

"There's a chill in here," Lex says, and her devious grin suggests she's not talking about the temperature. Seeing the joke fall flat, she says to Deka, "Are you well fed and rested?"

He instinctively rubs his belly. "Yes. You are too generous."

"Well, you've certainly earned it," Lex says. She gestures toward the map. "So, you were saying…"

"The Giza Gate is damaged." Deka can't help but spare me a quick look when he says this. My body tingles at the memory of smashing all those stone blocks with my fists.

"It can only power a short jump," Deka says, and he actually sounds sure of this. "Only on-planet transits, like the one that brought me here."

"These gateways…" Lex says, her voice softening as lust grows in her eye. "If they allow you to leap across Space, then that's where the Time-jump must come in, right?"

There it is again. All this time travel talk is getting worrisome.

Deka frowns and rubs a hand over his head in contemplation.

I need to get us out of here the first chance we get. I'll be strong enough to carry him from the window to the river below. Those boats down there will offer us a quick getaway, with Deka being a mariner and all. Sliding one down that steep slope without crashing it may prove difficult, but we'll worry about that when we get there. And it seems our mission here is not yet accomplished.

"You should worry about the present," I tell Lex. "What's happening now and what will happen in the near future are all that matter."

Lex picks up on my irritation and gives me a conceding nod. "The *present*, of course." She stares longingly at the 'mountain' on her map. "So our gate here is the planet's backup."

"It's not *your* gate," I say.

"Then to who does it belong?"

"The Magister governs it."

"Who?"

Of course. I'd gone through this with Deka. "He's a cosmic authority. It's his job to find refugee races new homes."

"Why doesn't he just go back in time to stop whatever destroyed their old homes?"

I grit my teeth in frustration. She's not even trying to hide her motives now. "That's not how time travel works. The Magister is powerful, but he can't stop a meteor from smashing into a planet!"

"Settle yourself," Lex says.

I loosen my hands and realize how worked up this has been making me. Diplomacy doesn't prosper through screams, so I must measure my words more carefully.

Deka doesn't contribute much. He rubs a hand over the varnished table edge as if admiring the shiny wood, but his distant stare suggests he himself is doing a bit of time traveling right now. I must have rammed him pretty hard into that tree.

Lex presses her hands on the table and resumes leaning over her map. "So they're coming for this gate. What will they do with it?"

"Summon reinforcements."

"And then?"

"They'll snuff out all life on Earth," Deka says.

"Why?" Lex asks.

The answer to this makes me shiver and sweat at the same time.

"There's a great darkness that lives past the edge of infinity," Deka says, "where not even starlight dares to wander. That darkness loathes all that is good and light. It craves eternal darkness, but it can't do much in its current form. Not on its own, anyway, so it charms the hearts of corrupt mortals to do its bidding. The Marshal of Watchers is one of its possessed. *Jexa* is her name, and her mission is to ensnare as many souls as she can."

I watch Deka with growing confusion. How has he come to know all of this?

"So she thinks she can end the Universe by exterminating all life?" asks Lex.

"Not quite," Deka says. "The energy of consciousness can never be truly destroyed. The closest way to accomplish that end is to feed them into a black hole—*The Dark*, some call it."

A shiver rocks me good, and I'm glad it's Deka telling this story instead of me.

"The more light those agents of darkness feed into that crushing void, the more unstable the balance of existence will become. And worse, Jexa doesn't need to send all light into the Dark. There's a point when the Dark will swell with so much energy that its gravity will pull the whole Universe in on itself. With less matter to resist the pull, everything will submit to it—all Space, all life, and even Time itself."

Lex had been staring off in deep thought until that last part.

"There's a name for that end," Deka says. "It's called—"

"Omega," I say.

Deka gives me a dark and knowing look. It seems

knowledge of this fate is rooted in all conscious life, these unenlightened *sapiens* included.

"So that's what this invasion is really about," Lex says. "We stand at the precipice of the Omega Point." She folds her arms and rubs her chin while evaluating her map. "That gateway is in Regulus's domain. This threat will darken his skies first."

I roll my eyes. Not this again. "Don't you see—"

"I must be ready to reinforce his army."

My heart skips a beat. Did I just hear that right? When my heart resumes pumping, it plays a rhythm of hope and admiration for this Wolf who grows tamer as the night darkens.

"Yes," I say, but I am cautious. "If he won't accept your help immediately, you must be ready to ride in when the Watchers overwhelm him. It's your only hope."

"Okay," Lex says with a nod. Her lustful stare at the gate's position on the map concerns me, but that's a problem for another time. For now, I count us lucky she's even interested in that mountain. Her passion will go a long way toward its defense.

A knock at the door echoes across the room.

"Enter," Lex says.

The door creaks open, though much slower than our previous visits. So much that it raises Lex's intrigue. "Well, come in. What is it?"

A boy peeks his head in from the corridor. His stricken stare suggests he drew the short straw to deliver whatever message he now carries. "You—Your..."

"What? Come on, boy, spit it out."

"You're wanted in the stables. There's an important v-v-visitor here."

"Then why are they in the stables?"

The boy clings to the door edge as if it's the only thing keeping him from running to hide.

Lex huffs, then looks to me and Deka. "You'll have to excuse me, I must see what this is about. I shan't be long."

She rubs Deka's arm, then smiles at me over her shoulder as she leaves.

I rush to the wooden door and ease it shut, then make my way to the window as I throw away my robe. "Come on. This is our chance."

I fling open the window and step aside for Deka to climb up, but he remains standing across the table.

"Hurry," I say.

"I'm staying."

These words hang heavy in the air. I don't even know what they mean. "The Wolf is all in now," I tell him. "She's going to fight the Watchers. We're free to go."

"My place is here."

What is he talking about? "Your place is with me."

He responds with the nastiest look I've ever seen. "Really? Then why did you leave me alone in the forest?"

"I came here to get help."

"You left me!" he screams, his face twisted with pain. A teardrop slides down his left cheek. "You left me."

"I had to, Deka. What's gotten into you?"

"I'd *never* leave you like that. When you were hurt, I didn't even think of it. Not once."

Oh, father of darkness, that's not even the same thing! He had nowhere to go to find help for me, and if I hadn't come here he might still be unconscious in the cold dark woods. But I see his emotions have seized him on this.

"I'm sorry, Deka. Just come with me and I'll make it up to you."

"How?" He struts around the table toward me, his eyes fierce with anger.

I find myself backing away, because his glare warns that he wishes me harm.

"Are you going to use me to make all your problems go away?"

"What? No," I say, my voice never sounding so meek.

"How do you hope this will end? Wait— Let me guess. You'll use me to open a gate home and leave us here to clean up your mess. That's all this is. It's all this bond of ours ever was to you—a ride home." He looms over me, his breath shuddering. "Tell me I'm wrong."

A lump balloons in my throat. "I'd take you with me."

"So I can be your plaything? Or will it be to share your guilt after we abandon our people? Well, either way, I'm done being your puppet. The Wolf fights for my people. My place is by her side now. You and me..." He shakes his head in disgust. "Our hearts will never be aligned."

I slide down the wall and sit with my knees to my chest. For the first time in my life I have nothing to say, because he's right. Nya, the great Rebel Marshal, defeated by a few words from a human boy.

Deka returns to the table and leans over it with his back to me. His hunched form blurs through the tears flooding my eyes.

So that's it? This is where our road together ends?

Lex bursts through the door carrying a leather sack, her face flushed and her eyes frazzled.

I'm on my feet in a second. Even Deka perks up at the sight of her.

Lex looks to me and says, "You came to Anterra with a friend?"

"Yes," I say, trying to interpret Lex's behavior. These humans are always so serious that it's hard to read what's behind their expressions. "Sheffa. She went to…"

I notice Lex staring wide-eyed at the bag in her hand.

My belly lurches and squeezes bile up into my throat.

Lex sets the bag on the table. A strand of brown hair sticks through the cinched opening.

No…

"Well," Lex says, "it seems your friend is now the *head* ambassador to Amyria. *This* is how Regulus greets outsiders."

My whole body goes cold, numb. But that can't be Sheffa. I just need a moment to work up the courage, then I'll open the bag to show Lex her mistake.

Deka turns and offers me a look of sympathy, every trace of anger extinguished from his eyes. It's all the confirmation I need.

No one speaks for a long while. It's so quiet I hear the candle flame wavering.

My voice is surprisingly calm when I break the silence. "If the King dies, will his people follow you?"

"They will," Lex says. "It's the people on this side of the border who need convincing. Too many of them see me as a foreigner. We share a common enemy, true, but many don't care to fight Regulus. They do not believe we can defeat him.

But if you bring me his head, that will inspire more faith in our cause."

I stare at the bag, rage swirling inside my chest and heating my body, drying the last teardrops in my eyes. With my target so far away I must store this energy for later, for I shall certainly need it. I've tried to sit out this war by playing puppeteer, but Deka was right. I've been blinded by my own pursuit. But I can make it right. And it all starts with a single word.

Revenge.

CHAPTER 30

DEKA

It doesn't matter how much distance I put between me and the cave where my mother was killed, her screams still find me in my sleep. Only, here it's different. Here I see the murder not through the eyes of a frightened child, but through those of a killer.

I fly in arrowhead formation high above a desert of rippled sand. To my immense discomfort, the companions to my left and right are the worst company one could ever find. Hair of black, blue and purple rattle upon two dozen heads like chimes in the wind—dark songs played out by the ornamental bones of a hundred vanquished races. These Watchers grip black spears that reflect no light to warn of our approach.

At the head of this hideous gang flies the most vile of them all—Jexa. Her two black wings flex slightly to leverage the southerly air current. In the midday sky, so close to the sun, it's a wonder her white skin doesn't blister and slough from her bones. Instead it takes on a waxy sheen, which I see clearly because I fly so close I could touch her feet if I dared to risk it. Luckily her stare remains fixed dead ahead, with not so much as a sideward glance.

Our destination calls out to us, luring us like the breeding grounds of migrating birds. Only, instead of mates and fair weather, this V-shape sweeping across the sky is out for blood.

Blue ocean sparkles beyond the desert ahead, where a seam of brown coastline joins a wet sea to dry land, and though I've never seen this place from so high up, I could never mistake that beach for another.

Jexa dives toward the breaking white lines of surf. I maintain perfect position behind her while the twenty Watchers flared back from her left and right also dip toward the coast to follow.

I don't want to go. I'd give anything to drift up toward the sun and disappear into its light, but an invisible tether keeps me in formation, close to the Watcher Marshal.

We zoom toward the ground at breakneck speed. When the dunes come within shouting distance we level our flight, and—

An arrow whizzes from a crevice and hits the Watcher leading our left wing.

She crashes into a dune as Jexa swoops toward the beach with me in tow. Our speed is exhilarating, with colossal dunes blurring by underneath. The left wing of fighters peels away to maintain a higher altitude, flying a circle over the crevice where the arrow had originated, four swirling in a halo while another four dive down in attack.

Jexa leads the right wing halfway across the beach and loops back to fly through a tall black cave entrance in the cliff face.

Arrows explode from the darkness of the Fisherman's Gate. They drop two Watchers behind us as Jexa and I glide through unharmed. I stay on her like a tail as she weaves through our defenders, cutting down any who stand in our way and leaving the rest to her followers. Steel rings and shouts echo as Watchers root out those in hiding.

When we reach the Grand Gallery, everything takes on a mint-green illumination. Screaming warriors emerge from shadows wielding crude melee weapons, the terraced pit now a battle arena. Some faces I recognize, others I do not. It's a disorganized rabble, cavemen brawling with a goddess of war as she bounds between terraces to make quick work of them—every kick and punch a one-way ticket to the afterlife.

Then we're following the orange glow of candlelight down a passageway. We stalk the wavering light to the end, where my mother waits with a knife in hand.

I've witnessed this scene more times than I can count, through the eyes of the child cowering behind a desk against the far wall. I'd only ever seen my mother's backside when Jexa took these fateful steps, which had been curse enough. Now, as she drives her spear into mother's chest, twisting the shaft to wrench her soul from her body, mother's scrunched expression of agony makes her hardly recognizable to me.

Her mouth opens wide to scream, yet nothing comes out. But there *is* a scream—a wail of despair from the black diamond spear shaft in Jexa's hands.

My voice joins mother's screeching. Our cries echo loud in a dreadful chorus, hers fading away while mine grows louder. I scream myself breathless, until the rugged cave walls flatten to stacked blocks of stone, and the floor softens to a grand bed propped high upon wooden posts.

I fling a swath of fluffy fabric away and stand to survey the chamber with raised fists. A window to my right opens to dark sky, where an armored warrior watches me.

I pounce from the bed and tackle him to the ground. He goes down without a fight, and on the floor I realize it's not bones holding the armor upright, but a wooden stand.

As the cold of stone calls my wits back to me, I realize I'd seen this display before falling asleep, by the glow of the fire now smoldering in the corner. I'd recognized the flex armor, its helmet with sloped sides that curl outward—along with the curved blade hanging from its belt—from the only book my father ever opened: *The Art of the Samurai.*

Steel rings from the corridor outside my chamber door and brings with it screams of pain.

Sweat slicks my skin despite the chill. I spring to my feet and pull the samurai sword from its scabbard and, like an appraiser of ancient artifacts, immediately sense the authenticity of this warfare relic. The steel vibrates with hymns of glory and anguish, of strength and honor, which beckon me into a trance.

I whirl the blade gracefully to test its balance, making my way across the room until the freezing stone becomes too much for my feet.

I hurry to my bed and slip into a pair of fur-lined sandals. The comfort they offer emboldens me. I tiptoe to the door and pull a steel ring to ease it open, and a blast of cold air shows me how little I'd appreciated the heat from my chamber's dying fire. To be fair, though, no flame could ever keep the chill from my bones in this place. And it's not just winter darkness that rattles me. There's a lot of bad energy around this mountain. The rock seethes with it. I suspect that even when summer daylight shines outside, these halls remain dark and its chambers cold.

Growls echo down the corridor to my left.

I grip the sword hilt tight with both hands and creep into the hallway. Instincts beg me to flee right, away from the fight, but, as ever, curiosity prevails. I slink down the corridor toward the skirmish, sword held back with both hands ready to swing.

White flakes drift through an opening in the left-hand wall ahead. Whacking and ringing grow louder as I approach the wide window, which overlooks the courtyard where my recovery team had delivered me to Lex.

Snowflakes fall into the roofless space, where two lines of shield-bearers square off against each other. Twenty warriors make up each side, ten males and ten females in black undergarments standing shoulder-to-shoulder. Each side works in unison to press their shield wall against the opposing force in an effort to shove them outside a red square marked on the ground.

Men grunt and women growl as their bare feet dig at cobblestone for purchase, their bare calves flexing in their struggle to gain ground over their opponents. Sweat glosses their skin despite the snow falling onto their shoulders and shaved heads.

A short girl in the middle of the line closest to me lowers her head and drives her shoulder into her shield. Her thighs bulge with muscles thicker than my waist and produces enough power to shove her counterpart back, and with it goes the entire opposing line.

I watch the display in wonder. These people are beasts, with even the smallest making me a frail child by comparison.

No doubt the food Lex had sent to my chamber contributes to their vigor. Whatever that seasoned red meat was, it was the greatest thing I ever tasted, no offense to Horus. I'd stuffed my belly to illness, yet I'd have gone begging for more if sleep hadn't beckoned me so forcefully.

Lex observes the skirmish from the side with her hands on her hips.

"Incoming—up high!" she yells.

Both lines break and spin back-to-back to form an out-facing circle. They raise their shields and join them overhead as a large object drops from the roof. The boulder crashes onto the dome of shields and bounces off to the side.

Lex draws a curved sword and shouts, "Left flank!"

The warriors rearrange their shields to form a wall facing Lex. Seven silver stars make up each of the three stacked rows that cover each warrior from knees to scalp.

Lex swings her scimitar down with all her might. It whacks the upper left shield, lifting its right edge briefly. She breaks into a rampage like this, testing their cohesion with wild swings, prodding their defense for weakness. When a sustained effort fails to break their hold, she resorts to kicks and shoves.

This heartwarming sight is not enough to stave the chill from my bones, and the comfort of my bed demands my return.

As I retreat down the corridor, an orange glow lures me past my chamber toward the end, where a half-open door permits the escape of a bright hearth's warmth. I sense Lex is not one to pry upon, but when I catch a glimpse of what's inside I cannot restrain myself.

Curved bookshelves line the circular walls of this round

chamber, breaking only at a glowing fireplace, a shuddered window, and the doorway in which I stand. A worn leather chair sits beside a crackling fire, the flames of which cast orange light over rows upon rows of the colorful spines that fill each shelf from floor to ceiling.

I lean my sword against the wall and wander inside, where a soft mat of bear fur welcomes me to the center of the room. But the cold floor has become a distant bother for me.

The sheer volume of books surrounding me is a marvel in its own right, but it's their condition that leaves me awestruck. I can make out the words on every spine, the titles and names of every author, and even their publishers in fine print.

I pull a random book from a shelf left of the fireplace. *The Life and Trials of Duster Hughes*, reads golden letters over crimson backing. When I crack open the cover I need not take care, for this is no frail artifact of times past.

"Are you much of a reader?" asks a voice from behind.

I slam the book shut and turn to see Lex in the doorway. She holds the samurai sword I'd leaned against the wall when entering, a silver shield strapped to her back.

"Sorry, I—"

"Don't apologize."

Lex saunters into the room, sizing up her own collection with admiration. "It should be a crime to deny the curious mind such wonders. I find it a tragedy my followers take no interest in these books. Even my own great father, Polaria's last elected chancellor, failed to appreciate their value. In his day, to possess even one of these editions would earn you a walk to the gallows."

Part of that I can relate to. My father would have burned

all our books for warmth if not for my mother's defense of their worth, but to execute over them? My tribe saw books as useless, never dangerous.

My confusion must be obvious.

"After the Decimation," Lex says, "the first settlers of this land brought with them a great distrust of knowledge. They blamed science for destroying everything they loved, so they took great pains to ensure it didn't do so here. That included banning all travel into the old world. Mother-forbid we ever happened across nuclear arms to defend ourselves with."

The room darkens. A look at the fireplace reveals it's not a smaller flame that gives rise to the shadows growing around us.

I return my attention to Lex. From what I'd witnessed in the courtyard, her support of technological advancement does not match her current tactics.

"I've seen your enemies," I say. "The King's warriors bear arms that kill from a great distance."

"And they reveal themselves from such distances as well. Whenever they trespass upon these lands, they find themselves at a great disadvantage. They'd sooner hide in trenches waging battle through their gunsights. My warriors, on the other hand, are masters of close combat."

Swords having the upper hand against firearms? I have trouble picturing it unless the gunmen are caught in an ambush.

"And when you attack them on their own ground?" I say. "How do your swords and shields fare then?"

"Our current shields can take pistol fire well enough, but heavier weapons are a different story. Until yesterday..." Lex's eye flashes bright with enthusiasm. She unslings her shield and stares at it in wonder. "When a simple gift showed me how I'd been looking at the problem all wrong."

She flings the shield at my chest. I fumble to grab hold of its smooth edges, baffled by this unexpected move. Terror joins my confusion when Lex draws her pistol and aims it at my face. A flick of her thumb and a *click* of the hammer warn of what's to come, so I raise the shield just as her finger pulls the trigger—*BANG!*

I scream and try to shrink behind the shield, trembling in anticipation of the bullet's close-range impact. Some time passes, too long for a bullet's journey yet enough for the shield's energy to radiate through me. It's a mix of Watcher hate, subservient defiance, and something else I can't quite place. When I lower it to assess its surface, I find no dent or sign of impact.

"Why take the hit at all," Lex says, "when you can avoid it entirely?"

She points to a blown-up book on the shelf behind to my left. I drop the shield, the *Watcher* shield, and step away from it. Lex scoops it up and hugs it to her chest.

"Where did you get that?" I say.

"Regulus. Yesterday, he sent me a warning upon a silver platter. What he did not realize was the significance of the platter." Lex stares at the shield wolfishly. "Just the technology I've been looking for. Two thousand more of these and we'll be an unstoppable force."

"That thing is not of this earth. You may not find the metals to replicate it."

Lex's smile flattens, but a devious smirk then curls to take its place. "Well, that was my plan until your friend arrived. If she succeeds in killing Regulus, his border soldiers will allow me to pass unchallenged. So, tell me, Deka, do you think she will succeed?"

"She wields incredible power," I say, anger swelling in me. But it's directed at my own heart for having opened up to her. I'd failed to recognize her for what she is: a weapon of mass destruction who cares only for her own desires. "I think Regulus will soon regret provoking her."

Lex gives a satisfied nod. Together we stare at the map of Anterra pinned to her wall. The crackling fire is the only noise for a long while, then I notice Lex's attention has shifted from her map to me. Her intense stare makes me sweat.

"You know," she says, "you remind me of someone I met long ago—out in the old world."

The heat in her glare suggests this was not a pleasant encounter.

I turn my attention to her books. "Where did you get all these?"

Lex breaks from her dark trance, and when her gaze shifts to her collection, her eye softens. "Come," she says.

She leads me down the corridor and into the mountain, where overhead lamps cast purple light onto endless rows of plants. Here grows crops I'd thought long extinct, food kept alive by a Wolf's ingenuity.

At the far end of the cavern stands a steel blast door. Lex swipes a wristband over a smooth black square in the rock face to the right, commanding the door to slide sideways into the mountain.

If there is an afterlife of paradise, I'd imagine my mother's would resemble what lies in the next cavern. The books covering the walls appear in the same arrangement as in Lex's study, but somehow their condition seems newer. Their uncracked spines suggest this library is a backup collection, which means Lex takes the preservation of knowledge very seriously. She'd have gotten along famously with my mother.

A machine with a great white drum occupies the center of the room. A closer examination reveals the drum is actually a roll of paper.

"You printed all these books yourself," I say. "But... how? From what?"

"An old friend of mine had a collection of digital archives," Lex explains, tossing her samurai sword casually from hand to hand. I'm unsure of her meaning, so she clarifies. "Back before the Decimation, the people stored their knowledge on computers. Harvesting this data was a great crime until a few years ago. Our government at the time feared we'd rediscover blueprints for toxic machinery or nuclear weapons, or maybe revive barbaric ideologies that died away during that civilization's final hours.

"Anyway, this friend of mine had a hobby of searching shipwrecks for treasure. Among his bounty were hard drives. When he stored all those articles onto the circuit boards of a single plastic box, he had no idea he'd created the world's greatest library of lost literature." Lex's expression hardens. "*Pandora's Box*, he called it. And he kept it all to himself."

"Why?"

"For one: it was illegal to own. Possessing just a sliver of what he had was enough to get him hanged. And two: he feared the knowledge in the wrong hands would cause more harm than good."

"So you stole it," I say, and this accusation leaves my mouth without thought or warning.

Anger wrinkles Lex's face. "I *borrowed* it. When the usurpers assassinated my father, I knew that box was the only way to get an edge over my enemies. So when I fled Polaria, I took Pandora's Box with me."

Lex's tackling of Anterra's unbalanced equation with an inferior class of weaponry puzzles me. "Then why waste this knowledge on developing shields? Why not just fight fire with fire?"

Lex frowns and twists her lips. "I'd be lying if I said I wasn't tempted to. But you must understand, Deka, those soldiers across the border are my own people. When I march, it will be to liberate them from tyranny, not conquer them. If my return home is done through slaughter, Polarians will see me as an invader to be resisted." She shakes her head and says, "That simply will not do. With deflective shields, though, we'll hit the border like a tidal wave. There'll be nothing they can do to stop us when we wash over their trenches. Their firearms will do little in the close quarters fight, and they will quickly surrender. I will stand over their trenches, and with the blades of my warriors at their throats, I shall offer them mercy and freedom. They will rip off their crown patches, and together we shall rid Polaria of its monarchy."

The smile forming on Lex's face looks almost unnatural.

A far door slides open, through which a man wearing a long white coat emerges. Machinery whines and casts streams of sparks across a great white space behind him, but the door slides shut before I can see what they're working on. My presence stops him dead.

"Doctor Cotter," says Lex, "this is Deka. He's the foreign visitor I was telling you about."

He ignores me and shows Lex a board with a paper document clipped to it.

Lex's face remains neutral as she reads. She nods faintly and says, "I see. Doctor, please escort our guest back to his chamber. Make sure he's well fed and rested."

Doctor Cotter frowns at this. I know the look. It is that of a man given a task beneath his station. Yet he does not protest.

"Of course," he says with a slight bow. To me, he says, "This way."

Lex steps up to the door he'd just emerged from. I wait for her to open it so I can steal a peek beyond, but she stands there watching me, waiting for us to leave.

The doctor outside the opposite door clears his throat. He watches me with great impatience, so I turn to follow.

As the blast door slides sideways to seal off the library, I hear the far door open to unleash a screech of grinding steel from beyond.

"What's in there?" I ask the doctor.

"None of your damn business."

His response doesn't faze me, for I have come to a profound conclusion here: Alexandra Arcturus is the most extraordinary human to have ever walked this Earth.

CHAPTER 31

DEKA

Endless hours of darkness make it hard to tell when the time for sleep comes here, so I wait until the castle grows quiet. I suppose I could ask Lex for permission to explore her library, but I've seen how particular she can be about what she wants me to see.

I lie under my blanket until the echoes of chatter die out. Soon after, when the hourly patrol passes my door and their clunking footsteps fade and then disappear around the corner, I slide from my bed and lean against the door to listen.

Silence.

I crack open the door to see someone standing there.

I stifle a yell as I fall back in fright.

The boy, who is not much younger than myself, fights to conceal a mischievous smirk. "Did I frighten you, fearless prince?"

I vault to my feet. "Were you spying on me?"

He straightens, eyes wide in panic, as if the mere accusation might land him in trouble. "Of course not. Lord

Arcturus sent me. She's invited you to the ballet. I'm to escort you there at once."

I have no idea what a ballet is, but I sense Lex's invitations are simply orders in disguise, so I slip into my boots and follow her attendant down the corridor.

"My name is Hector," he tells me without my asking, "personal steward to Lord Alexandra."

"Where did you say you're taking me?"

"The ballet. It's a dance."

This gets my alarm bells ringing. Am I expected to perform some home ceremony for Lex and her chieftains? That's how wanderers who stumbled upon the caverns of my home earned their meals—by offering us providers some much-needed foreign entertainment.

"Don't worry," he says, "it'll be far from boring. It's actually called the *Blood Ballet*."

His smirk when he tells me this fails to put me at ease.

He escorts me to a sunken pit around which rings of seats shrink toward a round floor. My place is above it all, on a private balcony. Lex sits on a similar balcony to my right, secluded from all others. She doesn't spare me a glance.

Two warriors enter the pit through opposing doors. They carry spears and shields, and each wears a band over their head that covers one eye. They fight until one slices open the arm of the other, drawing blood. The bleeding man is declared the loser. Guards enter and remove his eye patch, then drag him away while an attendant drapes a violet long coat over the winner's shoulders. The winner bows to applause before leaving through a door under Lex's balcony.

"Try-outs," Hector explains. He stands behind me, to my right. "Only the best may serve in the Lord's house guard."

I've seen how Lex treats her warriors. To endure such hardship, I assumed they'd been forced into service. "What does she offer in return?"

Hector gives me a puzzled look. "The honor to serve at her side, of course." He looks to her balcony with an enchanted stare. "Some say she is the All-father born again."

"All-father?"

This draws an even more befuddled look from my attendant. "You really aren't from around here. Well, *Odin* is what they once called him. Lord of all the gods. He disappeared for a long time, fallen into a great slumber some say. Others will tell you he wandered the darkness beyond the edge of eternity, but only he can really say. We just know that he wasn't around seven hundred years ago, when our ancestors destroyed the world.

"Survivors struggled for decades to survive in the blistering aftermath. A smart and daring few saw this last bit of land as our only salvation—a lonely continent at the bottom of the world, far from the radiation and merciless heat of the wastelands. It was on that journey that the first settlers rediscovered the Old Way. It came through a trial of blood and salt, of sea and stone. Some say the Sage Abelia used Odin's magic to grow Anterra's first tree. By using his runes, she cracked the code to nature's mysteries. You really haven't heard of her? She founded Polaria. Imagine that: the first Polarian, the first of *all* of Regulus's people, used our ways to ensure their survival. They declared her a Sage, the honor they give to the rare few righteous among them. Funny thing is, she was more like us than them. That'll just tell ya. And they wonder why they haven't had another in over three hundred years."

I imagine my ancestors watching the last ships flee our home in search of something better. I wonder how many of those ships risked coming here. For all I know, I may have ancestral cousins wandering these lands. Perhaps under this very roof. Might even be the next contender to walk through that door. Is it possible one could be a warlord somewhere, weighing his decision to join Lex's cause?

Goosebumps ripple my skin at the possibility.

The next duel lasts about a minute and includes a few impressive exchanges. In the end, the bigger lass beats the scrawny girl. The loser tosses her eye patch onto the ground and stomps out.

I wonder how Marlok would fare in this pit. Or Huxley. Would either leave here wearing a new purple coat and a patch on his eye?

"So this All-father was a god?" I say.

"Yes, he was the god of gods, like I said."

"Why do you believe Lex is him?"

"I said *some* believe that. Others say she is his prophet, that Odin works through her. Either way, she does the all-important work that only gods dare pursue. She has walked the same path as him in many ways. She even sacrificed her eye like he did, for the sake of all mankind."

"A god with only one eye?" I'd assumed gods were perfect, or even boasted extra appendages or strengths. Never less.

Hector crouches beside me. He props an elbow on my armrest and leans in.

"It was the cost to drink from the Well of Knowledge. He did it to save his people, just like Lex had done in her youth, when she ventured to the old world in search of our salvation.

She succeeded and returned a hero, back when Polaria still valued such people. They tire quickly of their gods over there. The days of those blasphemers have been numbered for some time now. Soon the ways of old shall rule Man once more."

"There are worse enemies than Polarians," I say, "believe me. You'll see soon enough."

Hector nods knowingly. "Ragnarök — the end of days — twilight of the gods. The Valkyrie have been busy of late, urgent in their search of our battlefields, selecting the finest warriors to serve at his side for when the beast of chaos rises to devour the world. Odin will fight the beast, while his hand-picked warriors battle the legions of Hel."

If I'd not seen what I have in recent weeks, I'd say this lad has spent too much of his life in the wilderness listening to myths. Crazy as the story sounds, though, it carries far more truth than fantasy. I've encountered too many 'beasts of chaos' of late to dismiss his claims for superstitious ramblings.

The next match ends swiftly, just as it begins, and gets a nod of approval from Lex.

"What do you think?" I say. "Do you believe she is a god?"

"Do you think she's not?" He stares at her, transfixed. Everyone here is, in some way or another. As if sensing me notice his gawking, he breaks his stare and stands. "Have you seen her dam? The things she's created here? Is it all not born of magic?"

I'd call it science. Clearly this kid hasn't figured out what all those rectangular things occupying Lex's bookshelves are. Admiration and caution duel inside me. The cunning Wolf has used her reputation and the magic of science to build herself a cult in this deep dark land.

I watch the next round in silence. When the winner receives his violet long coat, the vanquished surrenders his eye patch.

"What happens to the losers?" I ask.

To this I receive no response. I look over my shoulder to see Hector staring at a strip of purple cloth in his hand, the fabric stained white from sweat. It seems the resourceful Wolf finds other uses for her defeated contenders.

The next warrior enters the pit alone. He watches the opposing gate, awaiting a challenger who does not come.

Lex shifts impatiently in her chair. Someone will pay for this delay.

When the door finally bursts open, the warrior who emerges is unlike any who has come before her. Rather than dull, loose-fitting garments, her black attire clings to her body with a sheen that gives her a flattering shape. Matching black hair hangs down between her shoulders, over which two crisscrossed bands wrap to cover both eyes.

Gasps rise from the stands. Everyone sits on edge, leaning forward to whisper to the spectators sitting before them, or turning to hear the mutterings from those seated at their side.

The contender stumbles in her blindness, then draws a beautiful scimitar that rivals any other weapon of human craft. She swings the curved blade before her in search of her foe, and this is enough to subdue him. I watch in amazement as he drops his spear and raises both arms in surrender.

Laughter and ovation prompt her to remove her makeshift blindfold. Seeing her disarmed opponent, she smiles with feigned wonder and raises her sword in victory, then gives Lex a mocking bow.

"*Raven*," says Hector.

The venom in his tone raises my curiosity. "Who is she?"

"Some would say she's the greatest warlord in all of Ortaria. I'd call her a murderer."

Lex stands and applauds. The smirk on her face and the twinkle in her eye tell me she's genuinely happy to see this master of warlords. She signals Hector with a jerk of her head. He races down to the pit to escort Raven through the winner's gate as Lex takes her leave out the back.

The show ends with her departure. Many of the audience, veteran guards who'd earned their coats long ago, stand and disperse.

As I make my way back to my quarters, I ponder it all. Even warlords with reputation enough to disarm the fiercest of Lex's contenders travel to her court. I sense Raven is not one who typically pays visits for pleasure, but the look in Lex's eye had suggested that may be the case here.

Though I don't consider Lex to be the most attractive specimen of my kind, I cannot deny her lure. What is it about her? Perhaps she does wield some form of magic, casting spells of charisma on all who enter her presence. Or perhaps Raven sees in her an equal, a hero in her own right, for at mid-thirties she is no older than Lex. Raven will have gained her reputation through some fantastic feats of her own, and yet here she is, possibly paying some sort of tribute in her own strange way. And so I can't help but wonder...

Do I spend my days now in the halls of a god? Or is all of this splendor the work of a con artist? It's more likely Raven sees a threat and has come on an assassination mission of her own. Something about her presence does stir a sense of unease in me.

I'll have to sleep with one eye open, for if the alpha wolf should be slain on this night, this fortress will become a prison of mayhem.

CHAPTER 32

NYA

The southern air is cold, but my thirst for revenge heats my blood.

Kill the King.

That is my mantra, and I shall say it until I hold his severed head in my hands.

Kill the King, and this fractured land will be whole again.

Kill the King, and we shall gain a formidable ally against the Watchers. *Kill the King...*

Yes, my path is clear.

A silver thread meanders through black wilderness below. From this height the mountains look like frozen waves stretching from sea to sea, splitting the continent where a red line marks the border on Lex's maps.

As I near the edge of the mountains, the winding river that reflects silver moonlight descends toward the lowlands in a remarkably straight line. It's almost unnatural, an artificial feature like the dam holding back Lex's fortress lake, as if some great machine had dredged it out.

Gliding closer to the mountaintops, I notice what appear

to be enormous claw marks scarring their slopes. They funnel down into large gullies, which flow into half-pipe valleys that descend into the lowlands toward the distant sea. These forested channels tell of a devastating melt that once dumped a crown of ice into the ocean. The loss of that great frozen sheet had forever changed this planet, much like the removal of a golden crown that we shall see in the coming hours.

I marvel at the spectacle below. From my view up high, this rugged land that sits alone in darkness at the bottom of the world shows me there is magic and beauty to be found even in darkness. It is in the hearts of its inhabitants, who offer so little fear to the dark and unknown. Admiration for them swells in me, and no doubt their resilience is why the Watchers have left them alone all this time. Any attack must come during summer, when the regenerative sunlight graces the sky, but even then its energy has less to offer here. But that's not all.

Having met Lex and witnessed Regulus's behavior, Jexa's scouts have no doubt concluded that these two countries would eventually wipe each other out. It was only a matter of time, an annihilation destined to happen well before the planet's new inhabitants happened across this distant land. The discovery of their bones and artifacts would fuel debates among their scholars. History itself would need to be rewritten, depending on what the Magister had them believe when transplanting them here.

But no. They'll never step foot on Earth if I have anything to do with it. This place belongs to Deka, and *maybe* Lex, *if* she smartens up, but certainly not Regulus. He's already taking his final breaths.

The divisive mountain range slopes down to the lowlands

of Polaria. In the foothills, between steep slopes and vast plains, sits a dark seam stitched into the earth. Glints of red light reveal heads bobbing up and down this line. Border soldiers.

Crown soldiers.

When I cross this line, I know I've entered Regulus's domain. I am an invader. An assassin out for blood.

A dome of yellow light brightens the distant horizon. Amyria, Capital of Polaria and Regulus's seat of power, will be the place the great *sapien* king meets his end. I'll rip off his head and pulverize whatever remains of him, then Lex will lead both great armies to face the Watchers on the Southern Gateway. There we shall wage the final battle for Earth.

Goosebumps ripple my skin, and it's not the chill air that rouses me. Sure, you could argue we'd lost the Battle of Giza, but there we denied Jexa what she wanted, and I've been eager to put another villain in their place ever since. Regulus's death shall satisfy that craving. For now.

Even without the city lights beckoning me in the clear night, I'd still know where to go. The river flows straight for the capital and bends toward the sea a short distance before, with the lights casting a golden glow over the sharp river elbow.

As I sweep over the lowlands of the King's dominion, it becomes clear this river is the lifeblood of his people. *The Artery*, it's called on Lex's maps. Columns of gray smoke rise from settlements spread along its banks. The orange glow of firelight reveals humans dancing in open spaces boxed in by brick dwellings, and happy music tells me they are celebrating.

Have they heard of their tyrant's impending doom? Do they now rejoice over the approach of their rightful leader?

Their reliance on the river does offer Lex a mighty hold over them. The head of this vital waterway begins at her fortress, where she'd need only to seal up the dam and cut them off, causing untold suffering.

Do they know how deeply they are at her mercy? That she is the lord of their currents? The unseen heart to their artery?

I risk gliding low over a village for a closer look, and here the smell of burning meat assails my nostrils.

Bile creeps up into my throat as my jaw quivers in revolt. These people are beasts, and yet this reminder makes my heart throb with hope. Lex's folk are well fed, their muscles hardened and able. On the mountain gateway, where the gravitational Anomaly will deny flight to every Watcher, forcing them to rely on their underdeveloped legs, these rugged *sapiens* will put a real beating on them. But first...

Regulus and I must dance.

My wings are eager for the fight. I've not heard them buzz this fast since before the Battle of Giza. I've not had the energy, nor the purpose to inspire me. This, though... killing kings is something to get excited about.

The rest of the flight is boring but easy. The calm before the storm.

Square patches of black earth mark where Polarians grow their food during summer. Lone domes dot the landscape, where people hide from the smothering darkness of winter in orange light. The closer I fly to the capital, the bigger and more frequent these clusters of golden light become, leaving me with a striking realization.

The Southern Sapiens do indeed fear the dark.

As I near Amyria, I cannot deny the splendor of Regulus's capital. It takes immeasurable strength to survive so far from the Sun's light, but to actually thrive as a defiant beacon against threatening darkness... Yes, it is undoubtedly inspiring. And in a few minutes, I shall turn their entire world upside down.

The city glows from under eight colossal domes. Through their clear walls, rectangular silhouettes stand above lumpy clusters of forest, each dome a world unto itself.

I stare in awe at the city of golden light. If Deka could see this, he'd no doubt feel a sense of pride his tribe must sorely lack.

Soon enough, I tell myself, knowing he'll be at the head of Lex's liberation parade.

It doesn't take a genius to figure out where I might find King Regulus's throne. Neon spotlights cast a green glow over a tall pointy tower that stands at the center of the dome cluster, giving the spire an emerald sheen.

As I fly closer, this green light turns to purple. Its vibrant energy infuses me with comfort and warmth, luring me close with a growing sense of peace. I glide along carelessly toward the domes and nearly reach them before I snap out of it.

I stop my flight and check myself. I'm only a short whisk from the nearest dome, my target of assassination almost within reach, yet I'd been gliding along in leisure flight as if I've come to visit a longtime friend.

I narrow my eyes on the purple spotlights illuminating the spire, bewitching lights that had caught me in a spell.

What a cunning ruler this king must be. Rather than demand obedience through a heavy hand, he uses light to control the collective mood, and with it their individual minds.

Feel safe here in my haven, he tells them. *Here you will find comfort and shelter from the abyss. Together we shall fight the darkness of extinction, and under my watch we shall endure.*

I shiver with a new appreciation for my foe. He is a clever manipulator, which means I should approach him with more caution than I'd been planning.

CHAPTER 33
NYA

Despite Sheffa's recent incursion, the King's capital defenses remain woefully scarce. In fact, from what I see, they are non existent. Bright patches in the geodesic domes invite me through perforations in their roofs, so access is just a matter of gliding through a hole a third-way down the wall, and when I do...

I slip into another world. One second I'm flying in the cold dark night, the next I find myself soaring across a warm blue sky. A canopy of green leaves sprawls out below, divided by a grid of grassy lanes that section clusters of glass housing into neat city blocks.

A scream of delight explodes from my mouth. *I can't help it!* After so many days of endless night, this place is a welcoming paradise. Truly.

I glide over rooftops and manicured forests, over grassy lanes where parades of celebrating citizens dance, and it's almost enough to make me forget we're under a dome in the dead of winter. In fact, when I look to the ceiling I can't even see the geodesic grids.

Euphoria swells in me.

Is it the same for the humans dancing on rooftops below? How deeply does this fake blue sky foster ignorance to the harsh world outside? Do some forget their reality by winter's end, only to be reminded by a blast of true light from the rising polar sun?

A grid materializes in the sky before me to break the illusion for me. Beyond the dome wall, at the city center, a purple spire bends high toward the sky.

I glide over a wide grass boulevard that leads to the tower through an arch doorway exiting the bubble. The celebrations seem to be moving in that direction, but they'll have to sing a good few more songs before they reach it.

As I land before the archway and stare out into the open space where there stands the spire, I can't help but feel like the villain here. Life here is good for these people. By the way they dine at eateries and indulge on fermented fruit, you'd never know there was crushing darkness waiting outside their doors. Regulus controls this ecosystem and everything in it, and here he offers them the wildest of comforts. And me...

I've come to take it all away.

When I step through the archway and back under night sky, I'm immediately confronted by an angry dust maiden. My sister stomps toward me with great urgency, and by the way her raised fists glow red before her chest and her clenched jaw bulges, I know she wants to hurt me. Her top lip curls in rage as a firestorm of hate swirls in her eyes. This threatening glare sends a wave of dread through me, and is enough to stop me dead.

My approaching adversary does the same, in precise unison with me, and it's now that I realize the figure staring back at me is my own self. A *reflection*, complements of the tower's sleek exterior.

Oh, Great Darkness! Anger had gripped me with such passion I'd not even recognized myself. And worse, what I saw actually frightened me, for I'd witnessed in me a wrath with a life of its own. At least I'd not lost my wits and gone Berserk. This force has the potential to possess me if I'm not careful, but now that I'm aware of it, I am able to channel it into my fists, which throb with swollen rage.

I continue marching toward my reflection in the tower's silver base. I feel like a flea as I near the narrow, three-sided pyramid, with its sides that twist to a point that pierces the dark sky. Regulus's guards no doubt keep watch from the beaming apex that overlooks the eight domes around me, and surely they see my approach here in the open.

I slow my pace. Anger had emboldened me to the point of madness, and, with it now in check, I feel deflated.

I remind myself why I'm here, and the memory of Sheffa's bagged head channels a flood of scalding rage to my legs that keeps me marching forward.

Why not just fly to the top, you ask? Sure, I could do that. But I think the occasion calls for a more dramatic approach. Picture this...

You're sitting on your throne, high and mighty in your tower, ruler of all you can see and beyond. And then, this little brat begins the longest climb of her life toward the greatest showdown of your nation's history. With every fourth step up your spiral stairway she punches your impenetrable steel walls with her vibrating fist. Each strike sends a pulse funneling up to the apex so that, when it reaches your ears, it's deafening. The steady rhythm rocks your world, an endless earthquake playing out the deep dark song of your funeral.

And that's exactly how it goes.

The steel bars blocking the entry offer me pitiful resistance, exploding at a flick of my finger. Inside, I find a spiral stairway that does indeed circle up the tower, and a light tap of my fist sends a thunderous boom toward the pointed ceiling. As promised, I do this every four steps to play out a steady and ominous tune, the image of Sheffa's head weighing heavy on my heart, and by the end I wish there were more stairs.

The cadenced pounding must've lulled me into a trance, because before I know it I'm walking across a great hall atop the tower. Starlight slips through slits in the walls, providing the gray space its only illumination. At the far end of the hall stands a throne, and on that throne sits a ruler of men. Shadows obscure his face, but I feel his eyes watching my approach.

White flakes drift through the air and melt on my skin. I suppress a shiver and strut forward. The slap of my feet on checkered tile echoes loud across the great hall.

The King looks so regal in his pose, with a ten-foot chairback standing tall behind him. With myself being five feet tall, it's twice my height!

But I've crushed greater seats with my hands.

I spread my arms wide and say, "Greetings, mighty king. I hope you've enjoyed your reign here, for your end has now come."

I stop a stone's throw from the throne and await his

response. My fists squeeze tight at my sides as I resist the urge to say, *Well, go on... tremble!*

He must be scared witless, because he sits in silence for a good long while. I still can't see his face, so I'm about to advance when he extends both arms toward me and claps slowly in mocking praise. The taunting noise echoes loudly across the hall and stirs a foul energy inside my chest.

My whole body blisters with rage, my fists clenching so tight my hands feel like they're about to combust. I'm about to lunge at him when he rises from his seat, and his face emerging from shadow sends me stepping back in surprise.

Whenever I've heard Anterran's speak of King Regulus, the way they said his name had conjured an image in my mind of a bearded old man slouched on his throne, his values warped by tradition and his only satisfaction reaped from the oppression of his subjects. The fair-skinned boy on the dais before me, however... He is no older than Deka. His rosy cheeks boast not a whisker, and his only crown is a mat of curly red hair that hangs down to his eyebrows, with the sides and back of his head shaved to his skin.

He descends the dais stairs, his long gray coat brushing each step behind as his black knee-high boots clunk out an ominous, defiant beat. Starlight glints over a row of metal ornaments decorating the left side of his chest.

He spreads his arms wide in welcome and says, "Bravo! What a riveting performance. And that costume..." He squints and leans forward for a closer look at me. "How did you get those wings to stick like that? They look so real."

Okay, this is not the reception I'd been expecting.

I suppress a shiver as the boy king circles me while sizing

me up with fearless green eyes... Eyes that tell me he knows something I do not. His confidence whispers of a trap from which he's sure I have no escape. Perhaps it is the same trap that had ensnared Sheffa and sent her to her fate.

I turn to remain facing him as he studies me.

"You know," he says, "I think those wings are real. What do you think, General?"

Shuffling bootsteps draw my attention to the dais, to where an old man emerges from behind the throne. A black cloak covers much of his face and his right hand, which grips a cane that wobbles in its struggle to keep him upright.

"She is another demon," the General says in a raspy voice. "An assassin brought into this world by a Wolf's magic and sent here to kill you."

Regulus gives me a casual and unbothered look. "Is this true? Are you a demon sent here to kill me?"

"I am no demon, but I am here to kill you."

"Hah!" The young king wags his finger at me as he veers out in a wider circle. "You've got fire, girl. A lot more than your friend had."

His outright confession hits me like a slap. "So you admit to killing her?"

Regulus clutches his chest and recoils. "Kill? Is that what she told you?"

Is that what she told you? he says. Does he take me for one who speaks with the dead?!

My throbbing fists ache for violence. This boy king is clearly deranged, and Earth will be better off without him. I'm about to punch this royal sack of pigswill into a trillion pieces when something stops me. This something holds greater sway over me than revenge or anger ever could, the very thing that's always gotten me into trouble.

"What were her last words?" I ask, my curiosity too great to deny.

"Who? Sheffa?" he says, and him saying her name hits me strangely. He clasps his hands behind his back and squints at the ceiling in contemplation. "I think it was something to the effect of... *I'll bring your message to the Wolf at once, Great King.*"

"Liar!"

I must look something fierce, because Regulus cannot hide the worry in his eyes. He holds up both hands and, almost pleadingly, says, "Okay, you got me. She never called me a great king. But the rest of it was true."

He takes me for a fool. I should smack him for his audacity but, with his death now within my grip, a sudden urge seizes me. If I can convince him to mobilize his army to defend the gate, that will avoid the mayhem that's sure to follow a coup. And more, it'll get *sapien* boots on Mount Tuck much sooner, perhaps within hours. Yes, that might serve me better. I can always just dust him afterwards.

Regulus steps onto the dais' bottom step. "What form of magic did Alexandra use to bring you here, anyway?" he says. "*Pixie Assassins.* It's a fresh angle, I'll give her that."

My face burns red hot. *Did he just call me a pixy?* This boy is really trying his luck. "Alexandra didn't send me," I say. "I came from the north to warn of an invasion."

Regulus clutches his chest and feigns surprise. "Invasion? Well, please, don't spare the details. Go on."

"This enemy is greater than any danger you've ever faced. To survive, you must join forces with the Wolf—I mean, *Alexandra*. You must combine your armies if you wish to see another summer."

"What makes them so dangerous?"

"They've come from another galaxy, and killing is their nature."

"We are no strangers to violence here."

Yes, I've witnessed their ways too well. "They can fly and heal grave wounds within seconds. You must fortify a strategic location in your realm before they arrive."

"And I bet you know just the place."

I squeeze my hands into fists. He's mocking me, and in doing so he plays a game with his own life. "Mount Tuck. That's where they'll attack."

"Mount Tuck? Really? Who would've guessed that's where Armageddon was scheduled to go down."

Armageddon... Ragnarök... The humans have foretold their fiery fate a long time ago.

"You need to send all your warriors there," I say, my top lip twitching with anger. "Every capable human must show up for this, or we will all fall."

Regulus steps close to me and leans in while eying his surroundings conspicuously. "Don't tell my enemies this," he says in a low voice, "but I can't afford to pull any of my troops from the border." He clenches his teeth in a mocking cringe. "They're spread pretty thin as it is."

A tornado of fire whirls inside my chest. This is entertainment to him, and he believes he can subdue me as easily as Sheffa.

"Your border is safe," I say. "It's just an imaginary line where your soldiers waste away in boredom."

Regulus gives the General a sly look. "Is that so?

Casualty reports tell me otherwise. So long as Ortaria still calls itself a country, there'll be no lack of excitement to keep my troops occupied. Outside these domes waits a cruel world overflowing with enemies, lawless outlands harboring unspeakable terrors."

The fresh memory of village celebrations along The Artery fail to support this claim. King Regulus has been misinformed, and I suspect his cloaked adviser has had something to do with it.

"Excuse me, Sire," I say to the King, "but have you ever visited your outlands?"

He frowns at my question. It's quicker than a blink, but long enough for me to catch it. "I have no need for such excursions. My trusted counselor here keeps me well informed."

I lean in close to Regulus and, with my voice lowered, I say, "Has *he* ever been?"

In the corner of my eye I notice the General's lip curl in anger.

"He takes monthly trips to the border," Regulus says, "and returns with worse news each time."

I step back and say, "Then he is a liar."

"You watch that foul tongue of yours, *dust maiden*," hisses the General.

That old man's last two words hit me like an unexpected slap. I step around the King and approach the dais. "What did you just call me?"

The General straightens and squeezes his cane. The wooden handle groans in his grip.

"How do you know what I am?" I press.

The old man growls and bares his teeth in anger, and

when he does, his white human eyes bloom with a tint of reptilian-yellow.

The sight hits me like a punch to the heart, and knocks the breath from my lungs. I know of only one intelligent species that sees the universe through vertical slits in two yellow eyes. The King's court has been infiltrated by the Watchers!

No wonder Jexa never wasted time attacking these *sapiens*. All they need do is turn their leader against his own people to further their cause, making total extinction inevitable. But their method involves more than just mutually-assured destruction. The Watchers use these people for sport, inciting wars for entertainment and research. Jexa no doubt sees the value in studying the warfare strategies of all races, and places like this provide ample learning opportunities.

The General points at me but speaks to Regulus: "Throw this creature into the dark cells, wise leader. Show her what happens to those who insult your reverence."

Regulus crosses his arms and rubs his chin while giving me a good look over. He watches me, yet he speaks to his adviser: "I'm curious, General. Why *did* you call her 'dust maiden'? Nothing of her appearance warrants this title."

The General's jaw goes slack. "I... I seem to have mixed up my words. Please forgive me, my lord. Just give the order and I'll—"

Regulus raises a hand to demand silence. To me, the young king says, "Are you called a 'dust maiden' by others?"

"Yes."

"Why?"

My heart flutters with excitement, for I have been dying

to dust something for too long now. "I think it's best I show you."

Regulus spreads his arms in approval and steps back. "By all means..."

I scan the room for the best prop through which to display my ability.

"Sire," says the Watcher in protest, "this is—"

"Silence!" shouts Regulus. His cheeks glow red with anger, but he quickly composes himself with a smile. "I've been in dire need of some entertainment around here."

The Watcher's host lowers his head and wrings his hands.

I continue scanning the great hall in search of something solid and valuable, something that will blow up in spectacular fashion. My search brings me in a full circle, back to where I started, and here my eyes lock onto the grand seat of steel occupying the dais. I give Regulus a taunting smirk and brush past him to begin my ascent to his throne.

The Watcher backs away, his shaking arms raised before him. "Sire, this is not wise."

"Why not, General? What harm could such a delicate creature inflict upon forged iron?"

My heart sears with rage. I can't wait to turn this king's world on its head, then carry *his* head out into that world.

I stop beside his throne and wind back my fist. My burning knuckles vibrate with a frequency capable of pulverizing the hardest iron with ease, so that when I swing with all I've got—

Something slams into my waist and knocks me to the ground. The hit nearly breaks my neck with a snap, but this is minor to my surprise when I see it's the frail old General who now pins my arms over my head. He's amazingly strong, so strong I can do nothing as he sinks his teeth into my neck.

Pain shreds my every nerve from my toes to fingertips, and it's only the beginning. His bite tightens, fraying my nerve endings to induce the most hideous sting ever! It's blinding and suffocating, too much for any mind to handle.

My consciousness coils tight to shield against the assault, leaving my body to convulsions. Searing pressure builds inside me, swirling the anger inside my chest to an expanding tornado of rage with nowhere to go, each second growing more desperate for release. Panic joins the havoc, for I know how this will end.

CRACK!—I explode in a flash of light.

Only...

I'm painfully aware of my body arched upward, muscles wound so tight my molars crack and fill my mouth with the sweet taste of blood. Sizzling sparks shower me as my hips lower to the floor. My chest heaves for air, but even suffocation cannot stifle my satisfaction when I roll my head to the side and see Regulus's playful mood has evaporated. *Poof*, gone, just like his dear adviser. His wide eyes and gaping mouth infuse me with a joy greater than any romance ever could.

I can't speak, so I shoot him a look that says, *You're next.*

Through his state of shock, the young king does manage a question: "How many more of you are coming?"

I spring to my feet, my muscles pulsating with fury. This boy king assumes too much by thinking he'll live long enough to witness the Watcher invasion. My fists clench so tight my elbows pop, which signals my better sense to rise in protest, but rage quickly swats this foolishness aside, and soon I find myself stomping toward the royal brat.

He stumbles back and trips over his own two feet. He sprawls onto his back and, though he raises his hands defensively, he manages a defiant yet very human stare.

I stop dead. My fists loosen as an insight reveals itself to me. Why hadn't that Watcher infiltrated the King himself? Why use a middleman when malicious influence may fall upon deaf ears?

The answer comes swift and clear: A Watcher cannot hijack a host who is pure of heart. Which means that Regulus...

An explosion of red light blasts my face with a *BANG*.

I stumble back but do not close my eyes against the attack. If this be the weapon of my demise, I shall face it with all the strength of my ancestors. My heart, on the other hand, is something I have less control over. It races in terror at the supernova illuminating the night sky. Sparks from the exploding star fall through the atmosphere, and I'd think it the Sun's death if not for the stink of sulfur in the air.

A blue streak launches from the ground and explodes in the sky before me. The blast shoots dozens of blue streams in every direction, which disintegrate as they sizzle toward the ground in the shape of a colossal palm tree.

An orange streak explodes to the right of it, forming its own tree of sizzling leaves. And then comes a red, and then another orange, and soon the sky is filled with exploding stars.

Screams rise from outside.

I leap over Regulus and sprint to an opening in the far wall, where a balcony overlooks the city of gold-lit domes.

Directly below, in the open-air ring around the spire base, gathers a crowd. But they are not screaming in fear as I'd thought.

Regulus appears in my peripheral. He joins me in admiring the display of exploding light in the sky before us.

"Word spreads quickly," I say. "They're already celebrating your death."

"It seems you timed my assassination well." Regulus allows a low laugh, but it's more sad than anything. "But no, they do not wish me dead. You've come at the hour of Winter Solstice."

A barrage of fireworks rises from the ground, exploding to hurl dazzling arms of light through the year's darkest night.

"The first settlers of this land started these annual gatherings to smite the face of darkness," Regulus says. "That's how it started, anyway, but it's since gained popularity for a far better reason."

I turn sideways to give him a curious look.

He nods to the crowd below. "Until fourteen years ago these people suffered under a rigid class system. When my grandmother won the revolution, her first order was to extend military service to all highborn citizens."

The King waves down at the crowd flooding around the base of his tower. At this distance I wonder if they can see him, and an eruption of cheers swiftly provides the answer.

Regulus smiles and throws up both arms to encourage more applause, and the mass gladly gives it.

I watch the spectacle with great bewilderment. When I try to picture Lex overlooking this gathering, the first image that comes to mind involves her warriors plowing their shields through the crowd to break up the festivities.

Regulus slouches over the rail and plants a boot on its footboard.

"In the old days," he explains, "every recruit owed twenty years to the defense force. They spent most of those days at the border, and a good few never made it home. When my grandmother forced a flood of upper-class citizens into service, that allowed those regular soldiers to rotate away. Suddenly a lifetime in the trenches became one month at the border followed by one month to do as they pleased. That policy guaranteed her the army's loyalty after the revolution. Only a few zealots resisted, mostly highborns with half their freedom to lose. Or those looking for—"

"Revenge," I say.

Regulus nods. "There's one who would see this city burned to ashes just to soothe her broken heart."

"Her plight is about more than just vengeance. They want democracy, too. Many don't like the idea of serving a king."

He smirks and looks below. "Could have fooled me."

My gaze lowers to the growing crowd of admirers. "So, most of them folk are warriors?"

"At one point or another, yes. Any who've already served their time can still be summoned for emergency service."

"Then you need to summon them all to Mount Tuck, *every* able body. That's the only fight that matters, and its hour is near."

Regulus nods absently. "I can rally my county militias and call in the regulars from their monthly leave. That'll give us fifteen thousand on the mountain without softening the border."

"No!" I shout, and I squeeze the rail until it explodes.

Regulus wails and flails in terror as he falls through the gap. I snag his collar and haul him back, then dump him onto the floor. I loom over him and scream, "You have to *open* your border! You'll need Alexandra's fighters at your side."

Regulus stands and jabs a finger at my face. "Hah! Even without the wings and pointed ears, I'd know you're not of this world. If I let Alexandra cross those mountains with an army, my people will drag my corpse through the streets. No, it's not even an option."

"But you must. The Watchers thrive off of division. The only way to beat them is through unity."

Regulus grits his teeth. "How do I know you're not trying to fool me, huh? Sure, I could pile my whole army onto that mountain. And when the Wolf rides in to sack the capital, there'll be no one here to stop her. That's how things go on Anterra. Like I told your friend before, we don't play nice together."

My face burns hotter than the sun. How dare he bring up Sheffa while standing so close to the edge! Only divine self-restraint keeps me from flinging him over the balcony, and that's wearing terribly thin.

"Says the boy who beheads peace envoys," I say.

Regulus gives me a quizzical look. "I assure you, your friend was in one piece when she left here."

"If you're going to do something so despicable, then at least have the guts to admit to it."

Regulus steps toe to toe with me. He leans in until our noses nearly touch, where his mossy-green eyes lock me in an angry stare.

"I sent your friend with a message for the Wolf," he says. "She was to let Alexandra know that no matter how many demons she sends to kill me, she'll never subdue the people of Polaria."

The conviction in his eyes suggests he believes his own outrageous claim. Either he's an excellent liar, or the General had Sheffa ambushed as she was leaving.

A volley of cheers erupts from the crowd and fortifies a suspicion growing in me—that King Regulus is not the wicked ruler I've been led to believe. Not only that, but seeing this city light up the dark after having spent so much time in the Wolf's stronghold leaves me wondering if I can say the same for Lex.

Regulus steps away and straightens his disheveled coat. "I'll send my domestic units to Mount Tuck," he says. "If they become overwhelmed, I'll pull some troops from the border."

Cold pain grows behind my eyes. I lower my head and rub my temples. "They won't get there in time," I say, frustration simmering inside me. "The Watchers move too fast and they won't let up! This is an all-or-nothing fight."

Regulus narrows his eyes in the direction of Mount Tuck. His conflicted stare tells me he's torn. It's hard to gage by his expression which way he's leaning, and my chest tightens the longer he deliberates.

Finally, he steps back through the balcony doorway, where he stops to address me. "I won't allow the Wolf to roam freely across my lands. If she wishes to help us, then she'll surrender her weapons at the border. My legions there will escort her army by train to Mount Tuck, and there they'll have their weapons returned. I'll assign them the lower ground to defend. That way, if she plans to betray me, at least they'll be at a disadvantage."

The tightness in my chest loosens. Given the history

between both countries, Regulus's verdict is measured and reasonable, and is the best decision I could have hoped for.

I place a hand on my belly and bow, relief swelling inside me. "I shall bring your terms to Alexandra at once, wise leader."

CHAPTER 34
DEKA

The long night brings many visitors to the Wolf's door. Warlords ride to her fortress from all over Ortaria, adding their warriors to the camp growing in a nearby valley. They pledge their swords to her cause, to ride into Polaria and reestablish order in the chaos that's to follow King Regulus's death. But whispers in the hallways reveal their true motives.

They have come to kill and plunder.

Lex accepts every one of them with open arms. She holds a banquet for each arriving party, meals which, in this long night, seem to stretch on into one endless feast.

Workers had begun harvesting the underground crops upon Nya's departure, for Lex has a growing army and new subjects to feed. This harvest keeps her banquet tables overflowing with food, so much that her feasters waste enough to feed my whole colony for a decade.

Her victory is certain. Every hour sees a bed chamber occupied by a newly swayed dignitary or war chief. Every day, this empty fortress fills with warriors who already count their rewards.

It's hard to sleep. The halls echo constantly with shouting and singing, which gets worse during the high feast. This is the hour each day when Lex introduces her new allies and the numbers they promise. Many attendees shout cheers of praise and welcome. Others give sullen looks over their cups, their glowers airing histories of bad blood.

Sometimes fights break out at the tables. Sometimes for good reason, but often it's from nothing more than an unwelcome look.

Lex watches it all from the raised head table with a satisfied smirk. She insists I remain at her right hand whenever she's in attendance. At first she introduces me as an esteemed guest from a far-off land, an assassin's handler who has infiltrated the king's court. My assassin now brings us his head, and Lex will take it to show his border troops. Seeing proof of their monarch's demise, they will invite her across to restore order to their capital.

Many in this rowdy hall had at first questioned her claims. They laughed when she told them of my African home, but when they see me in the banquet hall they all stand corrected, for exactly what reason I have yet to figure out. One thing I know for certain is that my invitations to these dinners serve one key purpose for Lex.

I am here on display.

All eyes watch me and everything I do. When I eat, they watch. When I examine my silver dining utensils, they watch. I smell my food before eating it, they watch. When I ask Lex a question, they watch and silence themselves to listen. It's all a bit much for this modest envoy. Trying to figure out how to eat half the food on my plate is enough on its own, but at least they don't expect much else of me.

Lex has strict rules about how her guests interact with me. None are to ask me questions or address me directly. She assures them it's all a matter of security, because I am in possession of sensitive knowledge. Occasionally, she leans close and assures me it's because her alliances on this side of the border are fragile. But when I'm alone in my bed chamber, the cold corridors carry echoes of her claims to my ears.

She tells them I am prince of a vast Nordic empire. My great emperor father has sent me to barter a trade agreement with Alexandra: our precious metals for Anterran food and fishing rights. Regulus had our previous envoys executed. This has made him an enemy of my people and, by consequence, an ally of The Wolf.

As the festivities drag on and Lex falls heavy into drink, her words become sloppy and her promises great. She appoints Ortarian dignitaries to esteemed positions in Polaria's forthcoming government. Their armies will receive farmlands and hunting rights. Lex backs her generous promises by sending wagons overflowing with food and drink to these warriors who are camped at a place called the Polis. It's a fort at the nearby South Pole, one of symbolic importance. Many of the banquet attendees have ordered their forces to gather there. Some boast of outrageous numbers that grow with every drink. Their political rivals dispatch scouts on the spot to check their claims.

As the party winds down, something always happens to Lex. Her mood darkens with the dying firelight, a sour stare scanning the crowd with resentment. This assembly is missing a face she believes should be here, I see it plain as day in her one good eye. By the end of the meal, this anger turns to sadness. She is the saddest person I've ever seen, actually, and part of me pities her.

Then, when the fires have died and the castle falls into sleep, I hear her pleas. Her radio room sits directly above my bedchamber, and if both our windows are open I can hear her voice. It always carries the same words.

"Commander Centaurus, are you there? Come in, Commander Centaurus. Can you hear me? Please, Toris, come in."

That last line always gets me. It makes my heart bleed for her, because this severed connection reminds me of Mali. Only, the other half of this dear companionship still lives. And he ignores her call to arms. I cannot imagine my pain if Mali ever shunned my summons for help, for I'd expect her to be the first to fall in by my side.

The Wolf always arrives to the next dinner composed and in good spirits. But I see her scanning the crowd, giving each new face on the bench rows a deep appraisal.

I understand Lex's desire to avenge her father too well, so I hope Nya delivers. We cannot afford distractions of the heart, and I do believe with Regulus gone the people of Polaria will follow Lex to the fight. From what I have gathered, Clarian was one of many who loathed serving the king. But Lex... She is different. People volunteer to fight for her. With science she tames this harsh winter realm, providing food and light for her people. She is the greatest candidate to command a human defense against the Watchers. The only thing standing in our way is a tyrant king.

It's our fifth banquet when Lex's chatter shifts from small talk about my homeland to the future.

"What do you see yourself doing after I liberate Polaria?"

Honestly, I've not thought much about this.

"You've read more books than any guest I've ever had," Lex says. "*Combined.* I'd say you're among the most literate people on this continent."

"I'd like to return home," I say. Perhaps Lex can provide me a means to create my own library in Africa, so that I may use her knowledge to usher my people toward prosperity.

"When I release you," she says, "you may go wherever you wish. But my country could benefit greatly from your wisdom. You'd have a loud voice on my council."

"Until then, am I your prisoner here?"

"You're my esteemed guest, nothing less. These lands are too wild and ruthless for you to roam freely. They will remain so until I dissolve the border that separates our two great nations, which, luckily for you, is on our horizon."

Lex takes a drink and watches me in the corner of her eye, and I sense she sees I'm not convinced. "You can walk out that gate right now if you wish. No one will stop you."

I shiver at the idea of wandering out alone into that abyss. Sometimes I sit in the window of my bedchamber and stare out at the sprawling darkness, wondering how long I'd survive out there on my own.

Lex's mouth twitches with a smirk. She knows it's not her stone walls that keep me here.

"When we liberate Polaria," she says, "I'll support you in whatever you do. I'll have a ship return you to Africa, if that's your desire. I'd like to visit your homeland myself, but I'll have my hands full restoring order here. But if you decide to stay, this castle will be yours."

I choke on my wine. This generous offer conjures in me a strong sense of suspicion. "Why would you offer me something so great?"

"You brought me a gift far greater than masoned stone," Lex says. "That friend of yours is the key to our swift victory. With Regulus gone, my place will be in Amyria. I'll need to give this castle to someone who appreciates all that it holds—someone who will devote his life to honoring the precious treasures within."

The treasure Lex speaks of must be her library. I'd be lying if I didn't think the offer tempting. My people have no future in Africa, but Lex does have the means to bring them all here. This fortress could house my entire colony in comfort, and the underground garden would see the word 'hunger' fall into extinction from disuse.

Seeing my consideration, she adds, "I'll make you lord of these lands, Deka. With Nya by your side, you'll govern fairly with strength and wisdom."

Suddenly I'm aware that Lex and I must look much the same at this table, each of us searching the crowd for a beloved face. Nya's absence leaves a chill in my heart, and this feeling makes me want to smack myself. She left me alone in that forest, and when this war is won she'll leave me to this planet as well. We have no future together.

"You seem to be placing a lot on Nya," I say.

"Regulus will not see her coming."

"Like Sheffa?"

Lex shifts uncomfortably. "I've seen warriors of all sorts, young Deka. Nya is different than them all. After this night,

Anterrans will call her a goddess of war and reckonings. If you serve me loyally in the coming hours, I'll see they call you a prophet for summoning her. Would you like that?"

I've seen the power words have on people. A partnership with Lex could restore humanity to its former glory, and the image forming in my head—of laughing with these people in the six-month summer and guiding them through the long winters—could be my highest destiny. Sure, Lex is blinded by lust, but she is not lost. Her heart is wounded, but I can use my position to guide her should she stray.

To be sure, I close my eyes and seek some validation. It comes quickly in the form of a warm breeze on my face as I ride across a sunlit valley. Ori scramble away from my mount's pounding hooves, while Fori wave from the nearby trees as I travel to advise the council.

When I open my eyes, I see Lex staring at me expectantly, awaiting a reply.

"I will follow you."

She gives me a crooked smile. "Good. Now swear it."

I give her a curious look.

"Get down on one knee," she explains, almost forcefully, "and pledge your life to mine."

The hall falls silent. Everyone watches me in anticipation. We're at the point in Lex's drinking where her mood may sour to anger, so I must choose my next words carefully. "Where I come from, a man's word is promise enough."

My words of resistance echo loud for all to hear. Lex's expression becomes neutral, denying me any hint of what's happening inside her head when she turns to the crowd. I'm expecting a backhand when Lex rises from her seat, her eye fixed on something that takes her breath away.

I trace her stare to the end of the hall, where there stands the most beautiful creature to have ever sprung into existence.

Nya stands in the doorway, looking very uncomfortable from all the attention. But it's my stare that sends her gaze to the floor and her cheeks glowing red.

Lex's chair screeches over stone as she steps back from the table. "Nya, darling, back so soon. Have you been to Amyria already?"

Nya's face brightens with a wide smile. "Yes, and I bring wonderful news."

"The King is dead, yes?"

Nya steps between rows of long tables to approach the dais. "Even better. King Regulus has sent half of his army to protect the gateway. I saw them mobilize on my flight back. He's really doing it."

Lex's jaw goes slack. "Regulus... He's... He's still alive?"

"Yes! He says he'll join forces with you."

Frantic murmuring echoes through the hall. Lex sinks slowly to her seat, her face pale with shock.

Nya frowns at the crowd's reaction. "Didn't you hear me? I said he wants to form an alliance."

"He wants a truce?" says a burly man with a forked gray beard. "His scouts have seen our mighty host and are soiling their britches. The hour has come. Let us ride to the border in force!"

"Yes!" Nya says with an enthusiastic nod. "His warriors are waiting for you to join them there, then they'll escort you to the battle."

This draws many confused stares to Lex.

"Escort?"

"The hell is she talking about?"

Lex leans forward with renewed intrigue and shushes the others with a dismissive wave. To Nya, she says, "You're saying he'll allow us to cross into Polaria?"

"Sure. You just have to surrender your weapons at the border, but you'll get 'em back at Mount Tuck."

The hall erupts with shouts, every one of them directed at Lex, who sinks low into her seat. Lex has gathered these Ortarians with the promise of victory over their rival, King Regulus. They have no idea about the Watcher invasion.

"What is this creature talking about?"

"Sounds like we were summoned here for a mass surrender!"

"You need to explain yourself, Alexandra."

Lex rises slowly from her seat. The ruckus fades to silence.

"Nya," she says, her jaw clenched, "I'm afraid you made a grave mistake. Regulus is a great deceiver. He *must* be killed. Return to Amyria at once and bring me his head."

Nya's jaw bulges as her fists tighten and crack before her chest. It's taking all her sensibility to restrain herself, I see it in her bloodshot eyes that turn redder by the second.

I jump onto the table before this turns into a brawl and raise both hands. "Brothers and sisters, the hate you bear for King Regulus is well placed, and his day will soon come. But right now, a greater threat approaches. They will wipe us all out if—"

"Ah, sit down!" shouts a man. "We can't defend our land against foreigners if we control only half of it."

Nya gives me a desperate look, urging me to continue, but I don't know what else to say. Human politics are strange to even myself. My lone tribe's only adversary has been the Watchers, and in that I see our lives had been simple.

"Go back to Amyria and kill Regulus," Lex commands.

"No!"

Lex's eye and nostrils flare. She storms around the table with a wine glass in hand and stops at the front of the dais before me. She leans forward with a hand raised to her ear and says, "I'm sorry, Nya, I didn't hear you. Please, say that again, and speak louder this time."

Nya's hand looks as if it's about to explode when she points at Lex and screams, "You killed Sheffa!"

Lex smashes her glass off the ground. "Seize her!"

A dozen warriors lunge at Nya, but before any can touch her she drops to a knee and punches the floor.

Dust and stone explode up to the ceiling and clouds the entire hall. A rock chip smacks my forehead and sends me scrambling for cover behind my chair. Coughing and shouts rise in confusion as pebbles patter onto the wooden table and stone floor.

The dust clears to reveal a large hole where Nya had been standing, in and around which many warriors now sprawl in a daze. Nya must have slipped back through the door in the chaos, because she is nowhere in sight.

Lex jumps onto the table and pulls a sword from the back of her chair. She sweeps it over her stunned audience and shouts, "Initiate Plan B! You have your targets—move forth to the border at once!" To a nearby attendant, she says, "Send word to Doc Cotter. Tell him to prepare 'Little Boy' for his trip to Amyria."

A throng of dusty warlords spills out from the banquet hall.

I slip away with the crowd, but I do not follow them to the courtyard stables. I race up a spiral stairway that leads to my bed chamber on the second floor, but I don't stop there. Instead I carry on up to a forbidden room.

The ceiling of the upper floor is low, so low I must crouch to avoid whacking my head off cobwebbed rafters, but thankfully it's a short walk to Lex's communication room. Here I find a radio set on a dark wooden desk. A braid of cables runs from the set to the window, where they slip outside and keep the glass open a crack. There must be an antenna out there, and if there's an antenna then there must be a way to access it for maintenance.

I whirl around and spot a ladder behind the door under a hatch in the ceiling. I climb up and shove open the wood covering, inviting an icy breeze inside. But even the coldest Antarctic gale could not chill the warmth in my heart when I see Nya.

She crouches on the turret opposite mine, the cylindrical fortification nearest the mountain, hugging her knees to her chest while she rocks back and forth on her heels.

Chains rattle from the gate rising between us. Riders stream out across the square and through the grand archway, warlords making haste to rally their warriors for the invasion.

Nya lowers her head and shakes it in distress.

I cup my hands around my mouth and hiss out a quick, "*Psst.*"

She perks up and looks straight at me. Her breath catches in relief, and she wastes no time leaping from her perch to flutter over and into my embrace. Her body radiates enough heat to stop my shivering, and her soft hair against my face smells like a fresh spring breeze.

Her bottom lip quivers as she watches Ortaria's war chiefs string out along the trail. For each of those riders waits a company of followers chomping at Polaria's bit. When the last horseman gallops across the beaten grass and through the trailhead's grand archway, she looks to me with defeated eyes.

"You need to get out of here," I say.

"They're going to attack the border?" she says, her voice meek and cracking.

I squeeze her tight in my arms.

"Who's *Little Boy*?" she asks.

This I do not know, but the order to Doctor Cotter tells me Little Boy has something to do with Lex's secret underground laboratory.

"Get as far away from this place as you can," I tell Nya, for she has made herself an enemy of Lex.

"I'm not leaving without you." She wraps both hands gently around my wrist. "I can carry you down to the river. There's boats there, and—"

"My place is with Lex."

Nya's jaw goes slack and her eyes gape wide in disbelief.

I grab her shoulders and hold her at arms length. "Don't worry, when this is all over I'll remind Lex that you're a friend. I'll make sure she sends you home."

Nya grips my wrists, her eyes so soft they water. "I don't want to go home. I want to stay with you. I don't care where that is, as long as we're together."

I twist my arm from her hold and hug myself. She's pulling on my heartstrings to manipulate me, and I'll not be deceived. What's happening on Anterra is a war of minds. In this fight, Lex will emerge our champion.

Nya joins me in watching the long stream of riders stretch out across the mountain face.

"We have to stop them," she says as she fidgets fiercely. "Regulus's soldiers are expecting them to surrender. It'll be a slaughter."

My heart sinks. Indeed we will lose many if we clash at the border, but it is a long ride between here and there. I'll have plenty of time to talk Lex into accepting Regulus's offer. The trust I've been building between us will soon pay off. Lex's broken heart blinds her, but her values remain sound. She believes I am under her control, and over time I can sway her.

Nya sizes up the warriors strung out across the trail. She holds in each of her hands the power to stop Lex's orders from reaching her army. I watch her survey the steep cliff face above them, from where she can send an avalanche of rocks down upon their heads. Or do a sidelong swipe below the path to blow the trail out from under them.

Her watery eyes harden with determination. She sits up on her haunches, ready to spring into action.

I grab Nya's wrist to anchor her. The resolve in her stare softens when she meets mine, and I seize the moment by pulling her close for a kiss.

Time slows...

All meaning of loyalties and survival that have consumed me in recent days fade away. Cold air nips at my ears and the back of my neck, and though goosebumps tighten my skin, I do not shiver. Her touch is all I need.

Nya's breathing falls into rhythm with mine, her belly

rising as mine falls, then falling as mine rises. Her fingers slip under my tunic. Their warm tips skim up my side, fingernails prickling my skin and summoning a tingly wave that cascades over my head and down my spine.

I'm not sure how long this spell lasts, but when I pry my lips from hers the riders on the trail are nowhere in sight.

Nya gives me a dazed, dreamy look, her half-parted lips inviting me in for more. I'm about to plunge back into that blissful escape when something stops me.

On the large square of grass between the gate and grand archway, where the hooves of a hundred horses just pounded a muddy trail across the lawn, now sits a giant blue balloon. A basket hangs underneath, from which ropes anchor each corner to the ground. It's the same hot air balloon that spotted me in the woods and directed Lex's rescue wagon to my location.

Wheels rumble like thunder over wood below.

I lean over the ramparts to see Lex strut out from the gate with a team of warriors pushing a steel cart behind her. Its U-shaped deck rolls on four tiny wheels, and upon this cart is something that sends an icy dagger through my heart. The green object resembles a sideways hot air balloon in shape, but it is no balloon. That cylinder of steel contains enough power to bring a whole country to its knees.

"Hurry!" growls Lex.

Men in white coats rush to strap Little Boy to the basket's underside. In their haste, Doctor Cotter urges them to handle the bomb with more delicacy.

Cold sweat slicks my skin from head to toe. I'd seen a similar weapon during my return to the Earthly realm, through images inside the Great Pyramid. The man-made catastrophe of ages past had unraveled threads of space-time unseen to human eyes and yet felt in places beyond our comprehension.

Whatever force had shown me that scene had also made a point to show me one last thing. The image of a wolf attacking that peasant girl has haunted me since I'd witnessed it, and now it's clear what I've come here to do.

CHAPTER 35

NYA

Deka has something crazy planned. I see it in his eyes.

He crawls to the roof hatch and sticks his legs down through.

I cling to his back and hold him in place. "Where are you going?"

"To talk some sense into her."

My hold around him tightens. "She's gone rabid. Come with me, please. I can get us both out of here."

Deka pauses to consider my offer.

Worry and doubt grip my heart. Can I follow through if he accepts? It had taken most of my strength to dust the Watcher in Regulus's court. Whatever remained after my return flight had gone into blowing up Lex's floor, and now I'm feeling woefully sapped. My arms tremble to keep hold around him, and we're not even moving. If I try to carry him down to the river we're likely to end up splatting on the rocks instead.

He takes my hand and guides it down over his belly toward his waist.

My heart races as I near his... his...

I gasp as my hand brushes over the hard object of his interest, and I waste no time yanking it free to see it's a knife from the head banquet table.

Deka seizes my wrist and twists the silver blade free. He returns it to his waistband and pulls his shirt over it, then says, "You're right. She's gone rabid."

"But... killing her? They'll kill you right back!"

Deka's mouth twitches with a smirk. "Not if someone swoops in to save me."

I look to the square below, where the Wolf supervises the loading of her bomb. It's not too far from the cliff edge over the dam. If I glide down from the turret closest to the mountain and pick Deka off his feet, we could be over the cliff before they realize Alexandra is dead. I can only hope the adrenaline rush gives me enough strength to carry us to safety.

"Okay," I say. Then I give him a hug and bury my face into his neck. "Be careful."

Deka forces a smile, then climbs down through the hatch and into the Wolf Den.

"Nya!" Lex's voice paralyzes me. "Nya, listen to me very carefully. I know Deka is still in this fortress. There's no way he could ever leave without me knowing. But so long as you do as I say, he'll not be harmed."

I jump up to reveal myself on the roof. Lex's stare had been already fixed on this spot, waiting, like the fifty warriors holding their star-blazoned shields behind her. They wear black garments under indigo long coats, with dark masks concealing their lower faces. Lex's balloon pilot had probably spotted Deka and me kissing when he landed, then alerted Lex to our location.

"You've lost your mind!" I tell her. "The people in Regulus's capital don't deserve this."

Lex points forcefully down the mountain trail. "You have no idea what they deserve! Every one of them had their chance to do the right thing. For *fifteen years* they had their chance! And for fifteen years what did they do? They bowed to a monarchy. That's high treason where I come from, and for that their sentence is death."

"Even the younglings?"

"Those children carry the blood of traitors. Better to cull them out and start over clean." Lex backs up to the bomb and runs a hand over its surface. "This here is a reckoning. It's vengeance and mercy and new beginnings, all delivered in one brilliant flash of light."

I should glide down right now and kill her myself. We could end this right now. But Deka... he'd never leave this place alive.

I'm about to shrink back to sneak into my rescue position when Lex's gaze falls to the gate.

"Ah! There you are!" she says, holding out both arms in welcome.

Deka emerges from the gate and walks straight toward Lex. Her warriors race to intercept him, but Lex waves them off.

I watch nervously as Deka nears striking distance and reaches for his waistband. His nerves must have him fiercely rattled, because he pulls out the blade in full view of everyone, with Lex still a good distance away.

A shiver of dread rocks me. *What is he doing?!* Even if he extended his arm fully, the blade still wouldn't reach.

I kneel on the roof edge and prepare to swoop in for the pick up.

Though faced with Deka's blade, Lex keeps all of her weapons sheathed. Instead, she widens her stance with her hands half-raised to meet the attack with her fists, and apparently this is enough to subdue Deka.

He drops to a knee and lowers his head. And instead of stabbing Lex in the belly, he turns the blade on himself. He slides the knife over his left palm, then squeezes his fist over his right hand to drain blood onto the opposite palm.

My heart drops like a meteor. *He's lost his mind!*

An exchange of words results in Lex ordering him to his feet, where they grab each other's hands in a crossway double handshake, sealing Deka in a blood oath to her.

"Stand tall, Deka," shouts Lex for all to hear, "and be recognized as my distinguished bannerman."

A cyclone of rage and jealousy makes my head spin. *Deka lied to me.* But worse than that, he chose Lex over us!

That bastard! How could he? Lex is a monster who wants to condemn her own people to darkness, and I'm... I'm...

What am I? Am I any different when I lead my own people from the light?

Lex throws an arm around Deka and turns him to face her troops. "Everyone, meet my newest adviser. Deka here will ride at my right side, and he shall carry my family's purple banner when we reclaim what's left of Amyria."

Betrayal overcomes me. All I can do is curl onto my side and pull my knees to my chest. Even if Deka hadn't offered himself willingly, Lex is keeping him close to use as a hostage. But the danger doesn't stop there. The honor of his new position is not an empty gesture to Lex's warriors. I see the jealousy clear in their eyes.

Lex turns to usher Deka back into the fortress. "Now, let's get you into a nice uniform. Something worthy of your post."

I dive from the roof and swoop toward Lex. She wraps an arm around Deka's neck and swings him to face me, positioning him in front as a human shield. With her other hand she cranks his arm behind his back to maneuver him.

I swerve right to avoid hitting Deka and am immediately faced with a wall of shields. I'd splat amongst the three stacked rows of stars if not for a last-second rise, though my belly scrapes over a shield-top in my passing.

I carry on, banking right toward the archway, and by the time I loop back toward Deka I see Lex has already dragged him into the gatehouse.

Her warriors race to form a shield wall in place of the gate. In doing so, they've left something precious of hers unguarded.

I zip over to the bomb and grab hold of its cart. This 'Little Boy' is enormously heavy, so I reach up to grab the armor tail fin in search of more leverage. And suddenly I'm in love.

A tsunami of warm energy surges up my arms and spirals inside my chest. The intricate pattern of this energy matches my body's natural frequency, much like how I do when dusting an object, only not quite. It goes deeper, seducing my DNA and singing in harmony with my atomic makeup. This tornado of radiant energy spins with elegant ferocity, infusing my heart and muscles with more strength than I've ever known.

PING! The cart's brakes snap and fling off to the side, and the wheels wail out in protest as I drag the ten thousand pound death device toward the cliff edge.

"You'll kill us all!" warns Lex from behind her shield wall.

I keep hauling on the cart, but it's slow going. The wheels scream under the bomb's weight. It gets worse when crossing the mud trail, but power expands out to my buzzing wings to gain me more momentum.

Ten of Lex's warriors break from their line to charge at me.

"Halt!" Lex yells.

Her warriors slide to a stop on the grass. They wind back their spears to launch, awaiting Lex's command, while I hide behind the bomb for cover.

Lex shoves through what remains of her shield wall and marches to join her forward soldiers. Deka remains under the watch of her guards as Lex holds out her arms to expose her body.

"You kill me," she says, "and they'll kill him. There's no way around it."

She continues walking until she reaches the opposite side of the bomb as me.

"Now," she says, her voice calm and measured, "I'm going to ride to the border with Deka by my side. If you want him to make it through the coming days unharmed, I suggest you go ahead and scout for us. Make sure our way is clear at all times. When we attack the border soldiers, report their movements to my captains, and when this bomb drops on

Amyria, I'll release you both from my service. This to you I swear."

It takes everything in me to not fling Lex from the cliff right now. Though, I see her march to the border isn't all that bad. It'll at least give me time to figure out a way to disarm them so Regulus's soldiers can bring them to Mount Tuck. Or I may have better luck convincing Deka to slip away with me when the opportunity presents itself. Either way, my choices to end this here don't end well for anyone.

Stepping out from behind Little Boy, I say, "Fine, I'll be your scout."

"Good," Lex says, though her stare is rife with skepticism. "I'm pleased to have you on our side... Again. Now, let's go turn Polaria inside out."

To be continued...

BOOKS BY JR DEVOE

Onero's Hunt

The Dark Monarch Series
Prequel: The Light Ones
Book 1: Dust
Book 2: Ashes
Book 3: Sparks

ACKNOWLEDGMENTS

There are countless people who supported me throughout the writing of this book, and I could never fit them all into a few pages. Perhaps I'll try in the final book of this trilogy, but for now, I want to extend my heartfelt thanks to my incredible beta readers: Nikki Bocelli, Leslie Arambula, and Maciek.

As with my previous books, James and Julie Devoe deserve special recognition for their tireless proofreading of the many "final" drafts this story has undergone. Your dedication and sharp eyes made this book what it is today.

And of course, my deepest gratitude goes to you, the reader. Your continued journey with me is something I cherish more than words can express. Writing is a solitary endeavor at times, but knowing that these stories are finding a home in your hands makes it all worthwhile.

Thank you for being part of this adventure. I can't wait to share the rest of this journey with you. Until next time, happy reading.

About the Author

J. R. Devoe grew up on Cape Breton Island, Nova Scotia, in the town of Sydney Mines. He has since traveled to six continents, including Antarctica in 2013 to research elements of his debut novel, *Onero's Hunt*.

In 2014, he pedaled a bicycle across Canada to raise money for WaterAid Canada, a charity that provides clean drinking water and sanitation services to developing countries. In 2016, he pedaled a bicycle across New Zealand for the sheer joy of it.

J. R. Devoe currently works as a professional seafarer, where his voyages continue to inspire his writing and fuel his passion for exploration.